BETWEEN TWO WORLDS

Nov 21, 2008

Gail,

May you enjoy many more years of
Bluebirds over the white cliffs of Dover.

BARRY FELDSCHER

ISBN: 1-4196-9230-5
ISBN-13: 9781419692307

Visit www.booksurge.com to order additional copies.

This is a work of fiction based upon hypothesis. It contains some extrapolations of incidences either experienced by the author himself or related to him by others. Also major historic figures and occurrences are touched upon to reflect the times or perspectives of the characters. Other than these, the names, characters, places, and events included here are the products of the author's imagination, and any similarities to actual persons, living or dead, are purely coincidental.

This book is dedicated to my mother,
Mrs. Helen Legum Feldscher,
and her sister,
Mrs. Rose Legum Balser,
two of the finest ladies of their generation.

Preface

This story presents a view of today's world through the eyes of someone direct from an era when the technology which came to shape the world as we know it was in its infancy. It gives the reader a sense of opening an old trunk in the attic, and bringing to life the forgotten thoughts and feelings of a bygone time.

In 1973, a body is discovered frozen in an Alaskan glacier. Due to the unusual nature of this discovery, it is carefully removed and flown to a federal facility, the Institute of Consolidated Research in Los Angeles, where a medical team with a special heat induction device is standing by in an attempt to revive him.

Against tremendous odds, the project is successful. However, instead of being heralded as a major breakthrough in science, the recovery is immediately cloaked in a veil of secrecy and intrigue. And the young man at the center of it all finds himself thrust into a world for which little in his background has prepared him.

The premise may be fictional, but the human nature depicted is very real.

Between Two Worlds is a study in contrast between two subcultures separated by time and technology. It does not set out to paint a nostalgic picture of a bygone age, nor does it attempt to compare the purported virtues of a forgotten era with the uncertainties of today. Its main intent is to present through the eyes of a man suddenly cast from another time a unique perspective of our own, and, in doing so, give us pause to reflect upon how far we have come, as well as what we have gained… and lost.

Chapter 1

1973

Across the vast Malaspina Glacier bordering the Gulf of Alaska, a lone figure towed his loaded sledge behind his snow scooter. John Buck, a Tlingit hunter, had tracked the bear a long way. His patience rewarded at last, he was on his way back to Yakutat, content that he had provided for his family. As he crossed the barren expanse of ice, he could see the tree covered hills of the Sitkagi Bluffs slowly passing by while the distant peak of Mount Vancouver appeared not to move at all.

He stopped for a moment to inspect and readjust his sledge. Checking his tie lines for tautness, he was working his way around to the other side when he suddenly froze in his tracks. In the ice he spotted a strange form.

It was a body, frozen and entombed just a foot or two beneath the surface. Buck was unable to make out much detail, but with the bent knee and extended right arm, its human form was unmistakable. Probably fell down a crevasse, reasoned the hunter. And from the clear, hard condition of the ice, it must have happened a long time ago.

After he and his family finished skinning and processing the bear, Buck dropped by to see a friend of his, Bill Farnsworth.

Farnsworth, a middle-aged man with a full head of white hair, called Yakutat home following his retirement from the Coast Guard. Buck had come to know him from his days of having assisted from time to time on search and rescue missions.

As Buck related what he found, Farnsworth's eyes intensely fixed on him as if he were hearing for the first time an amazing tale.

Racing across the icy plain on their snow scooters, Farnsworth could not help but wonder how by the purest of chances, this vast desolate expanse could ever possibly yield one of its secrets. Furthermore, he wondered about his friend's ability to locate once again this tiny dot in a vast icy terrain.

But John Buck's keen navigational skills, upon which rested his reputation as a renowned hunter and tracker, brought them back to the site with not the slightest deviation or error.

For the next several minutes they stood in silence before this incredible discovery. Farnsworth crouched down and with his heavily gloved hand brushed away at the surface in an attempt to get a clearer look.

"Yep," he nodded in acknowledgement to Buck, "...looks like you found something interesting alright!"

He then took a pipe from his mackinaw and lit it. "John, this sounds a lot like those frozen Mammoth elephants they've found in Siberia."

Buck nodded in agreement, then he asked, "Shall we notify Sheriff Hardy?"

Farnsworth did not answer right away. He drew a couple of long puffs as he gazed down.

"If we tell Hardy at this point...," he said, "then he'll simply treat it as a routine matter - you know - establish identity, cause of death and so on, then they'll bury him. I think we have here some unusual circumstances which might merit a little more consideration."

"But Hardy'll really kick up a fuss when he finds out a body's been removed without his bein' let in on it," warned Buck.

"Oh, we'll tell him," assured the older man. "But first, I'm going to make a few phone calls to some people I know. They may have some idea who might be interested in this." He turned to his friend. "In the meantime, I think it might be a good idea if we keep this between ourselves. We don't want a lot of noses poking around at this point. After all," he quipped with a wink, "...since our friend has been here this long, I don't see why he can't wait here a little longer."

The Institute of Consolidated Research in Los Angeles traced its origins to the Second World War, when it embarked upon various scientific undertakings of importance to the military. Its heyday came in the fifties and early sixties when it provided a haven for some of the brightest minds in the country. The manicured lawns and prefabricated concrete buildings, gave it the look of a modern university.

But with the decline of the post-Sputnik boom, along with the Viet Nam War, funding for research became increasingly scarce. Attrition took its toll as many scientists and engineers found greener pastures elsewhere. Those who remained felt trapped by family obligations, choosing to endure the frustrations of being stuck in a dead end career over the uncertainties of change.

One such scientist who found himself pigeonholed was Dr. Reuben Abrams. Abrams had developed an electronic induction device which could uniformly raise the temperature throughout an object. It was the size of a moving van and resembled a stack of donuts lying on its side. Through the core of the stack slid a special gurney upon which the object to be thawed was placed.

Beginning with frozen animal cadavers he perfected his techniques with flash frozen laboratory fish, mice, and rats. He had also used it with success in surgery with larger animals in treating aneurisms. Abrams had come to see his inductor in terms of potential and highly significant contributions to medical science.

But any opportunities he may have had for personal enrichment had been stifled by the administration, and at this stage in his life, he had grown tired of fighting the system.

On this evening he received a strange call. He said a few words and then hung up.

His wife noticed the puzzled look on his face.

"Reuben, what's wrong?" she asked.

"I've got to go to the office," he replied as he opened the hallway closet for his jacket.

"At this hour? What is it?"

"Don't know for sure. They wouldn't go into it over the phone." Then he added, "If I'm late don't wait up for me."

He kissed her and went out.

When he returned several hours later, it was after two in the morning. His wife though in bed was not asleep and turned on the lamp by her nightstand.

"It seems the project's been suddenly given a new lease on life," he said anticipating her.

"What do you mean? What happened?"

"Seems they found a body - a human body frozen in the ice in one of those glaciers in Alaska. They want me to put together a team to fly up there and recover it."

"Why you?"

"They seem to think it might be a good candidate for the machine. Frankly I don't think it's worth all the trouble but-"

"It still doesn't merit all this hush-hush," she cut in with disgust. "Ever since they put that... that *dictator* in charge, he's run everything like it's some kind of top secret military operation!"

Abrams knew there was more to it than this.

"Phyllis, what's really eating at you?"

"Oh, nothing."

"Come on now, honey. We've always been honest with each other."

"Reuben," she cried, "you've got only two years left and then you can retire from that pest hole. Julie will be out of college and then we can finally begin traveling and doing all those things we've talked about."

"We still can, honey. This doesn't change anything."

"It doesn't? You'll start getting involved again with those late nights and long days. I thought all that was behind us."

"This may be the culmination of a lifetime of work. It's an opportunity which in all probability will never come again."

"I know about those *opportunities*. You put all your blood and sweat into it and then they take the credit if it works and blame you if it doesn't."

"Come on now. Let's not go through that again."

But Phyllis wasn't finished. "Every day they make it a living hell for you. They stifle you while they pick your brain. Then when you're of no further use to them, they'll throw you out like so much garbage!"

Abrams remained silent for a moment. Then, tenderly holding her, he looked into her eyes.

"I'm a scientist. You knew that when you married me. You also know that I can't stand by and pass this up because of some petty politics. They've always hated the project and want to scrap it, but they don't dare because too much money has been invested in it and too many questions will be asked. I'm the one with the best chance of making it go and they know it. I don't give a damn about them or their little intrigues. I'm not doing it for them. I'm doing it for us!"

The midnight stillness on the glacier was broken by the WHOP WHOP WHOP of a Chinook tandem-rotored helicopter approaching for a landing. As the turbines whined down, two heavily clad figures emerged. Armed with flashlights, they slowly searched the surrounding area when one of them suddenly stopped and pointed down. He was joined by his partner who immediately signaled the pilot. The after cargo door opened, and six more men emerged with jackhammers, a portable hoist and a generator. Floodlights were placed in a circle and soon lit up the selected area. Presently the din of the jackhammers echoed across the empty wasteland as trenches were dug to separate the section of ice containing the body.

Next, chainsaws were used to free the bottom. A grid of steel bars was assembled beneath the ice block and connected by chains to a portable hoist suspended over the hole. As the hoist was cranked, the ice block slowly rose until the bottom was level with the surface.

It was subsequently loaded onto a special sledge which was then dragged to the helicopter. There it was hauled aboard into the cargo compartment, where it was placed into a portable refrigeration unit. With the crew on board and the ice block secured, the Chinook lifted off for Yakutat, leaving behind a square pit as sole evidence of its presence.

At the airport, the unit was transferred to a waiting C-130.

Before boarding, Abrams turned to Farnsworth and Buck.

"I don't know at this point how things will turn out," he said offering his hand, "but whatever happens, I want you to know how much I appreciate your efforts."

"It was our pleasure," smiled Farnsworth. "Just keep us posted how things develop."

The squat bird lumbered to the end of the runway. As it revved up to full power, it began to roll slowly at first, then gradually accelerated until it lifted off, assuming an air of grace as it climbed into the sky and gently banked to the southeast.

As the two men watched the plane vanish over the horizon, Buck observed, "Didn't that strike you as odd?"

"What's that?" asked Farnsworth.

"You'd think he'd be real happy, excited at finding something like this. Instead he seemed to be way far off - like he wasn't sure what might lie ahead for him."

"Different folks react different ways," Farnsworth replied. But he wondered the same thing himself as he took a long draw from his pipe.

Edmond S. Johns, Major General USAF Retired, was the director of the Institute of Consolidated Research. An ambitious and ruthless man, he was determined to transform the ICR into a major player in the space program. Part of his campaign included staffing his departments with his own people of proven loyalty. Although this undermined the merit system thus further lowering morale, Johns justified his policies with the rationale that he was streamlining his organization by getting rid of the deadwood.

His prime target was the Radio Frequency Inductor. It could not fit into a space vehicle, therefore he could see no use for it. But because of the enormous sums spent on it in the past, as well as its prior visibility to certain key members of Congress, he could not simply make it go away.

In reality, he felt threatened by it.

Johns was gazing out the big picture window in his office when his console buzzed.

"Yes?"

"Dr. Halleck is here, sir," answered the secretary.

"Send him in."

A heaviest, jowled man in his late fifties entered. Thomas Halleck had served with Johns both at NASA and the Air Force. He now held the chair of Deputy Director of Science.

"Well, Tom, what did you find out?"

"I checked with Abrams, General, and he says he'll be just about ready in a few days."

"'Just about' doesn't cut it here," Johns snapped. "Hell, he's been sitting on the damn thing for two months now! Couldn't you nail him down any further?"

"That was as precise as he could give me, General. He said he had a few more tests to run on the computer."

"Damn!" muttered Johns as he paced the floor. "How in the hell did we ever get into this mess? All these years I managed to keep that white elephant on the back lot until those idiots took the hint and left on their own so we could get rid of it once and for all, and now some high-level jerk from Washington wants us to use Abram's toy on this corpse they've found. Obviously Abrams has been circumventing me, so now I have to put on a goddamn show of how enthused we are and what we're doing to ensure its success!"

"But if it does succeed, General, couldn't we turn it around as a fait accompli?"

"Tom, you seem to be forgetting that the name of the game is *funding*! If by the remotest chance Abrams succeeds in pulling this off, then his project will wind up with more money. And that's money taken away from us! You can kiss the augmenter wing and the reentry spoiler projects goodbye. Any recognition he gets will come at our expense!"

Johns picked up the phone. "Tell Abrams I want his ass up here right now!" His eyes narrowed as he turned to Halleck. "Bastard," he spat out. "Goddamn scientists think they're all a bunch of prima donnas! You've got to stay on top of them all the time, Tom! All the time! Let up for only a second and they'll screw everything to *hell*!"

"Der Fuhrer hast gesprochen," mused Abrams to one of his aides as he hung up.

"You'd better be careful," warned the young man. "He's out to get you. You've really crossed him this time."

"That's the only pleasure I've enjoyed around here lately. He won't do anything right now. He's committed on this as much as we are and I'm the one with the best chance of pulling his chestnuts out of the fire."

"But you know what he's capable of. It would be just like him to pull the rug out from under you - from under all of us."

As Abrams prepared to leave he turned once more to his associate. "Norm," he smiled, "…life's too short to be afraid of people. Once you show them you are, then they gain control over you. He's just a manager and goes to the toilet same as everybody else. He's not Jesus Christ."

As Abrams walked down the long hallway, the old thought recurred to him as it did quite often: if the ICR was a civilian government agency, why did the director's office carry the air of one more befitting the Joint Chiefs of Staff?

Johns wasted no time cutting to the point. "Abrams, how's the project coming?"

"Like I told Halleck here, General, it's coming along fine," he replied casually.

"What specific progress has been made?"

"Well, the inductor tests out. Most of the computer systems check out OK too."

"Can you give me a specific date which I can announce for the demonstration?"

"Not precisely at this point, General, but I'm sure it'll be just a few days. We still have a few minor bugs. You know how these things go."

"No, I *don't* know how these things go!" John exploded. "When we sink millions of dollars into a project, we set precise objectives, we seek precise results, and when for some reason we don't get these precise results, we'd *damn* well better have some precise reasons why!"

In a patronizing tone, Abrams spelled it out for him.

"Circumstances surrounding a project of this nature do not readily lend themselves to the neat little boxes you would have, General. We don't know what we've got here. There are a lot of variables to take into account."

"What are you talking about?"

"Well, for openers, the body has to be maintained in the condition in which it was found. For all we know, the individual may have already been dead when he was frozen. If this turns out to be the case, then there is nothing we can do for him short of a nice obituary in *National Geographic*. On the other hand, if he was unconscious, this opens up two additional possibilities."

"Skip the damn double talk and get on with it!"

"Most likely, we have a case of someone who died as a result of being frozen. If not - and assuming he exists in a state of suspended animation - he may have incurred irreversible brain damage due to oxygen starvation. Should this be the case, if we revive him, we'll have on our hands a total vegetable. Our big hope - and it's a long shot - is that when he fell into the crevasse and the ice caved in on him, the freezing process happened so quickly and thoroughly that all his metabolic processes were suddenly and simultaneously stopped. The brain did not have time to miss its oxygen. If *this* is the case - and we're proceeding on the assumption that it is - then we will have only a few seconds to get them going again. It will require split-second coordination between our team at the machine and the medical team standing by."

Johns sat motionless as he stared at his clasped hands.

"I will select the medical team," he declared bluntly.

"I've already done that, General."

"Without consulting me?" Johns raged. "I can have you fired for insubordination!"

"That's your privilege, General," Abrams replied, "but if anything goes wrong, it's your neck, not mine. If I am to have total responsibility, than I must be free to choose people whom I feel best qualified."

Grudgingly conceding Abrams' point, Johns' lips tightened. "That will be all," he snapped.

When Abrams had left, the director turned to Halleck.

"I'm gonna be on his damned ass every lousy second! As soon as he pulls the slightest butch so help me, I'll nail his arrogant hide to the wall so fast the bastard won't know what hit 'im!"

As Abrams returned to his laboratory, he was haunted by a nagging issue. It wasn't just the personality clash with Johns that bothered him; that was just part of life.

What now weighed most heavily on his mind was that Johns had found a philosophy to justify his greed. In recent years, Abrams had become aware of a new attitude pervading through the scientific community and he didn't like it.

The powers-that-be were becoming increasingly obsessed with predetermined results and short-term gains. In other words, immediate justification for the enormous sums invested. To Abrams, it was like being certain of the outcome of the movie before paying the admission.

This rigid attitude went against the grain of everything he stood for. Abrams too wanted the subject to be revived successfully. But whether or not this came to be, there was still much to be learned. He wanted to approach the task as a researcher, patiently and systematically unraveling the mysteries within. Discovery was the beauty of science. It was this which had drawn him into the field when he was a boy.

But if their "results or else" philosophy was part of the price of high technology then, Abrams concluded, the world of science was in for a new dark age.

For now however, the chief scientist would play out his role as a second-string end who had suddenly intercepted a forward pass. This was to be his last hurrah.

The countdown began.

Abrams' team of scientists began to systematically chip away at the ice. Little by little, the mysterious form within began to reveal its secrets. It was clad in a fur lined parka and wore laced high-top boots of a style popular during the years immediately following World War One.

It was a male Caucasian, estimated to be in his late twenties. Height: five feet - eight inches; Weight: between 130 and 140 pounds. There was a bruised gash on his right forehead, probably incurred when he fell down the crevasse.

Timing was critical now. The gurney was rolled into the induction core. As the remaining ice melted away, the team set about stripping away the clothing and inserting electrodes all over the body.

As the temperature within the body continued to rise, the bent knee was slowly straightened and the arm brought to his side.

A resuscitator mask was placed over his face as part of an effort to reactivate lungs which had not functioned in decades.

The temperature monitors were closely watched, for everyone knew that one miscalculation could bring irreversible brain damage - if indeed that had not occurred already. They were gambling on one chance in a million.

Conductive jelly was smeared on his chest and a cardiologist held two shock paddles on each side.

Abrams gave the nod.

The switch was thrown. The body convulsed. A pulse briefly registered on the EKG oscilloscope - then went flat. A second shock was administered, followed by another momentary blip. The cardiologist looked at Abrams and shook his head.

"Try once more," Abrams said.

Again the switch was thrown. This time the blip turned into a sustained series.

So far so good. The vital signs were weak at first, but became more stable as the minutes passed.

Meanwhile, soggy papers were removed from the pockets of his coat.

"Take them to the freeze-drier," directed Abrams. "Maybe they'll tell us who he is."

They recovered another interesting item - a gold Elgin pocket watch.

Under tight security he was transferred to a room on a closed-off floor of an Army hospital, where a small hand-picked medical team, sworn to total secrecy, maintained a round-the-clock watch.

Before long his vital signs grew stronger and color gradually came to his face. But as the days passed, and the electroencephalograph waves continued to indicate no brain activity, many of the staff began to have doubts. Had humane and religious ethics had been pushed aside in the name of science? Surely it would not be right if, for all the efforts which had been undertaken, he remained in a vegetative state. Would it not have been better to leave him where he was and let nature and death take their inevitable course?

The possible repercussions were never far from their minds either. As it was originally presented to them, they had been selected for a high visibility project with potential high level recognition. But the flip side had by now become painfully apparent, for should the outcome turn out negative, their careers would be sacrificed on the altar of political fallout. That possibility now seemed very likely.

Colonel Reardon, the senior Air Force physician assigned to the project, stopped by for a periodic status check. He was informed by the young nurse on watch that there was no change.

Her eyes registered deep concern as she looked down upon the patient.

"Do you think he'll come out of it," she asked.

"Look at what we've achieved," he replied trying to sound upbeat. "Given the circumstances under which he was found, we've come a lot further than we had a right to expect."

But as he looked at the young man lying there so still, he abandoned any further pretensions of optimism.

"We've done all we can," he said solemnly. "Now the rest is up to him."

Chapter 2

1922

It was late March. The plains of the upper Midwest were covered with a blanket of snow. Ice stalactites hung like daggers from the eaves of roofs, from the telephone lines, and from the tall iron girders which supported the town's water tank. By the calendar it was spring, but the subfreezing chill left no doubt that this winter had not relinquished its strangle hold.

Hardship was nothing new to the people who lived here. Winters had always been like this and the folks had accepted them as a matter of course.

But what concerned them now was the low water level in the river, very unusual for this time of year.

Warm air from the south had alternated with intrusions of an Arctic air mass, causing enormous ice floes to break loose and float downriver. Two miles upstream from the town of Kayesville, this ice had collected into a massive jagged pileup damming the river. The water behind this ice jam was backed up and rising, and if this blockage did not break up soon, the river would overflow its banks, inundating Kayesville and much of the surrounding farm area. To the townsfolk faced with losing all they had, it was a nightmare.

An emergency meeting was held in the courthouse. Judson Hobbs, the town's mayor, presided over an atmosphere heavy with tension as people shifted nervously in their seats, muttering to each other. It took several raps of the gavel before he could bring the meeting to order.

Hobbs took a deep breath as he struggled to conceal a sinking feeling in the pit of his stomach.

"The situation which confronts us…," he began, "is only a temporary one. We will deal with it as we have dealt with all the others before. If we keep our heads and pull together, we can quickly put it behind us!"

Andrew Adams, the town skeptic, stood up and took the floor.

"Who are you kiddin' Judd! Everyone knows the damn river's gonna flood and we oughta pack up what we can and get out!"

A rumble echoed through the courtroom as the mayor one again hammered to restore order. With all the patience he could muster, Hobbs answered, "Andy, I'm surprised at that kind of talk comin' even from you! We've faced worse before. Have you forgotten the drought a few years back? And what about Sam's farm when it burned down and all of us pitched in to help him rebuild it? Are we about to turn tail and run because of some goddamn *ice?!*"

He crossed the podium to roll out a large blackboard. On it was drawn a crude map of Kayesville along with the positions of the river and the ice jam. The room quieted down as he tapped on the map with his cue stick.

"If it hits flood stage, it's gonna happen right here," he declared as he pointed to a section of the riverbank. "We're gonna build a wall of sandbags extending on down past the ice jam, and any runoff'll be diverted back into the river channel. When it's done this levee'll gain us enough time for the spring thaw to break up the ice, and then everything'll be back to normal."

Adams still remained unconvinced. "This cold spell could go on for weeks, and the buildup'll only get worse. How long will your sandbags hold the water back then?"

"Aw shut up Andy!" one of the farmers shouted, "unless you got somethin' better!"

Hobbs went on. "I'll need able-bodied men to work around the clock until this emergency has passed, men on the line, twenty-four hours a day, as many as we can put up there. Okay," he proclaimed with a final rap of the gavel. "Meetin's adjourned. Let's get to it!"

As the mayor stepped down, a small boy of about twelve came up to him. "How high's it gonna be, sir," he asked.

"Just as high as we can make it, son," the old man said gently.

It was as if they were preparing for a siege. Men came from all around the nearby countryside to volunteer, and every available truck and horse cart was pressed into service hauling sand, burlap sacks, and picks and shovels to wherever they were needed. All through the cold days and the chilly windy nights sandbags were filled, then hefted from man to man in bucket brigades up and down the line. They worked until they dropped from exhaustion and were quickly replaced by others. Before long the massive levee began to take shape.

Taking a break himself, Hobbs returned to his hardware store where Sheriff Ed Gaines, his old friend and hunting partner was waiting for him. They went to the office at the rear and closed the door.

As they poured some coffee Hobbs remarked, "Ed, it wouldn't hurt to work out that evacuation plan in case we need it."

"Aw Judd, don't pay no mind to Adams. He don't know what the hell he's talkin' about half the time."

"We may have to give the Devil his due this time. There's really no tellin' when it'll warm up and it could hang on like this for quite awhile before the ice gives way on its own."

Gaines looked at him solemnly. "You really don't think it's gonna hold, do you?"

"Let's just say I want to hedge my bets. C'mon out here, Ed. I want to show you something."

The boots of the two men crunched in the hard snow as they walked to an underground cellar behind the store. Hobbs extracted a key from the pocket of his mackinaw and unlocked the door. They proceeded down the stairs into a small dark room which smelled of mildew. The mayor then focused the beam of his flashlight onto a pile covered by a sheet of moldy canvas. Pulling it back, he revealed a wooden packing crate. He picked up a crowbar and pried open the lid.

"Whew!" whistled Gaines. "I sure wish there was a way we could use this!"

The crate contained dynamite.

From his small hotel room, Dusty Dervin looked out at the rain pouring onto the muddy street below. One of a small troupe of pilots who barnstormed across the upper Midwest, he had been stranded for the winter here in Claremont by a mishap following one of his performances. His Jenny had hit a chuckhole upon landing, and flipped over on its back. He came away with a concussion and the aircraft suffered extensive damage.

He had put these months to good use fixing up his plane, and it would soon be ready for a test flight once the weather cleared up. It was beyond him why the weather was hanging on for so long and he was anxious to rejoin his friends for the coming tour.

The time spent here, however, had not been entirely devoted to work.

After he had been pulled unconscious from his plane, he was taken to the house of the town doctor where he was stretched on a cot in a small room beneath the stairway.

When he awakened, his head throbbed in pain. He reached up and felt the heavy gauze bandage.

"Please lie still," spoke a soft feminine voice. "You suffered a pretty nasty whack on the head."

He groaned a little, blinking his eyes as he tried to focus. He looked around the room until he found her.

"Where am I," he asked feebly.

"You're here with us. My father's the doctor. I'm Peg."

His brow knitted in a worried look. "The plane -"

"About as bad off as you are," she smiled. "But don't worry. Your friends took it to a barn where it's waiting for you. Are you hungry?"

"Yeah, a little."

"That's a good sign. Let me go tell father and I'll see what we've got in the kitchen, okay?"

Dusty had never met anyone like her before. Her long hair flowed gracefully below her shoulders and her blue eyes had a sort of penetrating look as if they could see into his innermost thoughts. For a moment he wondered if indeed he had survived the crash, or if this were merely a stopping point along the way to the Great Beyond.

It was several days before he could stand without the room spinning around. One day Peg returned home to find him sprawled out on the Persian rug in the living room. "Didn't I tell you not to move about," she said pretending to scold him. "Why do you fliers always think you have to prove how tough you are?" She helped him up from the floor, slung his arm across her shoulder and got him back to his cot.

As the days passed and his strength returned, he was able to take short walks around the house. Then with Peg at his side he graduated to longer ones, first along the block, then up the street into town. She had taken a liking to this soft-spoken young man with a certain dreaminess about him.

As they walked through the park, they could hear the chorus of crickets singing against the backdrop of the evening sky.

"You made pretty good progress," Peg said admiringly. "I think you will be able to join father and me at church if you want to."

"Oh... uh... sure," Dusty stammered. "That would be nice."

Detecting the hesitancy of his reply, Peg asked, "Dusty... don't you go to church much?"

"I'm afraid not," he admitted.

"How come?"

"Oh, I don't know. I guess I never really fell in much with that stuff."

She turned to him. "You do believe in God don't you?" She asked this not in judgment, but more out of curiosity as to how his outlook in these matters differed from her own.

"Of course I do," he said. "I just find Him in other places, that's all. Up there... why, He's all around you. You can see the wonders of His creation spread out in all their majesty. I don't need to go to church, Peg... the sky is my church. The wind and the engine are the choir. And if you know how to read it right, the sky can tell you a lot of stuff."

"Like what?"

"Do you see the Big Dipper up there?" Dusty pointed out. If you follow the imaginary line between those two stars of the cup, you'll find Polaris - the North Star."

"I see."

"And Polaris also makes the tip of the tail of Ursa Minor - the Little Bear. You see it?"

"Uh huh."

"They can tell you where you are. You see those clouds over there... the wispy ones kind of off the moon? They're called mare's tails. They can tell you when a storm's comin'."

They paused before a statue of a Civil War soldier. Peg turned to him and asked, "How did you get into flying, Dusty?"

"One day when I was little," he began, "I was fishin' along the creek when I heard this clatterin' sound. I looked up in the sky and there was this strange contraption, looked kinda like a box kite. Just a pair of wings held together with sticks and wires, but the pilot seemed so free up there, like he could go anywhere he wanted. If he was curious as to what lay on the yonder side of the mountain, all he had to do was point his plane in that direction and go there. From then on, I knew I wanted to do that more than anything else in the world. After the War, I got me one of those surplus Jennies they had. Then Jim Higgins came along and taught me to fly it. Soon after that, he introduced me to a bunch of his buddies and we formed this group."

She picked up a fallen leaf and twirled it in her fingers.

"Dusty, when you're up there are you ever afraid?"

"Gee, I don't know. Never thought about it. Maybe sometimes I guess."

"What do you do then?"

"It depends. If it's somethin' that requires quick action - like when the engine quits - you're so busy lookin' for a place to put down that you don't really have time to think about fear very much. But if you're caught in a storm or rough air, well then, that's somethin' else again."

"How so?"

"It's different with each of the guys - like Jim. Whenever he gets into trouble he takes a shot of whiskey. Says it steadies his nerves. He's been known to put away a whole pint at one time."

"And you," she asked inquired.

"Hmmh," he smiled. "So you want to know my secret, huh?"

"Uh-huh."

"Well... whenever I get *real* scared, I whistle that song they usually associate with Lincoln."

"You mean *The Battle Hymn of the Republic*?"

He nodded.

"Why that particular one?"

"This may sound corny I suppose, but for me, it sorta puts things into perspective."

"That's not so corny," she laughed. "It certainly beats Jim's whiskey."

They walked on for awhile. Then Peg asked, "How long will it be before your plane is ready to fly again?"

"First part of spring, I hope."

"When you get it all fixed, do you think you could show me some of those clouds?"

"I think so," he said.

When Dusty had sufficiently recovered, he moved back to his hotel room.

In the isolated small towns they visited throughout the country, barnstormers provided thousands of people with their first glimpse of an airplane. These gypsy pilots carried about them a certain mystique. Coming from the outside world, they were hero-worshipped by the young lads and adored by their older sisters. But there were also those who regarded these fliers with distrust and suspicion, particularly local peace officers who would often threaten them with jail if they didn't move on.

Dusty learned early in the game to be wary of uniforms and badges.

He was awakened by an early morning knock on the door. When it turned out to be Sheriff Gaines, Dusty wondered what kind of trouble he had gotten himself into.

"Uh - can I help you," he stuttered.

"Mind if I come in?" asked the older man.

He took off his hat and sat down on the flimsy chair. "I understand you're the fella who cracked his plane up at the fair last fall."

"That was me," Dusty replied. "Dumb chuckhole."

"How're the repairs comin'?"

"Just about finished."

"Then it's ready to go?"

"Should be. I've been waitin' for the weather to clear so I could take it up for a test run - you know - check out the riggin' and stuff. Then I'll be outta here to rejoin my friends."

Dusty was now curious about the direction in which these questions were going. Gaines got straight to the point.

"Son... I guess you heard about the problem we got in Kayesville."

Dusty nodded. "It's been the talk all over town the last couple of days."

"We may need your help." The sheriff then went on to explain to him what he had in mind.

Dusty looked at him in bewilderment. "I've never really done that kinda stuff before."

"I saw you drop 'em at the fair."

"That's different. Those were made with flour. Nothin' big and cumbersome like you're talkin' about. It would have to be carried outside the cockpit."

"My people would help you build it. I've had experience in these things."

"Have you ever dropped a bomb?" Dusty asked.

"Seen it in the movies. I'll admit it's more your line of work than mine, but it's the explosives I'm talkin' about."

"Please!" Dusty exclaimed raising his hands. "That word alone makes me shudder!"

Gaines' face now turned grim. "Our town's in grave danger, boy, and you're our only hope of savin' it and possibly many lives along with it too!"

"But what about the big berm you guys are buildin'?"

"We hope it'll hold, but mainly we're just buyin' time. We were countin' on the spring thaw to break it up, but now it don't seem likely that's gonna happen anytime soon. The water's gettin' higher and higher and the pressure's buildin' up. We don't think it'll hold much longer."

Dusty was silent. He walked over to the window and looked out. "I don't know," he said. "I'll have to go out and have a look-see before I could even make a *guess* what to do."

"Well what are we waitin' for," said Gaines. "Let's go!"

Chapter 3

1973

It was a few minutes past two in the morning. The nurse posted to watch over him had fallen asleep.

He began to stir. Slowly turning his head one way and then the other, he tried to determine the direction of the beeping sound. Slowly his eyes opened, straining to accustom themselves to the light. His attention then fixed upon the strange wave pattern on the blue screen. Never having encountered an EKG oscilloscope monitor before, he had no idea as to its purpose.

Beginning with the bottle suspended above his bed, he tracked the course of the intravenous tube leading to the gauze patch on his left arm. Next he noticed the wide Velcro tape strapped around his right arm with a mysterious bunch of wires and tubes leading out to all directions.

Then he slowly looked around the room, first to the door, and then toward the window with its curtains drawn. When his eyes focused on the young woman peacefully snoozing in her chair, at first he hesitated to disturb her.

But as his mind cleared and he became more awake, his curiosity soon intensified over his strange surroundings.

"Hello," he whispered.

She did not respond. He tried again.

"Uh… hi."

Her eyes popped open.

"Y-you're awake!" She cried.

He was puzzled at her sudden burst of excitement.

"Don't go away!" she stammered. "I have to get the colonel! I'll be back."

A second later she popped her head through the doorway. "Stay right there," she motioned with her hand. "He'll be here in just a few minutes."

"Where am I," he asked.

"The doctor will answer your questions."

"But you said 'colonel'."

"Please," she insisted, "Just be patient." She remained there holding the door open, anxiously looking down the hall.

Soon a thin, taciturn looking man in his late fifties entered.

"That's fine, Lieutenant," he said formally. "I can take it from here. Did you tell him anything?"

"No sir," she replied dutifully. "As I mentioned, he just woke up."

"Good," said the colonel as he studied the chart by the bed. He turned to the patient. "I'm Doctor Reardon. I'd like to ask you a few questions."

He then pushed the button on a small electronic device on top of the bureau.

"What's that," asked the patient.

"It's a tape recorder."

"What does it do?"

Reardon and the nurse glanced at each other.

"It records our conversation," he replied. "Shall we begin?"

"Sure. Go ahead."

"What's your name?"

"Dervin... Dusty Dervin."

"Where are you from?"

"You probably never heard of it; it's a small town outside of Muncie."

"Muncie, Indiana?"

"That's right."

"How old are you, Dusty?"

"Thirty."

"And what do you do for a living?"

"I'm a pilot."

Reardon paused a moment to jot down some notes.

"How do you feel right now?"

"A little groggy," Dusty replied. "I think I had too much sleep."

The nurse pressed her fingers to her lips to suppress a giggle.

"And I'm hungry as hell," he added. "What are these dumb tubes in my arm for?"

"Don't worry about that," assured Reardon. "We'll remove them shortly. I'd like to ask you one final question and then we'll be through for now."

He looked up at Dusty.

"What year is this?"

The pilot, curious at the triviality of the question, replied, "Nineteen Thirty-One."

With the successful outcome of the project assured, Johns now felt like someone whose white elephant had suddenly turned into a gold mine. His agency, having accomplished one of the greatest scientific feats of all time, stood to gain a badly needed shot in the arm.

But Johns was not ready for the sudden onslaught of publicity this was certain to bring. He needed time to go over all the implications and feared that premature disclosure to the news media could cause matters to quickly get out of hand.

Abrams had been his biggest threat, but with the successful outcome of the recovery, he was now out of the picture. Scientists outside of their fields were fools, Johns believed, and getting rid of him had proven easier than expected. Abrams had demonstrated the practical value of his inductor; with this done he was no longer needed. He accepted Johns' offer of early retirement in return for a waiver of any claims to possible rights to the project. In reality, both men knew that Abrams had no leg to stand on. The government had financed the entire development, and any attempts to contest it would involve long and costly litigation which the scientist was certain to lose. What's more, as Johns had correctly guessed, Abrams was tired of the politics and was anxious to put it all behind him.

Johns then issued a directive classifying the Revival Project Top Secret. Any disclosure of information would be based on a strict need to know. Ostensibly this seemed a legitimate concern. In reality it would become a license to steal.

Johns' console buzzed.

"Yes?"

"Dr. Verneer is here, sir," the receptionist replied.

"Good. Send him in."

Ronald Verneer was a psychiatrist. In his early forties, he was small, slightly built, and wore dark-rimmed glasses.

"I've gone over this preliminary report of yours," Johns began, "and I find little of it relevant to the matter at hand."

"But it's the only material I could find which even begins to approach what we've got here."

"What? POW's and their problems of readjustment to society? That hardly fits here. There are no parallels at all."

"Why isn't it appropriate, sir?"

"Because all throughout their captivity they were still living out their lives. True, they had to adjust to the deplorable rotten conditions of confinement, poor food and so on, but their minds were still functioning and their clocks were still ticking. We have here what amounts to a time warp. This guy flies along, fat, dumb and happy, then all of a sudden his engine quits. He lands on a glacier, walks away and falls into a hole. Suddenly the lights go out! No readjustment… no nothing. Complete limbo. Forty-two years pass and suddenly the lights come on. We have here a whole new dimension added to the field of culture shock, and we have a chance to get in on the ground floor!"

"Shall we start with the standard battery of personality and aptitude tests?"

"Yes," Johns agreed, "but I want special emphasis placed on the degree of his skill retention."

"I understand, General. I'll put together a syllabus right away."

"Good. And Verneer, I want a total lid kept on this. Since nothing of this nature has ever happened before, no one is more qualified than we are to exploit the possibilities here."

"Before we proceed any further..." cautioned Reardon, "I must remind you that you are no longer in Alaska in 1931. You are now in Los Angeles and it is 1973. You will see a world entirely different from the one you knew, and the changes will come upon you all at once. Do you think you are ready for all this now?"

"No better time to find out," replied Dusty. His muscles weak from years of atrophy, he was assisted to the window by Reardon and the nurse.

What he saw left him dumbstruck. The tangled serpentine ribbons of interconnecting freeways and the clutter of towering skyscrapers overwhelmed him - a far cry from the narrow two-way dirt roads and two-story false front and brick buildings he was familiar with.

His mouth hung agape as he saw a DC-9 Jetliner parading overhead on a landing approach. The immense size, the swept-wing configuration and the whining engines without propellers looked to him like an alien spaceship. As it continued its descent, it was soon followed by the giant Boeing 747.

Dusty suddenly felt faint.

"I think we'd better get you back to the bed," Reardon said, supporting his upper arm. "There'll be time for you to explore all this when you feel more up to it."

A few days later a tall man in his early forties entered the hospital room. With graying blond hair and a three-piece suit, he looked as though he could've been a model for Macy's.

"Dusty... Ken Reynolds," he smiled, offering his hand. "I work in Public Relations at the ICR. I imagine the past few days have been pretty overwhelming for you."

"You might say that," Dusty replied.

"Do you understand any better now what's happened to you?"

"Bits and pieces. They tell me I spent the last forty-odd years in an ice pack."

"That's right, Dusty. You're an incredibly lucky man. You were found at just the right time. In a manner of speaking, you're quite a celebrity."

The pilot looked down at his bed sheet. "I don't think so," he said glumly. "I'm afraid I gotta lotta catchin' up to do."

"Well, you really are. And we're here to help you learn your way around and ease your transition into this new world."

"There seem to have been quite a few changes since I last had a look at things."

"They're not all bad," reassured Reynolds. "As soon as the doctors say its okay, we'll check you out of here and into a hotel. You'll love the pool, the weight room and the Jacuzzi."

"Ja - *what?*"

Reynolds laughed. "I guess there'll be quite a few new words you'll be adding to your vocabulary as well."

Dusty paused for a moment to collect his thoughts. "Why are you doing all this," he asked.

"Why… you're going to be famous," Reynolds proclaimed. "You've been through an experience which no one else has ever undergone. We want to learn all about its effect on you… what the world looks like to you."

But the pilot was skeptical. "I'm sure there are plenty of old men around who can tell you just about anything you want to know about that sort of thing."

"True," answered Reynolds, "…but as they've grown old their objectivity has been compromised by having witnessed and participated in all the many changes which have taken place over such a length of time. However with you, it's going to be the sudden impact of a half-century of the most profound developments in the history of mankind!"

As Reynolds left the hospital he stopped by a telephone.

"Yes, General… so far so good. He's still befuddled by it all. It'll be interesting to see his reaction when we show him around LA and some of the regular tourist stuff… Yes, General… I'll have it all written up in my report."

As Dusty lay awake, the nighttime stillness only intensified his sense of loneliness. In his day he was quite an adventurer, flying off to distant points, meeting new people and discovering new horizons. He was right at home in a meadow, sleeping under the wing of his plane beneath a summer sky. That was his world, his element.

Chapter 3

But now he found himself in a strange new world, cut off from all he had ever known. And what loomed largest in his mind was the haunting realization that from this journey he would never return.

Chapter 4

1922

Dusty and Gaines walked along the dike of sandbags which now extended for half a mile as scores of men continued building and reinforcing it.

What the pilot saw filled him with utter shock. Downriver from the ice jam, the water flowed in a modest stream. Behind it the river was backed up and swollen into a giant lake. The rushing water formed spillways on either side of the jam. The strong treacherous currents made it impossible to row out to the ice, plant the dynamite, rig the detonation wires, and make it back safely.

"How much time you figure we got," asked Dusty.

"Can't tell for sure," Gaines replied. "A few days at most."

Dusty walked out to the edge, his eyes slowly studying the scene. His face turned grim at the magnitude of what he saw before him.

After several minutes, Gaines joined him. "Well, whaddya think?"

"Don't know yet," the pilot replied while rubbing his hands to keep the circulation going.

"Let's get some coffee," suggested the sheriff.

They sidestepped down the embankment and proceeded to an old army tent. There Gaines lit a lantern and closed the flap.

On a small folding table he revealed his plan. He knew a local ordnance expert who could construct two bombs from twenty-gallon milk cans containing powder from the dynamite. The plan was simple and straightforward. One bomb would be mounted under each wing to be dropped and detonated on impact. Dusty, intimate with the constraints and limitations of his Jenny, set about figuring out how to implement this.

It would be risky at best. There would be barely sufficient ground clearance beneath the lower wings, so the makeshift runway would have to be smooth. There must be no bumps during takeoff that could jar the bombs loose. A special quick release mechanism, which could be activated from the cockpit, would have to be built. It had to be simple to use, particularly in subfreezing weather where it would be operated with heavy gloves.

When they finished, Gaines took the plan to Mayor Hobbs, who turned out to have some misgivings of his own.

"Twenty?" exclaimed Hobbs. "You say he's only *twenty?*"

"Well, yes Judd," Gaines explained, "...but I saw him at an airshow, and he looked like he knew what he was doin'."

"But he cracked up."

"Hit a chuckhole... could've happened to anybody. Anyway he says his plane's jest about fixed up and he's waitin' for the weather to clear so's he can rejoin his buddies."

"I don't know," Hobbs said shaking his head. "What we *don't* need right now is some dumb fool kid blowin' everybody to Kingdom Come!"

"What choice do we have, Judd? You said yourself the levee ain't gonna hold much longer. That aerial bomb thing's the only chance we got, and he's the only one around who can pull it off."

"What if it don't work, Ed?"

"At least we can't say we didn't give it a try."

Gaines motioned Dusty to the mayor's tent.

"Ed here seems to think maybe you can help us out," said Hobbs.

"It might work, sir," the pilot replied. He felt awkward in the presence of men old enough to be his grandfather, expecting at any moment to be tossed out of the tent for wasting their time.

"Do you think you can have your machine ready in time?" asked Hobbs.

"It's practically ready now," said the pilot, "once we fit out the bomb release."

The mayor rose from his chair, walked over to the front of the tent and pulled back the flap. He looked out among scores of people - many of whom were old friends and their sons and grandsons - pitching in with all they had and contributing to a massive effort, all stemming from their unshaken faith in his judgment.

It was a curious contrast of two generations. Dusty saw in Hobbs a man with his back to the wall, forced to lead his people on a course for which the outcome was uncertain.

To these older men who had spent the majority of their lives in the horse and buggy era, Dusty was a mere boy, a bit naïve perhaps, but willing to risk his life for an unproven idea.

"Young man," Hobbs said, "if you need any help, just ask. That Ford over there is yours for as long as you need it." Then the mayor rose and offered his hand. "All I can do for you now is wish you good luck."

Dark gray thunderheads began to gather. With the river channel blocked like it was, a sudden downpour could push the pressure on the levee to the bursting point at any moment.

From the moment she found out what Dusty was planning to do, Peg was not in favor of it. The idea of playing around with explosives in a tricky flying machine under treacherous weather conditions filled her with grim foreboding.

"So even if this thingamajig works and you *don't* wind up getting yourself killed," she argued, "…what do you think you're going to get out of it - a pat on the back?"

"There's a lot of lives involved."

"And you think this will make a difference! I'm not sure you've gotten over that *bump* on your head!"

"It's the only chance they've got," he insisted.

"You know what I think? I think you've got one of those strange delusions of glory! You want to be a war hero… that's really what this is about, isn't it! Well if you want glory, I'll show you the Victory Monument in the cemetery! I knew personally several of the names on it! I'll introduce you to their families! *They'll* tell you all about *glory!*"

This made it all the more difficult for him. His tone now took on a gravity that seemed to add to his years.

"I can't back out now, Peg," he explained. "I've made a commitment to these people."

She looked at him as though he had taken leave of his senses. "I can't deal with this," she said. Then she abruptly got up from the table and stormed out of the kitchen.

The next day found him shuttling back and forth between Kayesville and the barn. He had designed a pair of quick release devices for the milk cans, and then determined the refinements needed to handle the additional weight and balance. In addition he had to implement a pair of restraints to ensure that the bombs would not vibrate or tear loose in flight.

He lay sprawled beneath the lower wing taking some measurements when he heard a voice from above.

"Need some help?"

Dusty looked up toward the main door where he saw a tall rugged looking man wearing a long leather jacket and boots.

"JIM!" he shouted as he jumped to his feet to greet his friend. "Boy am I glad to see you! What're you doin' down here?"

"Came to see how bad that bump on your head was comin' along," Jim said. "Won't be long before we hit the trail again." He examined the Jenny closely. "Looks like you've done pretty well here - hey, what's this," he said as he stooped to examine the restraints.

"It's a long story," Dusty explained. Then he began to brief him as they set off for dinner.

Jim Higgins was a flier's flier. Twenty-eight years old, he had flown in the Great War and had a reputation for daring and skill unsurpassed. It was he who had transformed Dusty from a bumbling novice to a competent aviator who had come to master his plane as an extension of himself.

At the cafe, Jim brought Dusty up to date about what the other members of the gang were doing. This latest news of his comrades came like a ray of sunshine in this gloomy and seemingly endless winter.

Then they got down to business. Dusty took a paper napkin and drew a map of Kayesville, the river and the ice jam. Jim went over it for several minutes slowly nodding his head as he went along. Then the junior pilot reached into his shirt pocket and produced a piece of paper showing his calculations for weight and balance.

"Looks good," Jim nodded as he went over them.

Dusty felt a sense of pride at having the soundness of his approach confirmed by someone whose opinion he so highly valued.

Jim then took Dusty's sketch and made two tiny dashes on it. "This here restrainin' bolt's a good idea, only I'd use two of 'em just in case one fails. You can pull two pins just as quick as one."

Dusty soon had another reason to smile when he saw Peg walk through the door; she was no longer mad with him. Both men rose to offer her a seat.

"You must be the famous Jim Higgins I've heard so much about," she said admiringly.

Jim blushed, for he could quickly see that she was a class above any woman he'd ever known.

She asked how his Christmas was. Jim replied that he had spent it with some friends, then went on to relate the experiences he and Dusty shared in the various towns they visited. Dusty enjoyed hearing his adventures related in the words of someone else, as if they enhanced his own credibility.

"So when does this tour start," she asked. "Ever since I've met him, Dusty has hardly spoken of anything else!"

"Soon enough, I'm afraid - that is, once we get done with this little show here."

The evening passed pleasantly. Jim looked at his watch; it was almost ten. He sensed that Dusty and Peg wanted to be alone. "It's gettin' kinda late," he said rising from his chair, "...and I've got a few things to check on." He threw a quarter on the table. "This should take care of it." Then he turned to Peg and added, "It's been a real pleasure t'meet you."

"Me too, Jim," she smiled.

"Your friend seems very nice," Peg commented on the way home. "Looks like you're going to have some help now."

"Yeah, I could sure use it. It came as quite a surprise when he dropped in."

Peg fell silent for a moment, her eyes fixed on the sidewalk.

"I don't think he just dropped in, Dusty."

The pilot looked at her curiously. "What do you mean?"

"When I asked him about Christmas, he seemed a little anxious to change the subject."

"I didn't notice that."

"I guess maybe a girl senses these things more than a guy does," she said. "He didn't want to talk about it because... well, I don't think he had much to talk about."

"That sounds almost like a riddle," he said.

"No... actually it's very sad. He didn't speak of any family - or for that matter any friends - just business relationships. He has no real home to speak of, so he just hops around. I don't see a dashing daredevil, Dusty. I see a very lonely man."

Such wisdom from one so young, Dusty observed. "Peg, you never cease to amaze me."

"You wouldn't want to know all my secrets now, would you," she said with a wink. Then she turned serious once more. "You know Dusty... when Jim came here, you showed him something he hasn't found in a long time."

"What's that?"

"A sense of purpose. He's needed now."

The magnitude of what lay ahead had weighed heavily on Dusty's mind, causing him to often wonder if perhaps he had gotten in over his head. The expectations of so many people and the realization of the dangers involved were beginning to take their toll on him, and Jim's arrival on the scene provided a tremendous relief.

Events now proceeded rapidly. The two pilots drove out to the site where Jim could inspect the situation for himself.

Jim took charge of the overall part of the operation, and under his supervision, volunteers arrived the following day with tractors, pickaxes and shovels. When they were finished, the area adjacent to the barn was transformed into a small airstrip. A taxiway led from the barn to a runway, smoothed, leveled and covered with duckboards.

With ground conditions no longer a major problem, the fliers set about testing their aircraft. They rolled out their machines - fitted with milk cans of the approximate weight of the bombs - out of the hangar.

As they lumbered to the runway, the two bi-winged creatures of sticks and cloth intertwined with miles of wire, looked like giant prehistoric bugs fishtailing one way and then the other to see where they were going.

The clatter of Jim's OX-5 engine grew louder as he eased the throttle forward. The Jenny's awkwardness began to disappear as it picked up speed. The tail popped up and soon this spidery box kite assumed an air of grace as it lifted off to begin its ascent to the sky. Dusty's plane followed right behind him.

They selected as a practice target a fallen oak tree, gnarled and twisted like the ice jam itself. Before long, they became experts in precision bombing as they homed in, dropped the milk cans and returned to the airfield to do it all again. Accuracy and wind effect had to be taken into account since the makeshift devices were to be dropped from a height sufficient to protect the pilots and planes from the blasts. The top speed of the Jenny was about 75 miles per hour. With the expected headwinds and the added drag of the bombs it would be a lot less. Therefore the pilots would have to come in high in order to compensate for being slow.

Jim was in cheerful spirits that night. On the way to the hotel, puffing his cigar, he remarked to Dusty, "You've done pretty well for yourself, kid. If we can pull this here thing off we could come out lookin' like real heroes. This could be our break into the *big* time!"

"I thought what we've been doin' at the county fairs *was* big time."

"Nah," Jim shrugged. "That's all a big circus! I'm talkin' about *real* stuff!"

"The War? The airmail? That seemed like pretty real stuff to me."

"Just the beginning. All the War proved was that airplanes can be used to kill people. Airmail? That's still in the toy stage. In fact this whole airplane thing's a big toy to most folks. That's what brings 'em to see us. But Y'know Dusty, barnstormin' won't last forever. I'd give it maybe another year or two. Then it's gonna be old hat just like those wild west shows. If we hope to continue makin' a buck in this business, we gotta be open to new angles."

"Like what?"

"Transportation... that's the first thing that comes to mind. Eventually they'll be buildin' planes to carry lotsa people like trains do. And when that time comes, we gotta be ready for it... you know...be in on the ground floor. And when the big-money guys are ready to step in, they're gonna want pilots with proven experience. They're gonna want guys like us."

There had been a big thunderstorm that night, but by morning it had largely dissipated.

Jim felt that one more practice run would do it.

Once again the rickety aircraft clattered down the runway, rising off into the dark gray sky. At four hundred feet, they began a gentle left turn towards the river.

It was like old times. They were in their element once again, flying over the patchy quilt work of snow-covered farms. Dusty squinted through his goggles scanning the horizon for the fallen tree. When he sighted it he turned to signal Jim.

Jim's plane was gone!

Dusty looked around and, about a mile back, spotted his friend's Jenny in a descending spiral. Engine quit, he muttered to himself as he banked into a steep turn and headed over there.

Engine failure in flight was a common occurrence and Jim knew what to do. After jettisoning the milk cans, he set up his glide, took into account the wind effects and available altitude, and then he picked out a spot to land. Over flat farm terrain like this, he expected no problem.

Suddenly out of nowhere, two small children chasing their dog darted directly into the path where Jim had committed to land! He spotted them and quickly shoved his plane into a hard left turn. But for a Jenny – particularly one overloaded with the modifications it carried - there was very little difference between the glide speed and the minimum speed at which she would fly. The plane went into a stall and violently pitched its left wing down, cartwheeled into the ground and exploded, killing Jim instantly.

The children ran screaming to their farmhouse while Dusty circled helplessly, staring in horrified shock at the blazing pyre below.

Chapter 5

1973

The briefing was scheduled for 0900. Present in addition to Johns and Dusty were Halleck, Reynolds, Verneer, and Reardon.

For the pilot's benefit, Johns had hoped to project an informal and relaxed atmosphere, but the inherent rigidity in their collective manner made any such pretense impossible.

In his characteristically clipped style, the director explained to Dusty how well he understood the problems facing the pilot, and how overwhelming the events of the preceding days must be. Johns went on to add that if Dusty needed help of any kind, all he had to do was ask.

"You have been through an experience no one else has ever undergone," he began. "You have come to us directly from a distant time, a time when the modern technologies as we know them were in their infancy.

"These changes which have evolved across several decades must seem to you sudden and abrupt. We want to understand - in so many words - how you are experiencing these changes, ah... cold turkey."

Dusty noticed a peculiar mannerism of Johns. The general would periodically flash a forced smile which would then just as quickly disappear as he went on.

"The course we have planned to ease you through your transition is threefold. *[smile]* First, there's the Psychological Evaluation. From this we expect to obtain an accurate picture of your - ah - perspective. *[smile]* This phase will be conducted through a series of sessions under the guidance of Dr. Ronald Verneer, one of the leading experts in his field. *[smile]*

"You will also attend a series of seminars which will cover the historical/political developments which have taken place since your – ah, disappearance. This will be your History Briefing Phase. *[smile]*

"Phase Three is the one which will probably be your favorite. *[smile]*

We want to determine to what degree you have retained your flying skills and overall dexterity. Towards this end we have arranged a series of tests in an actual aircraft."

The director then shifted to other more urgent concerns.

"Right now we have some papers for you to sign. Since we do not yet understand all the legal ramifications of your return, we have decided to keep the true nature of your circumstances under wraps for the time being. There will be no disclosure to anyone outside this room of anything concerning your past.

"We have assembled a personal dossier to which all matters pertaining to your background will be referred. You will sign these receipts acknowledging a birth certificate, high school diploma, driver's license, and private pilot's certificate. In addition, there's another paper to sign which indicates that you understand these terms and agree to abide by them.

"In short," concluded Johns, "you will still be Dusty Dervin. However, since you were thirty years of age when you disappeared, you will officially be that same age now that you have - ah - reentered life." *[smile]*.

Dusty now had a question of his own.

"The papers I had with me... - what's happened to them?"

An uneasy feeling came over the others present, for they knew that their boss was not accustomed to being questioned.

"We are keeping them for further study," replied Johns.

"How come?" Dusty asked.

"It will complicate what we have to do if the true nature of your identity is revealed at this time," answered the director. "Too many channels will have to be crossed."

To Dusty this didn't make sense. However nothing really made sense to him at this point, so he simply gave a shrug as an indication of acceptance.

"You will be given the designation of Test Engineer," Johns added. "If anyone asks either about you or what you're supposed to be involved with here, you will answer only in accordance with the references provided you."

"You're wrong about him," Reynolds told Dusty over lunch. "He's really quite remarkable once you get to know him."

"I'm not sayin' he isn't," replied the pilot. "He just strikes me as a bit rigid, that's all."

"If you had all the responsibilities he has of running a big organization like this, I think you would be, too."

Just then the hostess appeared.

"Has your order been taken?" she asked.

"No, not yet," Reynolds replied. "Have they got you on double duty again, Donna?"

"'Fraid so," she nodded. "We have an unusually large crowd today."

As she took down their order, Dusty could not help notice her sandy colored hair and blue eyes.

"You from the Midwest?" he asked.

"Why yes," she smiled. "Is it my accent?"

"Illinois, right?"

"No, Iowa."

"Bet you miss all that snow."

"Hardly," she laughed. "I'll be right back."

Reynolds took notice. "You're doing pretty good," he mused. "Our chief pilot couldn't get to first base with her."

Dusty's thoughts returned on the matters at hand.

"I'm still not sure what they want me to do," he said.

"Don't worry. It'll all fall into place before you know it. It's a new experience for everybody. They're not merely interested in what you know... they just want to know how you react to this radically changed world you've returned to."

Dusty had heard of Freud before, but psychoanalysis was for the most part a concept alien to him. Aside from sketchy accounts of wealthy people going to Europe for it, he had mainly come to associate it with treatment of the insane.

Reynolds tried to reassure the pilot by describing it as merely another branch of medicine like surgery. A psychiatrist, he explained, was after all a doctor of medicine and, as such, could help Dusty sort through his fears and concerns about this strange situation in which he found himself.

From the very beginning however, things got off on the wrong foot.

The psychiatrist began with the standard personality tests. To Dusty they made no sense whatsoever. He was asked to interpret ink blots, differentiate among similar pictures, determine word relationships, and invent stories about pictorial scenes shown to him. Verneer also probed him with questions of a personal nature, such as concerning his relationship with his mother and father, and also politics, morality and sex. Dusty's responses were jotted down in a notebook Verneer kept.

Although Verneer liked to ask questions, he didn't seem to like to answer any. As the session went on, Dusty grew more curious about how the information he was providing would be used. But whenever he would ask Verneer any questions, the latter would fend them off with evasive responses like, "Why do you want to know?" or "How is this relevant?", or even more abrasively, *"I'll ask the questions here!"*

It wasn't long before Dusty came to see the psychiatrist as a man hiding behind the trappings of his position, yet wary of giving away anything which might betray his own insecurities.

The pilot didn't like what he considered this "one-way business". He was especially concerned over what Verneer was writing about him in those notes he kept. It all came to a head when Verneer refused to show Dusty any of his notes or recorded tapes. A heated argument ensued, and Dusty got up and walked out of Verneer's office.

The historical briefing put together by Johns consisted of the general's favorite film documentaries from television. Dusty was tested on his comprehension following the completion of each session to determine his mental retention.

The Great Depression was presented as a period of major economic upheaval and civil unrest. This really hit home to Dusty, who had personally witnessed several foreclosures and evictions which had involved his friends and neighbors. The bitterness of those days was still fresh in his mind, and he bit his lip as he saw it all come back on the screen.

He saw old newsreels of the Bonus March and the big auto strikes of the day. The footage of the mobs of police and the army scattering demonstrators raised in him intense feelings of anger. For although these events had taken place after he had gone, it had long been a sore point with Dusty as to how a so-called free society could unleash such brutal force on its own citizens driven to desperation by hardship and misfortune.

Although the period of the thirties had held the most personal significance for him, the greatest emphasis in the briefing was on World War II. The great battles, technological advancements and leading personalities of the period were covered in great depth. Pearl Harbor ushered in a time of trial and testing from which this country emerged to its present position of world leadership. No other conflict, before or since, so clearly delineated good from evil.

Dusty was especially fascinated by the role and development of airpower. The Flying Fortresses fighting their way to the enemy targets and back, and the bravery and determination of their crews held a special fascination for him. He felt a twinge of regret at having missed out on what he considered the peak of Aviation's Golden Age.

Then came 1945 - the year the War ended. It was the year that changed the world forever. The horrible revelations of Hitler's death camps filled Dusty with shock and revulsion. He was especially shaken when he learned of the Atomic Bomb and the advances in guided missiles.

"So it's finally come to this," he said to himself, sadly shaking his head.

To Dusty the shopping mall seemed like a gigantic amusement park. The endless assortment of shops and merchandise was a far cry from the small downtown stores he was more familiar with.

He was especially intrigued by the pushbutton world of electronics. The dancing blue display lights of a stereo receiver mesmerized him. The television and stereophonic sounds emanating from them convinced him they were live and nearby.

As the intrepid aviator and navigator, he found it embarrassing when he got lost among the multitiered maze of floors and causeways.

The one store which intrigued him most was the Antique & Collector's Shoppe. Here he could find many familiar objects from his day. It puzzled him why the wooden wall phones, victrolas and coffee grinders commanded such high prices when these items were considered commonplace, but again they served as yet another painful reminder that the world from which these came, like his own, was a long time ago.

His curiosity took him on a study of far greater depth than that provided by the briefings. Artifacts of the period immediately following his disappearance awakened a deep interest into the "Lost Years."

In a souvenir magazine from the 1939 World's Fair, he saw pictures of the optimistic smiling faces of men and women looking toward a bright future. Did they go on to realize these dreams, he wondered. Or had the Second World War and the passing years taken them away?

As Dusty sought to piece together the world he had missed out on, one magazine story led to another, providing him added insight on the lives of the people of his generation who had walked their way and were now mostly gone.

On a corner table stood an old radio. Age had blackened the badly scratched finish, and the filigree in front of the tattered speaker grille cloth was now split and broken.

"Where'd you get this," Dusty asked the lady behind the counter.

"It was part of an estate sale," she replied. "Just came in. We haven't had a chance to send it out for restoration."

"It's a Philco," he observed.

"That's right... a Philco Cathedral."

He looked at her curiously. "What did you call it?"

"A cathedral... It reminds folks of a church."

"Oh... They used to call it a Baby Grand because you could carry it around from room to room."

"If I tried that I'd get a hernia," she remarked.

"How much do you want for it," he asked.

"Oh... considering its condition... I'd say fifty'll do."

Dusty was astounded. "*Fifty*! That's what they used to cost new! I'll bet this one doesn't even *work*!"

"Be twice that if it did. A fully restored one'll fetch two hundred easily."

He closely scrutinized this relic which had once been the centerpiece of some family's living room. What historic broadcasts had emanated through its now battered grille? How many years had the innards of this walnut cabinet served as their sole contact with the outside world? He would make it new again and, in so doing, bring a part of his own past back to life.

To get around town, Dusty rented a car, thus beginning his introduction to one of the most prominent icons of contemporary life. It was a Plymouth, fairly basic as cars went, but to him it was a major quantum leap from anything he was familiar with. Missing were the choke and spark adjustment controls, and since it was equipped with an automatic transmission, so was the clutch pedal.

In addition to the streamlined design, Dusty couldn't get over the handling. The steering was effortless and, with the state of the art suspension system, the car seemed to float down the highway. In the old Model A which he was used to, it was a major effort to get it up to 30 or 40 miles per hour. The Plymouth, however, could easily attain twice that speed in about ten seconds.

Nothing in Dusty's background could have prepared him for his first experience on the Los Angeles Freeway.

He was taking one of his exploratory trips. Everything seemed to be going well until he merged into traffic, when all hell suddenly broke loose.

Flying was one thing; driving in 70 mile per hour traffic was another. In the air he was his own boss. On the freeway he soon came to see himself competing with maniacs in a fight for survival. Whenever he found it necessary to change lanes, he did so with trepidation as he looked behind him to make sure that nobody was speeding down the lane he was trying to enter, all the while hoping that, in the meantime, none of the vehicles in front of him suddenly slammed on its brakes.

He cautiously edged his way into the adjacent left lane and proceeded for several miles when, suddenly out of nowhere, a car cut right in front of him while making a multiple lane change so that he could make the next off ramp. Then another car came up behind him and blasted its horn, the driver of which gave Dusty a dirty look and flashed an invective gesture as he sped past him on the right.

Dusty saw it as a kind of dogfight. He decided that the safest thing to do was to pass any automobiles he encountered in clusters. This meant watching for the next clear opening, punching the accelerator when he found the hole, and zooming out of there until he encountered the next group.

The next vehicle he did battle with was a large 18-wheel semi rig with two trailers. It was by far the largest truck he had ever seen, and he found it daunting. As he was coming up alongside of it, he noticed the rear trailer swerving from side to side, and began to wonder if the driver knew what he was doing. He promptly took evasive measures to give the rig a wide berth and wasted no time putting the Kenworth behind him.

Finally, as the sign indicating the off ramp he was looking for came into view, he began to slow down to approach it when he suddenly heard a siren and looked up to spot the flashing red and blue lights in his rear view mirror.

When word of Dusty's speeding ticket got back to Johns, the general found it very amusing.

"This is very interesting," he said with a smirk. "It's a classic example of adjustment to modern day life."

"Do you want me to bring him up to date on our traffic laws," asked Reynolds.

"Certainly not. He's got to learn these things on his own. If we mollycoddle him, it'll compromise the scientific objectivity of the study. He's making a good salary; let him pay for his own mistakes. Nothing motivates a man to learn like hitting him in the old pocketbook." *[smile]*

It happened at that moment that Dusty was walking by and overheard the remark. It was not so much what Johns said but the way in which he said it that irked him, for the general was gloating over something at the pilot's expense - an interesting observation to note down in some sort of scientific experiment in which Dusty was the guinea pig.

Thus Dusty received his first inkling that perhaps the director did not have his best interests at heart.

A Cessna 172 was used for the flight proficiency evaluation. The objective of these tests was to determine the extent of which Dusty had retained his flying proficiency. A certified flight instructor, unaware of who Dusty was or the purpose behind the evaluation, was brought in.

The maneuvers were the standard basic ones required of a private pilot. Dusty quickly demonstrated that he had not lost his touch. For him it was just good to be back in the air again.

As the hours passed and his radio skills improved, Dusty began to acquire a unique perspective. This aircraft represented tremendous strides in the state of the art. He found it lighter, more responsive and more efficient in that it got greater performance for less horsepower. He also discovered that the radio equipment, largely undreamt of in his time, did most of the navigational work for him.

But the more he thought about it, the more he came to realize that he could not really compare this plane to a

Stinson or any of the other early types he had flown. Being from a different era, it reflected a different philosophy.

Instead of being flown by feel or the "seat-of-your-pants", it was designed to be flown by the numbers; adjust the throttle to 2250 rpm, set the rate of climb to zero, trim it - the airspeed turns out to be 102 knots - and you're in cruise configuration. Radio navigation followed a similar track; push a button, dial a frequency and center the needle. These were all procedures, and once executed, there was little else to do other than, of course, watch out for other air traffic.

One afternoon when Dusty got back from one of his flights, Reynolds hailed him in the hallway.

"Well, what do you think of our little airplane?"

"It's okay," he replied.

The lack of enthusiasm aroused Reynolds curiosity.

"What do you find missing," he asked.

Dusty reflected for a moment, and then he said,

"The feel of the wind."

Whenever Dusty worked on his old radio, he found a brief respite from the cloud which hung over him.

The old finish had been stripped away and the peeled veneer glued back into place, and Dusty fashioned a new filigree which blended in so well with the cabinet that one could not see where it was joined. Before long the radio stood resplendent in its new finish enhancing its natural walnut.

For all his skill at woodworking, however, the primitive electronics of his day proved too much for him so he took the chassis to a radio-TV repair shop.

The technician, a man in his early thirties, was intrigued by it.

"I haven't seen one of these in years," he remarked. "When was it built?"

"1930."

"They made some pretty good sets in those days. What's wrong with it?"

"When I turn it on, it just hums."

"Just hums? Nothing else?"

"Nope... Just hums."

The technician stood the chassis on its side, got out his test meter and began probing around the spaghetti-like maze of wires running every which way among the condensers and tube sockets. After several minutes he pulled back.

"Sorry," he said. "There's nothing I can do."

"Why not," Dusty said curiously. "Somethin' this old should be child's play for someone who works on all these TVs and modern gadgets."

"For one thing, I don't have a schematic to work from."

"But it's a basic TRF circuit."

"Look-," the technician admitted with some embarrassment, "I've never worked with this kind of stuff. Everything you've got on this chassis can be put on an integrated circuit the size of a matchbook. They don't replace tubes and condensers anymore. They simply replace the IC board."

"They just throw it out?"

"Yep. It's no longer worthwhile to take the time to go into the complexities of a circuit and try to fix it. Nowadays I just troubleshoot what's wrong, look the part number up in the catalogue, and replace it."

To Dusty this didn't make sense. He saw electronics, like aviation, as an evolution of progressive ideas and improvements, the culmination of trial and error. As he drove back to his apartment, he wondered how someone could earn a living repairing such advanced state of the art appliances as stereos and color television sets without even having the slightest understanding of how they got there.

Chapter 6

1922

Gaines went up the narrow stairway and turned down the dimly lit hall. When he came to Dusty's room he rapped on the door. There was no answer. The sheriff tried the knob, found it unlocked, and slowly opened the door. The pilot was sitting on the edge of his bed gazing numbly at the floor.

"There's a young lady out there askin' about you," he said.

Dusty gave not the slightest acknowledgement of the old man's presence.

Gaines walked over to the window and looked out.

"Sure'll be good when this weather breaks," he said. "Don't look like it much right now, but it won't be much longer. Before you know it spring'll be here and this whole thing'll be all behind us."

He then turned to Dusty.

"Y'know son... as you go through this life... sometimes you'll find long stretches where the goin's fairly smooth. You go to work every day, and you come home to your family at night. You watch your kids grow up and as the years go by, you come to accept it all as part of the natural order of things. You find a sort of comfort in it.

"Then one day somethin' *big* happens- an upheaval. Overnight a man can lose his farm, and everything he's worked for all his life goes down the drain. Or a loved one can suddenly be taken from him. And what makes it all the harder to accept is that there don't seem any reason for it. When my Emma passed away, I felt this big emptiness inside me for a long time, and I *still* really haven't gotten over it. Prob'ly never will 'cause I counted on her so much, and she was always there for me.

"But y'see Dusty, that too is part of life. Those of us who are left behind... we gotta pick up the pieces somehow and go on. And sometimes there just ain't time to mourn our losses or figure things out."

Gaines' tone now took on a sense of great urgency.

"Son... things ain't goin' so good now. The ice jam don't look like it's gonna melt. The water's gettin' higher and the levee we built can't hold it back much longer. Right now lotsa folks are packin' what they can and gettin' out. Others are tryin' to shore up the levee although we all know it's a lost cause. Damn it man, our back's to the wall!"

The old man picked up a chair, placed it near Dusty and sat down, his face only inches away from the young pilot's.

"We have a chance - not much of one I grant you - but it's the only one we got. Many lives are hangin' on it. They're in church, man... prayin' for some sort of miracle. And you're the only one who can make it happen.

"This is one o' them times we gotta put aside our own personal feelings for a greater purpose. Your buddy Jim would've understood this more'n anyone."

Dusty suddenly looked up at Gaines. There was anger in his eyes.

"What the hell do you know about him," he shot back. "To you he was just a bum none of you guys ever wanted around!"

Gaines slowly nodded. "Oh yes," he said, "...I knew him. Maybe not as well as you, but I know he must've been quite a guy. He went off to fight for his country and came back disillusioned like so many of 'em did, and he drifted back to the one thing he knew. Then one day he dropped in to see how his buddy was doin' and found out that some folks needed help. And when he found himself in a tight spot with them kids runnin' out in front of his plane-."

The old man's voice suddenly choked up and he had to pause for a moment before he could continue.

"He made a decision not many of us would be big enough to make."

Dusty could not sleep that night. His stomach was tied up in knots. Tossing and turning until exhausted, he found he was soaked with sweat. A bad taste hung in his mouth and when he took a glass down the hall to the bathroom for some water, his hand shook so much that it slipped, shattering to pieces on the floor. After returning to bed he just stared at the ceiling.

It was early dawn. A crowd of about 100 people had gathered some 200 yards from the barn, around which a dozen deputies formed a safety perimeter. They were all trying to keep warm by huddling around fires lit in trash cans; for cold as they were, nobody wanted to go inside.

Dusty was driven to a point just beyond the crowd.

He got out and was making his way to the barn when he heard the soft cry of his name.

Peg had come out in the chill to see him.

She saw a certain nobility about him, like a knight about to ride off into battle.

"Whatcha doin' here, Peggy," he said managing a smile. "You shouldn't be out in this cold."

"I couldn't sleep," she replied.

This made it all the more difficult for him. How could he reassure her when it was all he could do to hold down the gnawing fear that was tearing at his own insides?

"This ain't no big deal," he said. "Just a little old milk run. It won't take long."

Then taking her hands in his, he said, "You know little girl, you were right. This hero stuff ain't all it's cracked up to be."

"You already *are* a hero to me," she said. "Even if you choose to back out of it now, I don't think anyone would ever blame you."

"I would... every time I looked in a mirror."

"Dusty, I want you to have this," she said reaching into her heavy wool coat. She produced a little charm in the form of a terrier dog which she showed him, then pressed into his pocket.

They held each other tightly for a moment, and then she kissed him. He saw tears running down her cheeks. Then he once again looked into her eyes as though they were the last beautiful things on this earth that he would ever see.

Inside the barn his numbing fear intensified. Slowly and methodically he walked around the Jenny, scrutinizing every wire and bolt. He found nothing amiss, yet there remained that painful gnawing in the pit of his stomach.

He clumsily banged his leg on the side of the fuselage as he swung over into the rear cockpit. He pondered for a moment, mentally going over everything once more. Then with a haunting look, he gave a firm nod to the man in front of the plane.

Woody, the deputy who had drawn the short straw, swung the large propeller through a couple of times.

Dusty reached for a switch on the right side of the cockpit, which operated the booster spark coil.

"CONTACT!" shouted the pilot.

"CONTACT!" Woody replied. He swung the prop through again, this time jumping clear.

Nothing happened. Dusty turned off the switch and instructed him to realign the prop to get the best leverage.

Woody gave it another swing.

This time the OX-5 responded, coughing forth a cloud of oily smoke from the exhaust manifold. After several sputtery revolutions, the engine caught.

His task done, Woody bolted out the door.

The biplane slowly rolled out the barn bouncing along the taxiway. As it did so, Dusty continued to be haunted by a nagging doubt - had he forgotten anything? Was there a loose wire or nut he'd overlooked? He had gone over it all many times but the doubt would not go away. The carburetor had been adjusted. The valve rockers on the cylinders greased. But still he knew only too well that he hadn't eliminated that fatal probability; he had only reduced it.

When he got to the end of the runway he stopped to check the play in the ailerons and rudder.

He paused for a moment to reflect, taking one last look at the world around him, a final glimpse of peace and calm.

It had rained again during the night. Black thunderheads towered into the sky, their rumblings echoing like heavy guns. The level of the river was now just a few inches below the levee. A volunteer inspecting it spotted a leak. He no sooner turned to sound the alarm when the entire section suddenly gave way unleashing a massive torrent of water.

Dusty lowered his goggles. As he gently eased the throttle forward, the spidery crate began to roll. Slowly gaining speed, the Jenny began to weave from side to side until the aerodynamic forces of motion took effect. The tail rose first, then a few seconds later the plane itself lifted off. The right wing momentarily dipped, but Dusty quickly countered with opposite stick and the archaic-looking craft transformed itself into a graceful dragonfly as it ascended into the sky. Before long, its wings became two parallel lines growing smaller as they faded from view.

Kayesville now felt the full fury of the deluge surging through the streets. Entire buildings collapsed on themselves or smashed against one another. One house floated off its foundation and began to be carried away by the current when it lodged against a large oak tree. A man, his wife and their small son climbed out their attic window onto the front porch roof. Carrying the child in one arm the father reached onto a large tree limb and crawled his way along it to safety. Then with the little boy holding on for dear life, the man reached out beckoning his wife to climb onto the limb. With fear and hesitation she had no sooner begun to clutch onto it when the house suddenly shifted, causing her to lose her balance. She screamed as she plummeted into the raging torrent, and all her family could do was cry out in horror and watch helplessly as she was swept away.

Dusty banked his plane into a gentle right turn. He wanted to be high enough to afford the best choice of a landing spot in the event of an emergency, yet he also wanted to remain below the base of the clouds.

He could see the triple silo in the distance. The river wasn't far off.

The biting chill and rain penetrated the cockpit and his flight jacket. Lightening suddenly flashed off to his right and his heart leaped into his throat. Amidst the crashing thunder he began to whistle his beloved hymn, all the while praying that if the next bolt had his name on it, he would never know what hit him.

Hobbs stood outside his tent watching the destruction he had proved so powerless to prevent when a young volunteer ran up to him.

"Sir," announced the panting young man, "the plane took off a few minutes ago."

The mayor directed him to join the others up on safer ground, and then he ran down the levee where he yelled out to one of his deputies.

"Get that fire truck into position and have the man on the other side light that trash can! I want to see plenty of smoke!"

As he followed the course of the river, Dusty could barely make out Kayesville in the distance. His mind began to drift back to his county fair days when they would fly over the towns to herald their own arrival. He could almost hear the faint strains of the music from the band, and the wind whistling through the wires sounded like cheering!

He was now at 5000 feet. He looked over the side, and when he saw the raging floodwater below, it made his heart sink. The worst had happened and despite everyone's efforts, he was too late. He had raced against time and lost. With all the setbacks which had befallen him, there was nothing Dusty could have done to ready his plane any sooner, but this rationalization provided small consolation.

The bend was coming into view - and yes, he spotted the smoke signal! Now he could estimate the wind direction over the target.

As he approached the bend, Dusty entered a gentle right turn. The ice jam came into view. He was too high; he would have to get lower. A little lower and a little faster. He would have to make his drop from downwind. That would provide the best chance for a hit without getting caught in the blast that would follow.

Atop the fire truck a man began to crank the siren; its loud wail sent scores of men scrambling for cover.

Dusty spotted the breach in the dike and the raging water rushing through it. He set course for the ice jam, and when he got there he began to circle.

One shot. That's all he would have… just one shot!

He took a deep breath as he gently pushed the stick to the side, banking the Jenny as it entered into a steep dive. The pitch from the wind in the wires grew higher as the airplane picked up speed.

He exhaled and took another deep breath, then clenched his teeth as his right hand groped for the bomb release. His eyes focused on the target point!

The target was growing larger and closer! It would now require a mixture of intuition and experience to determine the release point. He slowly exhaled once again.

At the point guided by his instincts he pulled the release. He felt a reassuring snap as the bombs fell free.

Dusty pulled back on the stick and the Jenny began to come out of its dive. He then banked the Jenny into a steep turn to clear the area when he was rocked by a bone-rattling concussion!

The blast shook the ground like an earthquake, and for what seemed like several minutes, everyone remained under shelter. Presently a few individuals began to emerge and climb up the levee, where they saw a huge gap in the ice.

The bomb had hit its mark, but had it weakened the ice jam enough?

Presently a small trickle of water appeared. It began to grow until it became a gushing flow. Then suddenly a deep rumbling could be heard as the ice began to give way under the vengeful onslaught of the water it had so long pent up. Massive chunks of ice and debris broke loose and were carried away down the river.

The flow channeling through the breach in the dike gradually subsided. In a spontaneous outbreak of frenzied hysteria they waved their caps as they cheered at the top of their lungs.

Hobbs, however, was too exhausted to cheer. As he looked across the river at the muddy widespread havoc it had wreaked, he could be heard quietly muttering repeatedly, "He stopped it."

Dusty did not fly all the way back to Claremont. Instead he put down in a convenient cow pasture and rolled to a stop. He was totally exhausted, and right now, people were the last thing he wanted to see. He shut off the engine, pulled off his helmet and goggles, and buried his face in his hands. The tears flowed freely now. At last it was all over.

The clouds parted to reveal the rays of the sun. It was quiet now, just the wind. A gentle wind.

Chapter 7

1974

With the winding down of tasks connected with the initial phases of his transition, Dusty was assigned temporary work assisting various engineers with their projects. He found it boring. Logging data, interpreting strip charts, and reading computer printouts made little sense to someone not sufficiently grounded in modern technology.

As the months passed, he continued his struggle to put the pieces together. Coming from a world in which he had done everything for himself, he found it difficult adjusting to the complex bureaucratic web of channels and restrictions. He also found the overall atmosphere at the institute stuffy and artificial. Other than Johns and those immediately around him, no one else was aware of Dusty's background or the reasons for his being there. Those with whom he came in contact seemed patronizing or aloof, responding as briefly to his questions as required, and then scurrying off. At first he had regarded these highly educated people with awe but before long he came to perceive them as narrow minded specialists living and operating in their own little worlds.

Reading provided him one escape from the loneliness and boredom. From his research into the period following his disappearance, he gained an entirely different perspective from his indoctrination at the institute. While the briefings had provided him with a dry chronological high school level history, his own endeavors provided him an insight into how the people of two missing generations looked at themselves. Beginning with books and magazines, his explorations branched out into other aspects of the popular culture of the lost years: music, motion pictures, automobiles and fashions.

He found another outlet in the way he furnished his modest apartment. To the extent that he could, he transformed it into a small retreat from the modern world. In addition to the radio, he acquired a reproduction Tiffany lamp, victrola, pendulum wall clock, and other pieces similar to those he owned at the time he vanished.

Whenever he would crank up the victrola, the scratchy strains of music from a bygone time would evoke memories of distant places and old friends whom, for brief moments, he could almost see once again.

But inevitably his thoughts would return to a question which had haunted him since the moment he had awakened into this world:

What had become of his family?

He submitted a request for a month's leave of absence, and two days later was summoned to Verneer's office. The psychiatrist began by praising Dusty on the amazing progress he had made in his readjustment. The bouts of depression were recurring less frequently now, and soon the time would come when they would cease altogether. There was no doubt, assured the doctor, that this phenomenal progress was attributed to the plane of reference established through Dusty's work and his outside interests.

Verneer felt, however, that Dusty was not quite ready to handle the impact of half a century of change. Most of his friends and loved ones were gone by now, and any still remaining would no longer be as he remembered them. He would be young while they would be very old. Confronting this grim reality at this time could possibly trigger a severe mental setback. It would be better to wait a few months until he gained more self-confidence before taking on such a venture.

It was a nice speech. It may have been a bit out of character for the usually rigid doctor, but his logic did have merit. Perhaps it would be too much for him to handle at this stage. From the Great War Dusty had heard stories of returning veterans whose personal readjustments had taken several years. Furthermore, in light of his own unique set of circumstances, no one knew what complications there would be.

Dusty was disappointed in the limited extent to which the Flight Evaluation Series had been carried out. This project turned out to be nothing more than a checkout in the Cessna 172 and the radio navigational equipment, and the purpose of it turned out to be nothing more than to toss out a few crumbs for him.

Soon he began to develop his own ideas about the Evaluation. Seeing the potential value and importance to these tests, he submitted a report to Johns outlining his own ideas about them. He defined two main objectives: determination of skill retention following over forty years of suspended animation, and a transition study through the progressively advanced aircraft types.

To accomplish the first objective would require aircraft of the various makes and models he had once flown. Obtaining them should not be difficult, he reasoned. From his readings, he learned about the widespread interest in the planes of his day. Many Jennies and other so-called vintage aircraft were being flown by people who had built and restored them. There was even a national antique aeroplane association with membership numbering in the tens of thousands. Surely many such individuals would welcome the opportunity for personal recognition by contributing the use of their aircraft to such a study.

A week went by, then two. Dusty heard nothing in response. He went to the deputy director to find out if Johns had a chance to look at it. Halleck said no and Dusty left. When the pilot again inquired a few days later, Halleck curtly brushed him off saying there were too many more important matters pressing. Dusty came away with the realization that they had no intention whatsoever of considering his proposal.

So he arranged to have himself checked out in the more sophisticated light aircraft available to him, all the way up to the twin-engine Cessna 310. He found these new aircraft cleaner and faster, like moving up from a Model T to a Cadillac. One feature which impressed him the most was the absence of struts which afforded an improved panoramic view. Aviation had indeed come a long way.

But along with their incredible advancements, he found that these modern aircraft lacked the charm and personality he had known in the old ones. Also changed was the art of navigation. In order to find out where you were, you no longer needed to study the rivers, towns or railroad tracks. You turned on a radio, got a bearing, and crossed it with another bearing; it was all done with buttons and dials.

One evening after one of his flights, Dusty was walking along the rows of parked aircraft when he spotted something which made him stop in his tracks. Silhouetted against the orange twilight sky was a Stinson, similar to one he had owned. She stood proud and immaculate with her polished mirrored spinner, seeming to smile at him and beckon him to take her up.

Later when he went home, he spent the night thinking about it, but when he returned to the airport the following evening to revisit it, the Stinson was gone.

An inspiration came to him. If Johns and those guys weren't really interested in his idea, why not write up his experiences on his own? Once he made up his mind what to do, the words, the phrases, and then the paragraphs all seemed to fall into place. Then before long, the paragraphs composed themselves into a theme.

The VINTAGE FLYER was the publication of the National Antique Aircraft Association. Each month featured a center spread on an aircraft someone had restored - often from little more than a basket of parts. It also served as a technical reference with articles covering the entire spectrum of flying.

Dusty submitted his article, appropriately titled *Aircraft and Their Eras*. In it he developed the concept of the airplane as an expression of the era in which it was designed. He presented numerous examples of characteristics of the planes he knew as if they had unique personalities. There was much to be learned from these venerable aircraft, he went on to say, for as planes became increasingly sophisticated, many pilots were lured into a false sense of complacency and overconfidence. In the face of recent technical strides, Dusty cautioned, some of the instincts of yesterday's pilots had faded over the years, and the lessons which they learned at great cost were just as important now as they were then.

His article was, in actuality, the hypothesis he felt would have been proven had his Flight Evaluation Series been carried out to completion.

One week later, Dusty received a letter from the editor requesting his permission to feature the article in the next issue.

There were many aviation buffs at the ICR, and several of them read *THE VINTAGE FLYER*. Although the circumstances behind Dusty's presence there were known to only a few, his name as an employee was quickly recognized. Before long, word had spread around the institute. People whom he had not met came forward to congratulate him. He felt a profound satisfaction over this accomplishment on his own initiative.

Dusty carried this sense of well-being as he walked down the hallway to the director's office. He was sure that what he had done would reflect proudly on the institute.

The secretary promptly ushered him in where the general and Halleck were waiting.

"Close the door," Johns said in an ominous tone as he pointed to an empty chair facing his desk.

With a curious look on his face, Dusty sat down. He looked first at one and then the other.

"What's goin' on?"

There was tenseness in Johns' face. "Dervin," he snapped, "What do you think of someone who signs an agreement and then openly violates it?"

"In reference to what?" inquired the pilot.

"Shut up when the general is talking to you," interjected Halleck.

"I don't think that will be necessary, Tom," Johns said. "Dervin here is still unfamiliar with the way we do things here. He's never encountered this type of situation where he came from."

"What are you talkin' about," Dusty asked.

"This!" Johns exclaimed as he threw a copy of the magazine on the desk in front of Dusty. "I issued *direct orders* forbidding you to discuss, write about or divulge in any way the circumstances surrounding your being here! You signed an *official directive* to comply with those orders, and then you turned around and *deliberately disobeyed* that directive!"

"I still don't know what the big deal is," Dusty shrugged. "All I did was..."

"What's the big deal?! I'll *tell* you what the big deal is," Johns lashed out. "You *violated* an *agreement* you signed with *your government!* Do you know what the penalty for unauthorized disclosure of classified information is, Dervin?"

Dusty shook his head in disbelief at what he saw as a couple of grown men acting like lunatics and he rose to leave.

"Sit down! We're not finished here," commanded Johns.

"When you start makin' sense instead of yellin' like a ravin' maniac, then maybe we can resume this discussion," Dusty replied keeping his cool.

"You'd better *watch* who you're *talkin'* to, boy," snarled Halleck who then got up and moved menacingly toward him.

"And just what the hell are *you* gonna do," said the pilot defiantly staring him straight in the eye. The deputy director stopped in his tracks.

Dusty then turned to Johns. "I asked you time after time about the flight tests. I even sent you a detailed report describing how-"

"How *you* thought they should be run?" Johns sneered. "What the hell does a dumb jackass like you know about reports or anything else?"

Dusty held his temper. "When I came to talk with you about it, you weren't interested! So with a few little changes I sent it to somebody who was! And now you bark like the dog in the manger! I didn't violate your stupid agreement. Lots of folks fly those planes and lots of stuff has been written about 'em. What's more, all the information I used came from the hours I put in and paid for myself! There's nothin' I wrote that couldn't have been written by anyone else who'd done his homework!"

Johns was livid at this blatant challenge to his authority. His lips tightened as he pressed his hands to his desk to keep them from shaking. "I don't give a good goddamn how many people write!" he snarled. "When I issue directives, I expect you to *follow them to the letter!*

Not *questioned* or *selectively followed* as they suit you! Now you'd better get that through your goddamned head right now, or there'll be hell to pay, because if it's goddamn trouble you want boy, I'll see you get *plenty of it!*"

"That doesn't scare me much," Dusty shrugged. He walked to the door, opened it, and then turned around. "I don't know what bee got under your bonnet, General, but I do know somethin' about human nature. And right now I'm gettin' this feelin' that maybe all this hush-hush isn't for government purposes so much as it is for your own!"

That evening in the restaurant, Dusty sat slumped in a chair before the big stone fireplace staring into the flames. He looked up to find the hostess standing before him.

"Is everything all right," she asked.

"Yes, Donna," he said. "Everything's fine."

"You look a little lost."

"Does it show that much?"

"Don't want to talk about it, huh?"

"It's not that. It's just not clear enough in my own mind to explain it to somebody else."

"Is it a big decision?"

"You might say so."

"Have you made any progress in resolving it?"

"Yes," he said resuming his gaze into the fire. "I think I have now."

"General," Halleck said. "I think Dervin may be getting out of control."

"What do you mean, Tom?"

"He's determined to pursue the matter of his relatives. I've done everything to discourage him, but he's made up his mind to go through with it."

Johns cogitated for a moment. "It was bound to happen sooner or later. We just bought ourselves a little time, that's all."

"You mean you were expecting this?"

"Of course," the general said smugly. "We take a man who's accustomed to doing things his own way and lock him into a routine he considers confining. What else would you expect him to do?"

"But once he's away from here, he'll be beyond our reach."

"I don't think so. I know where he's going and I have a pretty good idea what he'll find when he gets there. And by the time he comes back, he'll have seen the error of his ways. Count on it."

"Suppose he comes up with something he can use as leverage against us?"

Johns turned to stare out the window. "I've taken care of that, too."

Once Dusty's mind was made up, his choice of travel soon followed; he would go by train.

It was the mode of transportation least changed over the years, and although the majestic steam locomotive he had known and loved had been replaced by the moaning diesel, the railroad still best suited his purposes. In a world made smaller by jet travel, the train still managed to preserve the sense of distance, and the further Claremont seemed from Los Angeles, the better.

When he looked out the window at the rolling countryside, a sense of timelessness came over him. The beautiful tree-covered mountains had not changed, nor had the plains. Cattle still dotted the rangeland, and the fields of corn and wheat stretched out to the horizon as they had always done.

The rhythm of the rails had not changed either. And as he was lulled off to sleep by the familiar ageless sounds, he felt himself whisked away to a distant place.

1929

He was returning from California where he had completed a two-month aerial survey for an oil company. His plane was a Stinson, a state-of-the-art, high-winged monoplane powered by a Whirlwind engine with a performance and reliability undreamed of only a few years before. Dusty had found his destiny. Aviation was coming of age, and he along with it.

When he spotted the S-turn of the river, he knew that home wasn't far off. The harvested fields and the cumulus clouds, vivid orange in the evening sun, formed a spectacular grandeur which made him long for the open cockpit.

Peg and their little daughter Maddie waited outside the hangar. Their anxiety mounted as they strained their eyes scanning for a tiny spec on the distant horizon. But for the last hour or so there was only silence and the wind.

She thought she could hear something but she wasn't quite sure; it sounded like a faint sputtering drone coming from the west. Gradually it grew louder but remained difficult to see against the setting sun.

Then there it was - a tiny dot! It slowly grew until first the wings and then the crane-like landing gear became clearly recognizable.

They waved frantically as the Stinson passed over the field, and Dusty wagged his wings in return. He chopped the power and spiraled down until he was lined up on final. A row of tall trees lined the foot of the runway. The relative positions of the trees and runway remained unchanged as he grew closer. He knew that if the trees rose to block his view of the runway, he would be too low and would have to gun the throttle.

With only a few feet to spare he skimmed over the trees, dipping the right wing as he slipped to the runway where at the last moment, he righted it for a three-point landing. He taxied off the runway across the grass to where they were, and then cut the engine and rolled to a stop.

He no sooner climbed out when he was almost knocked down with their enthusiastic hugs and kisses. Peg mockingly scolded him for his recklessness.

"Dusty, why do you always have to do that?"

"Do what, kitten," he replied.

"You know what. Cutting the motor like that and then gliding in as if you don't have any power. One day you're going to misjudge and wind up *in* the trees instead of over them."

"It's good practice," he explained. "You get the feel of the plane and the wind. It's a good skill to know if your engine ever quits on you."

"But what if it's gusty? You can't figure it out then."

"Gee, if everything was all so predictable, it wouldn't be any fun."

It was the best of everything. Combining the freedom and independence of doing what he loved best with the warmth and contentment of a home and family.

Peg would have to wait a little longer for the private time with him she had been looking forward to, for now he was the hometown hero. The news of his return spread like wildfire through the neighborhood, and after dinner the local children gathered in the living room to hear Dusty relate his latest exploits. The storyteller transported them to a world they could only dream about. They sat spellbound as he relived his days on the circuit and the distant towns he visited, and they also shared the terrors of the treacherous thunderstorms he encountered as he threaded his way through the mountains.

One of his young fans was a twelve year old lad named Billy Myers. Bright and energetic, he had one ambition in life; he wanted to become a pilot like Dusty. Dusty was impressed with the boy's knowledge of flying and his determination. But a major obstacle stood in the way of Billy's dream; he had a club foot and had to get around on crutches.

There was hope, however. His mother learned of a specialist in New York City who could perform an operation with a good chance of success. Kate Myers, in addition to her working at the general store, took in sewing and other odd jobs to save enough money for the surgery. Ever the optimist, Billy never seemed to let it get him down.

Late that night as they lay in bed, Peg turned to her husband.

"Dusty."

"Yes, kitten?"

"I missed you."

"I missed you too."

"Did the survey go well?"

"It sure did," he replied hopefully. "They've promised me a follow-up for next year."

"That means more of these long trips," Peg said dejectedly.

"Come on, hon," he said, gently holding her hand and looking into her eyes. "That's not fair. Do you think all this is fun for me?"

"I just wish you could find work closer to home, that's all."

"Now kitten, let's be realistic. You know that in this business you have to go where the job is. We're not yet big enough to hire extra pilots and it's only by operatin' on a shoestring that we're doin' as well as we are."

"Are we, Dusty? I haven't seen you but five months in the last twelve. Your own daughter hardly knows you."

The pilot, aware of what was in her heart, listened respectfully.

"It's all part of the growin' pains," he said. "In a few months or so, we'll be in a better position to pick and choose."

"Do you miss your freedom?"

"Now what kinda question is that?"

"It's just sometimes I get the feeling that you miss the old days."

"Where'd you come up with a foolish notion like that? Was it that old busybody, Leona Fidgett?"

"Well-"

"Well you can disregard that nonsense right now! That old fussbudget is just tryin' to project her own miserable frustrations on you. I don't think she's ever seen an airplane up close. She doesn't need to; she gets around on a broom!"

"Dusty, you're terrible," Peg laughed.

His tone turned more solemn. "Honey, I love you. I wouldn't trade what we've got here for anything in the world - and you know what?"

She shook her head.

"Next year, Maddie will be three."

"I know," she replied. "What's that got to do with it?"

"She'll be old enough to travel then. When I go back to California, I'm gonna take both of you with me."

Chapter 8

1974

An eerie feeling came over Dusty as he stepped from the train, a curious mingling of past and present. He did not recognize the station, built in the mid-thirties by the WPA, but as he walked through it he could make out clearly in his mind the outlines of the former one which had stood on this site.

He strapped on his backpack and started for town. Along the busy boulevard he could see the ghosts of streetcars rumbling over where the tracks once ran.

Soon he spotted a more tangible relic of his world. A restored Victorian house stood resplendent in its coat of gray with black shutters and white trim. The doorknobs and porch light were polished brass. In current use as a professional office building, it amazed him how much newer it looked than when he'd last seen it.

Most of the other buildings he expected to see however were gone; they were replaced by later ones, themselves looking old and weather beaten.

The neighborhood as he had known it had been within easy walking distance to the stores and shops, but what was left of the former downtown was now rundown and deteriorated. His old former street was barely recognizable. Most of the weed-choked houses still stood although in advanced stages of neglect, and occasional stumps along the crumbling sidewalks were all that remained of the long graceful archway of maples which had once lined the streets.

He rented a car and drove out to the site where the airport was - or rather where he thought it was. The old narrow road he took to get there was now a four-lane boulevard, and when he followed it as far as he remembered, he found himself in the middle of a suburb, complete with its own shopping center. The only sign that an airport had ever been there was a bronze marker indicating that it had been closed in 1960.

Late that afternoon from the window of his hotel room, he could see how the town now sprawled for miles over what had been farmland. The outlying points were connected by a system of expressways and boulevards to the present center of town, now two miles westward.

The modern buildings standing faceless in their monotonous geometric patterns lacked personality. Instead of traditional adornments such as clock towers or spires, their tops were abruptly truncated. Dusty saw this style also reflected in the barren steel and Formica furniture in his room. He called it Contemporary Sterile.

He had left a small town and returned to a city. In his head, logic told him to expect major changes, but his heart could not really accept these. Almost half a century may have gone by, but to him it had been only a few months.

The hotel operator awakened him at seven.

Learning four decades of history from a book was one thing, but threading through the personal changes taking place over that length of time was something quite different.

To obtain the news of the day, one goes to the television or newspaper. For the events covering a week or month, there are magazines. But to determine the local changes occurring over a period of many years, the best place to begin is the cemetery.

The history of the town was written here. On a gentle knoll not far from the main gate stood the Old Victory Monument where every year on Armistice Day the local dignitaries would lay a wreath. The bronze plaque was still there, inscribed with the names of all the local boys who didn't come back. They called The Great War the War to End All Wars, but adjacent to this plaque was an even larger plaque serving as mute testament that this had not been so. This roll from the Second World War held a particularly poignant significance for Dusty, for with these names he could recall the faces of young lads between six and fourteen.

Further along the path, an old oak tree cast a shadow over the stones and markers beneath it. Passing among the rows he could feel the presence of other faces. He could recall conversations with friends he'd seen only a little while ago. The inscriptions indicated to him that most had gone on to live out their full lives while a few others had been cut short in their prime. But whatever courses their lives had subsequently taken, here at this moment they appeared before Dusty as they were when he knew them.

He began to experience a contrast of feelings. On the one hand he felt as though a part of him was buried here, yet at the same time, he also felt as though he had been left behind while his contemporaries had gone on to some distant, happier place. Suddenly he was held in the grip of an overpowering numbness. A large stone of red granite which he had not seen before seemed to spring up out of the ground and stare at him with haunting eyes, for on it, inscribed in big letters, was the name ROBBINS.

The following day the librarian checked him out on the microfilm projector and left him alone with the newspaper file of 1958. Slowly he turned the crank as the pages of each succeeding day passed in review. When he came to the obituary page of the edition of August 15, he found what he was looking for.

It was a feature story on Dr. Robbins of whom it was said had delivered half of the citizens in town. The photograph showed him considerably aged with whiter hair and a lot more wrinkles, but Dusty could still recognize the man as he knew him. He had made it to 83.

The last sentence leaped up at him:

> *Dr. Robbins is survived by a daughter, Mrs.*
> *Margarite Dervin, a granddaughter, Madelyn*
> *Griffin, and a great grandson, Mark Griffin.*

His heart beat fast. Peg was still alive and in the area - at least as recently as sixteen years ago.

There were two avenues now open to him. He could either look for Maddie first or directly track down Peg herself.

He considered the first option more logical and straightforward. What did Maddie look like now? What sort of life was she leading? What was her son - his grandson - like? She would take him to Peg. She could also be a big help in putting together a lot of the missing pieces. All he had to do was look her up in the phone book.

But then the more he thought about it, the more he began to feel uneasy. When he'd last seen Maddie, she was four years old. Aside from the photographs and whatever else her mother might have told her over the years, she would have no way of recognizing him. She had long since accepted him as dead and his sudden unexpected appearance might prove too much for her to handle. He didn't want to spook her if it could be avoided.

So Dusty decided to proceed along a more discreet path of inquiry.

He went to the church mentioned in the article. In the fellowship hall following Sunday Services, he approached the pastor, a kind looking man in his late fifties.

"May I help you young man?" the pastor kindly asked.

"Yes sir. I was wonderin' if you might know a... Margarite Dervin?"

"Hmm," the pastor said. "No... I'm afraid I can't seem to recall that name."

"Perhaps you might have known her father, Dr. Samuel Robbins?"

The pastor shook his head. "No, I can't say that I have. They were probably here before I arrived; that would be about seven years ago." Then noticing the disappointment on Dusty's face, he added, "I'm sorry I can't be of more help."

"That's all right, Rev'rund. Thanks anyway for your time."

As Dusty walked away, a sudden thought occurred to the minister who caught up with him.

"Uh-young man, do you see that lady over there with the white hair?"

"Uh huh," nodded the pilot.

"Her name is Celia Woods. She's one of our older members... knows practically everybody. If anyone can help you find your friend, I'm sure she can. Let me introduce you."

Chapter 9

When Dusty first learned of the Claremont Rest Home, he envisioned a dingy three-story building tucked away in some forgotten part of town, where unfortunate souls no longer wanted by their relatives were condemned to live out their days in isolation and despair. Upon arriving there however, he was surprised to discover a peaceful looking ranch style house located amid sprawling acres of lawn and trees, where residents could be seen actively going about various outdoor pursuits or merely enjoying the sun.

The cheerfulness of this atmosphere was further reflected in the smile of the receptionist in the front lobby.

"May I help you," she asked.

"Um, yes ma'am," he said haltingly. "Could you please tell me where I might find Margarite Dervin?"

"Dervin? Hmm - name rings a bell. Is she expecting you?"

"I don't think so. I just came into town."

She began looking through the rolodex file on her desk.

"Oh, *Peg*," she exclaimed. "I know her better by her first name! Lovely person, one of the sweetest. She's in 184. Just make a right and follow the corridor straight down."

As Dusty walked down the long hallway, his heart pounded with each step as the room numbers passed in a countdown back in time.

When he came to the door, he hesitated a moment, then taking a deep breath he summoned up his courage and rapped gently.

"Come in," answered a soft voice.

She was resting in bed. The wheelchair and crutches revealed part of the story; her white hair and pale gaunt features told the rest.

Her eyes registered a curious look as she carefully studied her visitor. He looked like someone in his early thirties, yet there was something strangely familiar about him. It did not make sense. She thought her mind was playing tricks on her.

"You remind me of someone I knew a long -"

Suddenly she cupped her hand to her mouth. Her eyes widened in shock, transfixed upon this apparition from a distant time.

He stood there completely frozen, now concerned over the possible effect his sudden appearance was having upon her.

A long moment passed while she continued to look him over. Then, slowly lowering her hand and in a voice barely above a whisper, she uttered, "Dusty?"

He bit down on his lower lip as tears filled his eyes.

"Yes, kitten...it's me."

Peg continued to study his features with incredible amazement. His clothes were up to date, but other than that, he stood there exactly as she remembered him.

Then suddenly, she felt the weight of her many years bearing down on her. A fundamental principal she had always accepted as the inevitable course of life now stood contradicted before her. She could not understand how he had remained so young while she had grown old.

But soon strange conflicting feelings began to stir inside her. So many years had passed since she had last seen him. So much change had taken place. Yet at this very moment, all her memories of his many endearing qualities surged back upon her as if in a flood.

She motioned him to come over to her and he did so haltingly.

"Come here, Dusty," she said in a tender voice, gently reaching out to him. "It's all right. Let me have a look at you."

He gently took her hand in both of his, then sat down on her bed. For several long moments, neither could speak. Though her body was now old and frail, Dusty could still feel the presence of the young girl he had known. She was real, still capable of imparting warmth and belonging. He held her hand to his cheek and kissed her hair, closed his eyes, and for a brief moment found himself carried off to a faraway place.

When the initial shock had time to subside, Dusty began to fill Peg in on the events surrounding his disappearance and return. As she listened to him describe his experiences in this strange world, her eyes widened in wonder.

"It was like a sudden change in time," he explained. "One moment, I was caught up in a blizzard and the next, I woke up in this hospital with all kinds of needles and tubes stuck into me, and strange people standin' over me askin' all these weird questions. And now it seems that the greater part of your life has passed by like only a sec-."

He broke down.

"Dusty," she said in a soft, soothing voice as she ran her fingers along his neck.

"We never had much of a chance, did we, kitten."

"We did all right," she smiled gently. "It was the times, hon. We were victims of the times. What *does* bother me is why they didn't have the decency to tell me you'd been found."

"I've been tryin' to figure that one out myself," he said bitterly. "Nothin's made sense to me since I've come back! If the Almighty saw fit to take me away, why didn't He just go ahead and finish the job?"

"Don't say that, Dusty." Peg said with gentle reproach. "Don't *ever* say that. God did not punish you. What happened to you was an accident. You did what you had to do. And because of what you did with that insurance policy and everything, we were able to make it through all those hard years. Don't be sad for me. I have no regrets."

Peg then tried to steer the conversation to lighter matters, talking about the beautiful surroundings and the kind people who cared for her. She no longer had to bother with cooking or doing the laundry. And whenever she wanted, she could always find something to occupy her time - or just enjoy the peaceful world around her. At this time in her life it was the best place to be.

But Dusty could not help wondering if this was all merely the rationalization of a once active woman coming to terms with the infirmities of growing old.

He picked up a photograph on her dresser. "Maddie?"

"Taken a few years ago," Peg replied.

The corners of his mouth turned down as he studied it. "She grew up to favor her mama."

"And that...," she proudly declared pointing to the other picture, "is your grandson Mark. He's a sophomore in high school."

He nodded his approval.

"Dusty, when you first got here...I suppose you looked the town over?"

The pilot nodded.

"Wasn't too pleasant, was it?"

"What's happened, Peg?"

She lay back on her pillow. How could she explain decades of complex changes she herself barely understood to someone whose entire reasoning was geared to another era?

"They called it *progress*," she sighed. "A lot of the boys who came back from the War - uh, the *Second World War*, Dusty - they decided they didn't want to go back into farming, so they left. Some went to the cities, others headed west. The town council grew concerned that we were all going to somehow shrivel up and die, so they got together and decided that manufacturing was the wave of the future. They launched this big campaign to attract industry. In those days, you see, growth was equated with progress, and everybody believed it was healthy.

"In just a couple of years our population tripled. Farmers began selling out in droves to land speculators and developers. Vast expanses of good farmland became housing tracts and business sites. Suburbs sprang up with their own shopping centers, and to connect them they built those god awful concrete freeways. The old neighborhoods got choked off and nobody cared much because it wasn't considered worthwhile to fix them up anymore. And downtown couldn't compete because it was no longer conveniently accessible to the mainstream clientele. One by one, the stores closed up and pulled out."

"Didn't anyone see this comin'?"

"A few of us did," she replied. "They laughed us off. Said we were trying to turn back the clock. You know, Dusty, one thing about clichés - they're always convenient for derailing any open minded discussion and logical reasoning which might call into question the prevailing opinion of those in power at the moment. That's when we woke up to find that we no longer had control of our town. A new faction had taken over, promoting their own self-interests. Do you know what twenty-five years of *progress* has given us? Smog and traffic jams, taxes that have driven many of us to the poorhouse, and a rate of crime so high, it's no longer safe to walk the streets at night. And Ojibwa Creek where you used to fish? There haven't been any fish there for years; it's an open sewer now! When you get down to it, all that growth and technology has done is to make us worse off than before we *had* growth and technology."

"Do you remember," Dusty wistfully recalled, "...the nights we'd lie awake listenin' to the whistle of the Old Wabash, and we'd talk about all those wonderful places we hoped to visit one day? And the little dial on the radio that lit up as we'd hear all those neat programs from across the country. It was like magic."

"Those dreams have grown old, hon," she said sadly, "...just like the rest of us. The world has become more complicated now. All the younger people have their own dreams, and ours have become corny and old fashioned to them."

"I suppose that's to be expected," Dusty acknowledged. "But somehow, with all these modern jetliners and sophisticated electronic gadgetry, it makes me wonder if maybe somethin' might've gotten lost in the translation."

"What do you mean, dear?"

"When we developed the airplane, the radio and all those other new wonderful things, they were all supposed to make things easier for everybody. But instead of layin' back and takin' it all in, I've seen lots of folks all runnin' around lookin' for new stuff to worry about. Kinda like they're not sure what it is they want, but they seem to be in such a big hurry to get it. Why can't folks just slow down a little, look around and enjoy the moment for what it is?"

Peg looked into his eyes with a gentle sympathetic smile.

"Life is no longer the desperate back-to-basics existence that you and I knew, thank God," she explained. "But what you see here now, I'm afraid, is one of those unfortunate consequences of the prosperity we've come to enjoy since then. As we acquired more and more, many folks lost sight of that fundamental virtue that sustained us – patience. The younger generations who never went through what we did can't possibly understand what it was like merely by reading books about it. They need to experience it first hand, and who in their right mind would ever want to do that?"

The room became quiet. Peg saw deep lines of sadness etched into his face as he gazed out the window. And she could also see that, at this moment, his mind was very far away.

1930

The late twenties had seemed like years of promise. It was noted at this time that more scientific and technical advances had been made during the preceding fifty years than throughout the last five thousand. Aviation rode the crest of this wave, having demonstrated its potential in war and in flying the airmail. The sensational exploits of Lindbergh, Admiral Byrd and other pioneers highlighted the latest improvements in reliability and endurance.

The airplane had come of age and Dusty along with it. Opportunity, hard work, and a little risk taking had made the American Dream come true for him, and there was no reason to believe that this great prosperity would not continue.

Then suddenly it all came apart.

The Crash of 1929 and the subsequent depression caused an economic upheaval of a scale unknown in the recollections of anyone who lived through it. Across the country factories closed. As the months passed, conditions worsened as massive layoffs, bread lines, evictions and foreclosures became widespread. Every day the papers carried news of suicides.

Dusty's extension on the oil exploration contract was cancelled. There would be no trip to California. As the months went by, his self-confidence began to give way to a deep, gnawing uncertainty in which all in which he had been brought up to believe no longer seemed to hold true.

Some held the conviction that the current economic crisis was the whirlwind reaped for the sins of over speculation and deviation from proper morality - a divine retribution.

This reasoning only intensified Dusty's anger and resentment. Divine retribution for what? His neighbors and friends had been honest, hardworking people who had remained in the backwaters of the postwar prosperity. What transgressions had they committed that they should suddenly find themselves facing total ruin?

Why was their neighbor Kate Myers being punished that the money she had so laboriously put aside for her son's operation had to be used up in staving off foreclosure and just barely meeting their day-to-day needs?

Peg and Dusty weren't starving. For his services, her father accepted payment in kind, in the form of chickens, eggs, and preserves. Dr. Robbins would often pass on to others in need some of what he collected. Just a loan, he would say, until things picked up.

Dusty grew restless and irritable. He and Peg often quarreled between moments of moody silence, stemming from his resentment of having to live off her father's charity as he watched his own sense of pride and self-esteem going out the window.

Torn by guilt and plagued with periods of self-doubt, he felt a loss of purpose. At times he found himself longing for the old days when his only possession was a rickety biplane and his only worry was his next meal.

He found escape at the airfield, where he kept his Stinson polished in anticipation for calls which never came. Although he could no longer afford to fly, he felt that just being near his beloved plane would somehow delay its falling into the hands of his creditors. But he knew that this too would be only a matter of time.

One night, he received a visit from two mysterious strangers at his home. One stood out impeccably dressed in an expensive tailored three-piece suit, top coat and homburg. He had a slick, self-confident air about him, and flashed a large gold diamond ring. The other, dressed in a wrinkled suit, was more solidly built with sallow, pockmarked features. The first man introduced himself as Peter McKittrick. His associate did not speak at all.

They had a business proposition.

Peg retreated to the kitchen and the men sat down. McKittrick began by extolling the virtues of money and success. He maintained that, contrary to the wails and whines of social reformers, money was what the world was all about. It could buy luxury. It could buy power.

Our very lives were *controlled* by people with money. This wasn't something new; it had been going on since the beginning of time. True, there was a depression, but even so there was money to be made if one had the vision to seize the opportunity when it presented itself.

There were two kinds of people, McKittrick went on, those who finished first - and the losers. It was the first-finishers who called the shots. The losers spent their second-rate lives competing for the scraps. He considered himself one of the fortunate few blessed with this wisdom and foresight.

Dusty saw the speech for what it was, a distorted view of capitalism twisted to the point of absurdity, yet lent an air of credibility by the harsh uncertainties of the times.

When he finished his dissertation on economic theory, McKittrick turned to the purpose of his visit. He wanted Dusty to fly up north across the border to Canada where he would take delivery of some special cargo. These trips would be no more than three or four days at the most, and with just a few of them, he could make enough to pay off his plane and the rest of their debts many times over. If the conditions were acceptable, further instructions would follow in a few days.

Dusty got up and slowly paced the room. The proposition sounded suspicious. He sensed what these men were really about, and under normal times would have thrown them out in a second. But with a family to support and the means to his livelihood within days of repossession, he saw no other alternative. He agreed to the terms and McKittrick advanced him some money.

When the strangers departed, Peg emerged.

"Dusty, what did those men want," she asked.

"They offered me a job haulin' some freight up north."

"I don't like them," she said bluntly. "I don't want you to have anything to do with them!"

"I don't think you understood," he replied. "They offered me a job!"

"It sounds more to me like *trouble* which we don't need!"

"You don't know what you're talkin' about!"

"You know damned well what I'm talkin' about - *Bootlegging!* As if the people we owe money to aren't enough, we'll now have to worry about the law as well! What will happen to us when you wind up dead or in jail! Dusty, I don't trust them! They make me cringe!"

"Peg, your imagination is runnin' away with you. The money's good and it's no different from what I've always been doin'. We've got nothin' in the bank and even less credit. You said it yourself..." he said pinching his thumb and forefinger. "We're *this* close to foreclosure. And I'm not about to sit on my behind waitin' for it to happen! I'm not smugglin' liquor; I'm haulin' freight. It's a regular job, and if I don't do it, somebody else will!"

"Now you're beginning to sound like *them*," she said with contempt. Then she stormed up the stairs.

McKittrick had stipulated one demand; the airplane was to be painted a pale green. It was one more indignity Dusty had to swallow. When he had finished he stood back to inspect it. It was a totally different machine, drab and devoid of any personality whatsoever.

Dusty was sorry that Peg could not see the necessity of what he was doing, but he had come to the grim realization that if he was going to continue to look after his family, he would have to place their safety and well-being above his own.

As an added measure, he took out an insurance policy on himself, entrusting it to an attorney with instructions to reveal its existence to Peg only in the event of his death or disappearance.

A few nights later, the call came through. Dusty was to fly to an obscure lumber town some fifty miles from the Canadian border, where he was to receive coded instructions on where and when he was to pick up the cargo.

It consisted of twenty cases of whiskey. While they were being loaded into his plane, he was given further instructions as to where to land and unload them. The map and coordinates had to be memorized, for if this information fell into the wrong hands it could have fatal consequences for all involved.

He flew to the designated spot at night, heavily loaded and over unfamiliar territory. One missed landmark or reference point could spell disaster.

But once again his skill came through for him and he found three pairs of headlights lined up in the meadow to mark his landing spot. Everything went according to plan; the cases were unloaded, he was paid in cash on the spot, and within a matter of minutes he was on his way home.

The chill continued between Dusty and Peg. The days he was gone left her on edge. Maddie could sense it from the way they spoke to each other - when they spoke at all. Its effects on the little girl often manifested themselves in nightmares, when her screams would awaken her parents. On those occasions when she would tiptoe down to the kitchen, it puzzled her why her father now slept on the couch in the front room.

It was no secret that Dusty was flying again, but Peg would explain it away as "odds and ends" work. They maintained a low profile, making no purchases which might give away any major upswing in their fortunes. Nor did they change their day-to-day living habits. Bills continued to be paid late; paying in full might draw suspicion.

There was one individual however who took an interest in Dusty's activities. From his years as Claremont's sheriff, Clem Edwards had developed a keen instinct for detecting anything out of the ordinary.

Airplanes intrigued him and he would often drive by the field hoping to watch one take off.

One day he saw Dusty roll the Stinson from its hangar, and something about it rang a bell in the back of his mind.

He returned to his office, where he began searching through his files. Before long he found what he was looking for. It was a news clipping, dated several months before, describing a plane crash in the northern woods. The pilot had been killed.

As they sat down to dinner, Peg remarked that Kate Myers had taken Billy to New York.

"Oh?" Dusty said raising his eyebrows.

"He's going to have the operation. Seems she was awakened in the middle of the night by a knock at her back door. Scared her half to death. When she got the nerve to go down and have a look, she found a brown paper bag which turned out to be full of money."

"That so," he replied nonchalantly drinking his coffee. "If anyone deserves good fortune, it's certainly them."

"And you know Ike and his wife? They're not going to lose their home after all. Seems like they came into some mysterious good fortune too."

"Well I guess it's about time," Dusty smiled. "They were pretty worried there for awhile."

Peg cast a suspicious look at her husband whose attention seemed focused on his meal.

"So the Great Flying Hero of the Twenties has now become the Robin Hood of the Thirties!"

"I don't know what you mean, Peg."

"Don't play innocent with me! Who else around here has come into that kind of money?"

"You'd better not spread that around," he cautioned. "People will descend upon us like locusts lookin' for a handout."

"You think I don't *know* you after all this time," she exclaimed. "How long can you go on putting me through hell not knowing from one moment to the next if you're still alive? These aren't thunderstorms or mountains you're dealing with! They are treacherous people who will do away with you like *that* if it suits their purpose, and they're the worst danger of all!"

She stormed out of the kitchen. He calmly rose and followed her to the front room where she gazed out the window, tears streaming down her cheeks. He put his arms around her.

"Our friends need help," he tenderly explained. "They just need a little time until things start to turn around. This is all we can do for them now."

Dusty had just finished checking over the Stinson's engine when he received a visit from Sheriff Clem.

"Gettin' ready for another trip?" asked the latter.

"Yeah," smiled the pilot. "Takin' off in the mornin'."

Clem reached into his jacket pocket for some photographs. "I was wonderin' if you seen any of these guys around."

Dusty recognized McKittrick's face among five others.

"Nope. Can't say's I have."

"Well," the sheriff went on, "...it seems this Mckittrick fellow's been active in liquor traffic around these parts. Brings it in from Canada. Trucks, automobiles mostly. But he's also been known to fly it in now and then."

Dusty continued wiping down the plane. "Sounds interestin' sheriff, but why are you tellin' me all this?"

"The other day, I was goin' through my files when I stumbled upon this article from a few months back. This pilot, Eddy Wheeler, was killed when his plane crashed in a wooded area up north. Maybe you knew him."

Dusty shook his head.

"Turned out he was flyin' whiskey. Smashed cases and bottles spread all over the place. Lots of peculiar angles to it, but most interestin' of all was the plane's color. Y'see it was this dull brown. I didn't pay it much notice, not at first anyway. But then when I saw yours, it suddenly hit me."

The pilot stopped and looked at Edwards. "Mine? What's this all got to do with me?"

"This color. Hell, Dusty, look at it! It shows no imagination or creativity. That's not like you... not like you at all! You've always taken pride in this airplane here, like it's a personal extension of you. When people see it, they identify it with *you*."

"I still don't see what all this has to do with some guy who cracked up in the woods."

"You have this here beautiful aircraft which you're on the verge of losin'. Then you suddenly come into some work. Very fortunate to find these days, that is, if it's honest. Then you make your plane look drab and nondescript? Now you tell me does that make sense?"

"The plane needed a new paint job," Dusty explained. "The green paint was on sale."

"Perhaps," mused the sheriff, "...or maybe convenient. It won't attract attention. If someone sees it, he's less likely to remember exactly when or where if he's asked about it later on."

Clem's voice now took on a more serious tone. "If you're into a new line of work, Dusty, there's somethin' you better know right now! You're dealin' with a dangerous bunch of people here. They won't hesitate to get rid of you when you're of no further use to them or they think you're some kind of threat. This may seem like a cute sideline to you but these guys here play for keeps! I've known a lotta people tryin' to make a little spendin' money that suddenly disappeared. And there's another danger, too."

"What's that?"

"Me!" snapped the sheriff, his face only inches from Dusty's. "Family or personal considerations aside, you bring any of that crap into my territory, and I'll come down on you so hard, you'll think you ran into a goddamn freight train!"

A passing weather front delayed Dusty's takeoff for several hours. With the phone lines down there was no way either to call ahead or be contacted by them. They would have to wait for him - one of the inconveniences in this business.

Peg had been right all along. He should never have gotten into it. Now he could not get out; he knew too much. He had come a long way from the days when, guided only by his heart, he had explored the distant horizons of his dreams. He had attained the ultimate freedom, feeling as much a part of the sky as the birds and the clouds.

But now this freedom was gone. He now found himself increasingly dwelling over the heavy toll it had taken. How had he survived when so many of his friends had not? They had skills and instincts, in some cases even better than his own. What had happened to them could very easily happen to him. It was not a matter of skill; it was luck. And he knew that his was about to run out.

There were many ways it could happen: the sudden onset of a storm, wing icing, malfunction of a fuel pump. In an overloaded plane flying at night in the dead of winter over a heavily wooded area, an engine failure would mean almost certain death. If by some remote chance he survived the initial crash he would most likely perish from fire or exposure.

It was daybreak. The cars and trucks were parked along the downwind side of the frozen lake. After circling to judge the wind angle, he slipped down over the trees, applying power at the last moment to slow his descent. Other than a slight bounce on touchdown the landing went smoothly and he began to slow down. He gave the engine a shot of power and a blast of prop wash blew the Stinson around. Then he taxied over to the waiting vehicles.

Almost immediately Dusty sensed something odd. No one came running out to meet him and help him unload, and they were always in a hurry to transfer the liquor to the ground vehicles and move out.

He left his engine idling and climbed out. A sudden jolt of shock and horror shot through him at what he saw next.

Half buried in the snow lay several corpses caked in frozen blood. Some remained in their bullet-riddled sedans where, apparently caught by surprise, they never had a chance. Those faces still recognizable as such wore ghoulish expressions of contorted agony, their mouths agape and their eyes rolled upward staring at nothing. A bloody hand dangled from the open side door of a

Cadillac. Dusty recognized McKittrick's gold ring, the symbol of his success.

Had it not been for the icy snow, the scene would have looked even more gruesome. Had it not been for the delay caused by the storm, Dusty would have been a part of it.

His face white with terror, he slowly backed away, then turned and bolted for the plane. He hurled all the cases out onto the ice, slammed the door shut, gunned the throttle and took off.

Chapter 10

1974

In the loft of what was formerly Fire Station No. 4, Foster Westwood sat in his untidy office concentrating on the EVENING TIMES. His face bore the worried look of someone engaged in a major struggle which didn't seem to be going well. An attorney in his early forties, he had given up a lucrative practice to devote his time to civic causes, the latest being the Claremont Society for Historic Preservation.

He looked up to see one of his volunteer workers, a girl in her early twenties, standing in the doorway.

"Wha'cha got there, Judy," he said trying to sound upbeat.

"The latest contribution checks," she smiled. "I just entered them in the ledger."

"Hmm," he mumbled as he counted the entries with his pencil. "This makes a hundred and twenty-six so far this week." Then turning to a nearby chart, he measured off a length of green tape and extended the graph to reflect this latest addition. "We've passed last week and it's only Wednesday."

"Look at the latest signature count!" Judy proclaimed. "We've got six thousand so far and at the rate we're going, we should wind up with half again that many before the next council meeting!"

Westwood, however, did not share her enthusiasm.

"I'm not sure even that will turn the tide much," he said.

"Why are you so negative, Foster?"

"Do you think it's just the Old Town Project? There's more to it than that. We've brought this up before the council many times over the years: affordable housing, small shops, preserving a piece of the past. You think they gave a damn? It's only now that the developers who have ruined this community want to finish their work on the last remaining section that it's become a major issue."

He held up a sheaf of letters. "Do you see these? They're just part of the sacks of mail I've been getting every day! The bulk of them come from older folks who can't afford to move to the suburbs, parents concerned over the environment in which their children are growing up, and young people rejecting what they see as material excess, not to mention the latest concerns over the oil shortage. We have become the focal point for every cause that opposes rezoning."

"But with all their support, why are you so worried?"

"For one thing, we're pitted against a firmly entrenched coalition with the financial resources to wage an aggressive campaign. They will resort to smear tactics designed to mislead and confuse an uninformed electorate always accustomed to voting with their pocketbooks. You've seen how they've turned the council meetings into an armed camp with the police looking for the slightest pretext to throw us out."

"Yes, I know. But that hasn't hurt our cause; it's *helped* it!"

"Sure it has," he acknowledged. "It's worked so well that they've now stooped to an even newer low - blackmail."

Judy looked at him in disbelief. "Blackmail!? Have they *threatened* with something?"

Westwood nodded. "Last week I received an anonymous phone call warning me to lay off or certain information would be leaked out that could prove very embarrassing for us just before the election."

"What mud can they throw that they haven't thrown already?"

"Enough to plant a seed of doubt at precisely when it would have its greatest impact. By the time it's shown for the lie that it is, the election will be over and they'll move in with their bulldozers. There's a lot of money at stake on this rezoning issue, Judy. Big money. You don't know the depths to which these people will crawl to get their way."

"Foster, you still haven't told me what they've got!"

"It's not what they've got, Judy, it's what they can make it *look* like! Just take my word for it!" The testiness of his tone made it apparent that he didn't want to go into it any further.

At the Crestmont Tennis Club where she had just finished a women's doubles match, Lynn Griffin was walking through the lounge on her way out the door when she noticed a young man staring at her.

"Do I know you," she asked.

"Maddie?"

Her eyes fixed on him in a peculiar stare. "No one has called me that since I was nine years old. Who are you?"

"I'm your papa."

She broke into a nervous half-smile. "Is this supposed to be some kind of a joke?" Then suddenly the smile changed into an expression of shock. "No..." she stammered, "It can't be!"

Dusty gently motioned her to sit down.

"No, no!" she cried backing away. She turned and ran out the door. He rose to follow her but then sensed the futility of doing so. When he got to the window he watched her start her car, back out, and then swerve to avoid an oncoming sedan as she sped away.

The grandfather clock chimed four as Lynn opened the front door. She found herself gazing at the pendulum as if in an hypnotic trance. Her normal surroundings seemed suddenly strange to her.

She ran upstairs to the attic where she began rummaging through a pile of belongings her mother had left behind when she had moved to the rest home. Presently Lynn came upon an old trunk containing her father's personal effects. Peg had often gone over their significance with her when she was growing up.

Her hands trembled as she turned the key in the rusty latch and slowly raised the lid. She pulled back the musty quilt. Suddenly she drew back and froze.

All of her father's letters and photographs were gone.

"So Lynn didn't know either," mused Peg. "Well, I guess the cat's out of the bag now."

"She was sure frightened," Dusty said.

"I bet she was. She must've thought she'd seen a ghost."

From Peg's tone, Dusty sensed that all was not well between her and Lynn.

"You didn't tell her?"

Peg shook her head.

"Why not, Peg?"

"We...haven't been speaking now for six months."

He looked at her with shock and disappointment.

"It must be over something pretty big."

"Oh Dusty, you don't know the half of what you're getting into."

"How will I know if you don't tell me?"

Peg heaved a deep sigh. "Maddie was very pretty," she recalled, "...bright and full of promise. But she tended to be rather weak in matters of judgment and common sense. She didn't have to worry about things the way that we did.

"She married Joe soon after high school. Big talker. Real pushy. He always knew what he wanted and heaven help anybody who got in his way."

"I take it you don't care for him much."

She scowled as she shook her head. "Never could stand him... always so damned cock-sure of himself. No one could ever tell him anything. Oh, they've done pretty well for themselves I suppose. His civic connections have brought him a lot of business from the powers-that-be. But no matter how much he's gotten it's never been enough."

"How has he managed to drive a wedge between you and Lynn," Dusty asked.

"I own some property he's trying to make me sell. She's caught in the middle."

"*He* wants you to sell it?" said Dusty indignantly. "What business is it of his?"

"He's in cahoots with some developers who want to raze the entire area for a massive commercial complex… you know, with offices and a shopping center. If he can deliver the five houses I own, it'll play into the council's hands and make it easier to push the rezoning through."

This was all new to Dusty and he didn't quite know what to make of it. Real estate and the complexities of city politics had never been a part of his world. But he could see the negative effect it was having on Peg and this caused him concern.

"Is it really worth all that heartache, hon? That whole section is rundown. Restorin' it would cost a fortune. It's not gonna make us young again, or bring back the laughter of the people we knew. All you'd have to show for it would be a hollow shell of memories."

"Oh *no*, Dusty, You don't understand," she replied. "There are lots of people who want to make their homes there. People from all walks of life - professionals, young first-timers, retired people - they all want to rebuild and restore to the area the charm it once had. Wouldn't you like to see maples once again grace the streets of our old a neighborhood with the dignity it deserves, knowing that after we're gone a part of us will always be around for others to see and appreciate?"

From the bright gleam in her eyes, Dusty could tell that she had discovered a sense of purpose which had given her life meaning.

There was a knock at the door. "Come in dear," Peg called out.

The door opened and a small boy of about sixteen entered. When he saw Dusty he hesitated.

"It's okay, honey," she reassured him. "Come here, hon. I want you to meet somebody very special."

Peg had spoken of Dusty to Mark over the years, and the boy's first impression of this legend was sheer awe. Before long, after getting over the shock of Dusty's return, Mark was eagerly pumping his grandfather for all the little details to the many wonderful stories she had told him.

To Peg this reunion brought a warm glow to her heart. Up to now Mark had been the only friend whose loyalty and love for her had remained steadfast. Now she had two.

At five o'clock the nurse stopped by to announce the dinner hour. As Dusty rose to leave, Peg touched his arm, pulled him to her and smiled.

"You said there weren't any more children to tell your stories to?"

He kissed her cheek and with a reassuring wink smiled, "I'll see you tomorrow, kitten."

Joe Griffin saw himself as a man of vision. One of the movers and shakers behind the scenes, he had played a big part in the transformation of Claremont, letting contracts for the Civic Center, the library annex, and a new hospital wing. Over the years Joe had managed to work his way into the inner circle of city politics which included the mayor, several of the city council, and other key businessmen.

If from time to time their opponents charged favoritism and corruption, these complaints would usually fall upon deaf ears. Voices contending that this "progress" came at the expense of the poor, the elderly, and many of the lower working class were shouted down by those who were swayed by the promises of continued growth, jobs and prosperity.

The crowning glory of this transformation was to be what they called the Superblock. A massive complex consisting of high rise office buildings and a major shopping center, it was to be erected on the site of the Old Town area.

To accomplish this, Joe had put together a holding company which had systematically bought up most of the property in Old Town. His strategy was simple: push the rezoning ordinance through city council, drive out the remaining occupants, and then raze the entire area before the opposition had a chance to appeal. Thus far, everything had gone according to plan. Only one obstacle remained.

Following lunch, Joe returned to his office to discover a note on his desk informing him that a man named Burt called.

A steel-gray limousine pulled up in front of the Metropolitan Building and Burt Cunningham, president of the Valley National Bank got in.

"Sunk anymore birdies?" Joe smiled.

"No, Joe... Haven't had the time lately."

"What's on your mind, Burt?"

"Oh, not so much me, Joe," Burt replied. "The others are a little concerned over this mounting opposition. Have you seen the polls?"

"Jeez, Burt, polls don't mean anything. Hell... we commission our own polls to gather and publicize the results we want. They're an advertising gimmick. Nobody puts much stock in those things."

"Oh I dunno...maybe you're right, Joe, but I'm afraid a few of the boys are getting a little concerned."

"About what? I told you the Council vote is all sewn up."

"Well the skeptics would rest a little easier if they felt we had all our ducks in line."

"What the hell do they want for christsake?"

"The houses, Joe. They want the deal closed on the houses before the meeting. They're concerned about the fuss the opposition is kicking up. If the papers play this up before we're ready to act, we could all come out looking foolish."

"That's stupid! How often do I have to keep telling you there's nothing to worry about? You just handle your damned end and I'll take care of mine!"

"Don't get mad at me Joe. I'm satisfied you've got a handle on this. It's the others who need convincing. Humor them."

His grandfather's stories stirred Mark's imagination as they had the children of two generations before, for their appeal was timeless. The tales of flying in an open-cockpit biplane, dodging thunderstorms through treacherous mountain passes, or racing perilously close to the ground alongside a speeding train brought thrills which never grew old.

For Mark they opened a whole new perspective on life. The world of his grandfather seemed simpler, less restricted. It seemed to him like a time when one's natural curiosity was satisfied by free exploration, trial and error - not stifled by deadlines, grades, and pushy teachers.

Had Dusty grown old along with his generation, his narratives might have grown clouded in nostalgia. But instead, they evoked fresh images of another age. The people he spoke of were not two-dimensional, stiffly-posed figures in yellowed pictures, but real down-to-earth folks whom anyone could have known.

"Dusty," asked Mark, "What do you think about the Apollo flights to the Moon?"

"From what I've read they seem very impressive," he replied. "With all that technology it looks like they've come quite a long way, haven't they."

"How do you like the astronauts?"

"They seem to be a bunch of fine, brave men who are dedicated to what they do."

"Would you like to be one?"

"Gee, I never thought about it much."

"How do they compare with the pilots of your day?"

Dusty pondered over the question for a moment. "Now that's kind of a hard question to answer."

"How come?"

"You can't really make such a comparison. The times were different. It was a whole different world back then which called for different skills; like for example, they're trained to follow a large set of complicated procedures. In the primitive airplanes we flew, we had to do it by guess or by gosh.

"I suppose I'd feel out of place too if they put me in one of those jet planes or space capsules," Dusty went on. "But then by the same token, if you put one of those guys straight into a Jenny or a DH-4, without a proper checkout he'd most likely get himself killed. No," he concluded, "it's not so much that one group is better than the other. Most likely it's just that they're a different breed of cat."

At that moment a large jetliner passed overhead. They looked up at it and watched it proceed on its course until it disappeared from view.

"Would you like to fly one of those," asked Mark.

"Seems like it would be a lotta fun. They showed me inside the cockpit of one of 'em. Jeez, I couldn't figure out what most of those do-dads they had were there for."

"It still must make you feel proud knowin' you were in on the beginning," the boy said admiringly.

There was a sadness in his grandfather's reply.

"It's all gotten so big now," he said. "I never thought it would turn out like this."

"What do you mean, Dusty?"

"It was all new then. Flyin' to distant towns and performin' for folks; that was the real thrill of it. We opened a whole new world to them. Now the skies are all crowded and regulated. They're not so free anymore.

"Sometimes a dream can become a victim of its own success," he went on. "Whenever the masses get a hold of somethin', they often tend to ruin it for everybody else. What many people don't seem to realize, son, is that back when it all began, the vast countryside, the small towns and farms, and the little flimsy wood-and-wire planes themselves... they were all part of the dream, too."

Chapter 11

The telephone awakened Dusty from an afternoon nap. The desk clerk informed him that he had a visitor in the lobby.

She wore a navy blue leisure suit with a gold chain necklace. Again he was amazed by the strong resemblance to her mother, but he still could not get over the contrast between the little girl he remembered and this sophisticated-looking woman, now fifteen years his senior! Dusty correctly guessed that from what Mark had told her, her curiosity had gotten the better of her.

They sat down at a nearby table.

Lynn slowly looked over his face.

"I'm sorry for the other day," she said. "You have to understand it was all such a shock."

"I suppose it would be a lot to have thrown at you all at once," he acknowledged.

"You've certainly impressed Mark. Since he met you he hasn't talked about anything else!"

"He's a fine young man, Maddie. You should be very proud of him."

She nodded. "I wish he would apply his imaginative mind more to his schoolwork. When he came up with that incredible story of his, I thought he'd really gone over the edge."

"That's okay," Dusty gently smiled. "I'm not so sure I've got it all figured out myself."

Lynn still didn't know what to believe. "Why didn't the government notify us you'd been found," she asked. "Isn't that what they usually do in matters like these involving next of kin?"

"They've clamped a lid of secrecy on it."

"Secrecy? I thought that's what they do for the military or something. I would expect that they would hail you as one of the greatest scientific discoveries of all time - big media coverage, interviews. Why, you should be an overnight celebrity!"

"Believe me, that's the *last* thing I want right now," the pilot replied.

She paused for a moment to collect her thoughts.

"When I saw you sitting there, it was like… well… like all those faded pictures in mother's old trunk suddenly sprang to life. When I got back home, I ran upstairs to the attic to look at them, but they've all disappeared …the photographs… personal papers… everything!"

Dusty's jaw dropped. "They're gone? All of them?"

"That *really* spooked me. At first I thought that… well, maybe you had sneaked in and taken them… You know, like part of some weird joke or something. But that wouldn't have made much sense. You couldn't have known where they were unless you were a ghost - and don't think *that* thought hadn't crossed my mind. Then it occurred to me that perhaps Mark had borrowed them to show his friends at school. No one treasures them more than he does and he would never be careless with them. His favorite was the one of you which we kept in the living room. That's gone too."

"Damn!" muttered Dusty, "That's why they did it!"

"Dusty... what is it? What did they do?"

"They tried to discourage my comin' here so they could buy some time for themselves!"

"Time? For what? What are you talking about?"

He looked at her. "Maddie, I don't know how those pictures got out of the trunk, but I have a pretty good idea where they wound up."

"You mean... those government people?"

He nodded.

"But why would they want to steal them? They're only of value to us. If they wanted to borrow them, all they'd have to do was ask."

"Knowin' these people, if it comes to a choice between an honest way and a dishonest way of doin' somethin', you can always be sure they'll choose the latter. It would've been a simple matter to track you down from the papers they found on me."

"I still can't understand why they would go to all that trouble."

"I'm not sure either, Maddie, but whatever it is, those people seem to think that, just because they pulled me out of the ice, they *own* me!"

Ghosts, political intrigue - it was the most bizarre tale she'd ever heard. Ever since their first encounter at the club, she had searched back into the dimmest recesses of her memory, but it was all so long ago - another world, another lifetime.

Yet baffling as it was, it all somehow dovetailed with what Peg had told her over the years about the Depression, her father's mysterious disappearance, the heartbreak her mother had suffered and the cloud that lingered over her own childhood.

As he described what had happened to him, the old bitterness she had carried down through the years the years over what she thought had been his abandonment of them began to dissolve away, replaced by empathy for a man lost and suddenly cut off from those around him.

Another issue troubling her now rose to the surface.

"How is Mother?"

"She seems to be doin' all right considerin'."

"Considering what?"

"Well... you haven't been by to see her. She isn't too happy about that."

"No...I'm sure she isn't," Lynn replied. "Don't you know...? I'm the ungrateful daughter who's trying to gain control of her money!"

"She didn't say that."

"She didn't have to."

"Maddie honey... lots of folks say stuff in anger they don't really mean. Can't you see what your mama's been through? What worse hell can there be for a woman, active all her life, who now feels isolated from everybody?"

"I don't want to talk about it!"

"It must've been somethin' really big for what all you two meant to each other. You were the most important thing in her life!"

"You think you know so much! You go in there and try to help someone who turns on you and accuses you of trying to steal from her and makes insinuations about everybody! You don't know her! She's become a sick and bitter old woman who thinks we're all out to get her!"

Tears welled in her eyes and she broke down. She had not counted on losing control like this. Dusty gently took her in his arms and held her, all the while puzzled at how, in a world of such profound change, a little girl still needed her father.

The time came when they had run out of things to say. He walked her to her car, and as she was about to get in, she paused and turned to him.

"Dusty...dropping in out of the clear blue the way you did... tell me...how did you ever get them to believe you?"

It was an odd question, one which had never occurred to him before.

"I don't know," he replied. "Maybe they just wanted to."

"Surprise," Joe's voice rang out as he poked his head through Peg's door waving a bouquet of flowers.

"Not really," she said sourly. "You're the only one who never bothers to knock."

"That's pretty good," he laughed. "I see that my favorite girl is in good spirits today."

"What do you want, as if I didn't know?"

"There you go on the defensive again. I come by to see how you're doing and all I get is that nasty attitude which drives all of us away who care about you."

"Cut the crap!" she shot back. "I know why you're here and my answer remains the same."

Joe looked over the top of her dresser where he had previously left a large manila envelope. "The offer… Where is it? Did you have a chance to look it over?"

"The trash went out yesterday."

His smile vanished. "What? You didn't even look at it? I went to a lot of trouble putting this deal together, and…"

"You did it all for nothing! I told you six months ago I wasn't selling and I haven't changed my mind!"

His tone now began to turn belligerent.

"You know Peg… you're too stubborn for your own good. I'm trying to negotiate the best price possible for you and all you can say is to hell with it! Are you so naive as to believe that the city is going to give up on a multimillion dollar complex because you choose to hang onto some stupid fantasies? Well you'd better wake up to some facts! When the rezoning is passed, you won't have any say in the matter. It'll be on *their* terms, not yours! The city will begin eminent domain proceedings and run over you like a goddamn steamroller, and by the time they're finished you won't have as much as a sou. You'd better face reality! This is *prime land*, and the wheels of progress are not going to stop because of the foolish dreams of a silly old woman!"

Peg propped herself higher on her pillows. "You keep talking about *progress!* Progress for whom… - those crooks you work with? Oh, I know all about this little empire you've created for yourselves at the expense of all the people you've cheated and robbed! This *doom and gloom* you keep talking about... the rezoning... the eminent domain condemnations! What's taken them so long? If they're so damn sure of themselves, why haven't they done it already? Are you losing your clout with the city council? Are you afraid that the people of this town are finally wising up to you?"

She reached over and picked up the telephone. "Suppose I give the papers the *real story* about your extortion! Believe me, it's something I wrestle with every day, and the only thing keeping me from doing it is that I don't want my daughter and grandson dragged through the mud! But the more you keep pushing me, the harder it is to resist. Now get out!"

Joe's upper lip tightened. "You're making a big mistake, Peg! If you think you've heard the end of this, you're in for a rude shock!"

"I'm not going to say it again," she warned as she began dialing.

Joe stormed out. Peg put down the receiver and pushed the call button.

When the nurse came in to respond, she found Peg exhausted and trembling.

The four-lane highway continued for a few miles beyond town, but as Dusty and Mark got further out into the country, the surroundings became more familiar. Here and there a few farm buildings could be seen that weren't there before and power lines now ran along the distant hills. Other than that, however, relatively little had changed.

When they got there, they discovered that Kayesville too had been affected by a half-century of change. All that remained were a few crumbling walls of buildings and grown over traces of what had once been roads. The passage of time and the Great Depression had done what the flood couldn't.

Walking along the bank, Dusty pointed out to Mark where the ice jam had blocked the river. It took a considerable stretch of imagination to reconstruct the scene as it was all those years ago.

Mark could see the shock and disappointment in his grandfather's eyes. The town for which he had risked his life and for which his buddy Jim had given his was no more. The courage and bravery shown by so many had now become one more part of his world forever lost.

Not much was said on the way back to Claremont. Dusty dropped Mark off at his house then went on to the rest home.

The moment he entered Peg's room, Dusty sensed something was wrong. Her normally brightened spirits were missing. He was shocked at seeing her now looking so tired, demoralized and dejected.

"Is everything all right, kitten?"

She did not answer.

"What is it, hon?"

She turned away. He sat down on the bed and took her hand.

"Please tell me what's wrong. This isn't like you."

"It's all over," she sighed.

"What's over?" His first thought was that she had received some bad news. He looked around her bedside for a clue - a letter or something - but he found nothing.

"Now somethin's eatin' at you and I'm not leavin' here till you tell me what it is," he said.

She looked at him. Then in a tired voice she began to speak.

"Dusty, a long time ago we shared something together which was very special. All of those beautiful memories are things no one can ever take away from me. I have often thought about how wonderful it would have been had we been able to live out our lives together. But mine is now over and yours is still ahead of you. If you try to look for something which no longer exists, you will only find sorrow. You are entitled to your share of joy and fulfillment...but ...you're not going to find it here with me."

Dusty gave her a puzzled look as if she were speaking in some foreign language.

"What kind of talk is this? This isn't like you."

"I can't help you, Dusty. I can't even help myself."

"You let me be the judge of that," he said gently.

He picked up the phone.

Peg, her brows knitted in a furrowed scowl, looked up.

"What are you doing," she asked.

"I'm ordering some of that - what you call it - *takeout pizza.*"

"I can't have any of that stuff," she protested. "I've already had dinner."

"It's not for you; it's for me. Anything good on the television?"

"Dusty... it's getting dark. Hadn't you better head off to your hotel?"

"Too quiet there," he said. "I'd just get depressed."

"You know I can't put you up here. There's no place for you to sleep."

"This stuffed chair'll do just fine." And with that he settled in and made himself at home.

Around half past two in the morning he awakened. Ever so quiet so as not to disturb Peg, he picked up his backpack and slipped out of the room.

Chapter 12

The console buzzed on Joe Griffin's desk.

"Yes?"

"There's a Dusty Dervin is here to see you."

"Uh... have him wait a moment."

An uneasiness suddenly crept over Joe.

Like an annoying fly, Dervin's name had been popping up quite a bit lately. It was the center of dinner table conversations. Mark spoke of him like a boyhood hero. Adding to this was Peg's intransigence. There seemed to be a heightened resolve in this tired old woman. And then there was that matter with those two men who had stopped by a few weeks before.

It was apparent to Joe that a strange chain of events had been set in motion, and all at a critical time for the multibillion dollar project he'd been putting together over the last two years.

Joe did not like coincidences.

It seemed too suspicious. He couldn't figure out what was behind the sudden reappearance of a man supposedly dead for over forty years. He didn't believe any of this scientific baloney, not for a minute. To him it had all the markings of a shakedown.

Joe had his own plans for meeting Dusty, but it would have been more along the lines of having the pilot jerked off the street, dragged off to a secluded location, beating the truth out of him, and scaring him off. But now it seemed that the little bastard had gotten the jump on him.

"Send him in," Joe said curtly.

He motioned the pilot to a chair in front of his desk.

There were no handshakes or amenities. As Joe looked over his visitor, he saw nothing in the smaller man's appearance to warrant all this fuss. There were no slickness, no polish. Just an ordinary man wearing jeans and a sport shirt, looking pretty much like a common laborer.

Dusty for his part saw the trappings of Joe's office as manifestations of extravagance and hubris.

"What do you want," Joe grumbled.

"Oh nothing in particular," the pilot smiled good naturedly. "I just thought since I came to town, it was about time we met."

"I don't have time for a lot of crap," snapped Joe. "Get to the point or get out."

"I understand you dropped by to see Peggy yesterday."

Joe gave Dusty a hard look. He leaned back in his chair and cocked his head.

"What's it to you?"

"You're kind of upsettin' her," the pilot replied.

Joe refused to be put on the defensive. "I understand you've been causing some concern among some people here yourself," he said.

"How so?"

"Oh, some dumb little charade you're trying to pull."

Dusty looked puzzled. "Charade? I'm not aware of any charade."

"Oh *sure* you are. Who put you up to it? Westwood?"

"I don't know anybody by that name," Dusty replied.

"Oh *come now*. Even a genius like you couldn't come up with a crock like that all by yourself. Oh well... it doesn't really matter because right now you can do us both a favor while you can still leave town with all of your teeth!"

Joe pursed his fingers together.

"You seem to have some influence with my mother-in-law. I don't know what it is and I don't really give a damn, but as we both know she's getting along in years and... well, she's given to certain - shall we say - fantasies."

"What kind of fantasies?"

Joe ignored him and pressed on. "Now I can understand how old people tend to live in their own little world of make-believe and - hey, I got no problem with that if it makes 'em happy. Live-and-let-live, right? However in this case, it turns out that the dear lady happens to own five houses in an area that's so rundown, even the coloreds won't live in 'em. We're prepared to offer her a good price for that land - at least ten times what it's worth! Yet for some reason I can't figure out, she stubbornly refuses to act on what's clearly to her own benefit!"

"What do you have in mind," asked the pilot.

"Get her to sign this form."

Joe passed to the pilot a legal looking document which Dusty recognized as a transfer of title. "You'll be doing her a big favor," he went on. "There's five thousand in it for you when you bring it back with her signature on it… all yours to take back to L.A. or wherever the hell you came from!"

"What are your plans for this section," Dusty asked curiously.

"Oh, it'll be razed and developed - but that's really none of your business."

"What if she still won't go along with it?"

"Then regrettably the decision will have to be made for her. Once Council rezones the land commercial, her property taxes'll skyrocket. She'll be forced to sell by which time she'll be facing bankruptcy. She'll have to leave that nice nursing home. Now don't get me wrong; the old gal has a right to her own little dream world, but she'd damned well better realize that she can't take on city hall by herself."

Dusty read over the document, nodding slowly as he went over each point. When he finished he looked up at Joe. There was a slight smile on his face.

"She won't have to."

Joe looked up at him with a queer stare as if he were not sure that he understood Dusty correctly.

"What do you mean?"

"It must be sad to grow old," reflected the pilot. "The years slip by, your friends die off, and your children, wrapped up in their own lives, don't seem to have much time for you. Then one mornin' you wake up and realize that you're all alone. No one's around anymore who knew you in your prime, and then you begin to feel as if you never really had one.

"But if you have somethin' they want," he went on, "*then* they hang around like buzzards waitin' for you to die or slip up in some way so they can find an excuse to take it away from you. They hire doctors and lawyers ready to prostitute their ethics to declare you insane or incompetent. I'd call that a kind of betrayal wouldn't you?"

He placed the paper on Joe's desk and rose to leave.

"We're not through here, you bastard," Joe snarled threateningly. "You damned well better stay away from Peg if you know what's good for you. That goes for the rest of my family, too. You hear me!"

"I don't scare very easy, Joe," Dusty replied calmly. "Y'know... I got this feelin' you're in way over your head."

As Dusty turned toward the door Joe rose from his chair to his full height.

"We're not finished with this, Dervin!"

The pilot turned to face him once more.

"No," he said, "I don't suppose we are."

The evening found Westwood alone in his office finishing up some paperwork. He was about to call it a night when he was alerted by the closing of the front door downstairs. He rose and walked out to the hallway where, looking down onto the foyer, he could see a stranger studying some watercolor drawings on the wall.

"Is there something I can help you with?" he called out.

Dusty pointed to one of the pictures, then turned and looked up.

"These houses - before and after...," he asked. "Are they part of the renewal project?"

"Yes they are," Westwood said politely. "Perhaps if you could come back tomorrow, one of our staff may be able to help you."

"Well, I've only got one question," Dusty said. "Do you know where I might find a Foster Westwood?"

"I'm Westwood. Who are you?"

"Dusty Dervin".

Westwood's eyes fixed upon his visitor for it was now apparent that the latter had not chosen this late hour by chance.

"You wouldn't happen to be related to Margarite Dervin, would you?"

The pilot nodded.

Westwood carefully looked him over for a moment, and then motioned him upstairs where he offered him a chair.

"Would you like some coffee?"

"Black'll be fine," Dusty replied.

After looking to his guest and pouring some for himself, Westwood returned to his desk.

"What brings you here," he inquired.

"To tell the truth," Dusty said, "I'm not quite sure. I had a chat with some people and in the course of the discussion, your name came up. I see you have an interest in fixin' up old houses. Peggy's been talkin' a lot about that, too."

"She's a wonderful person and a dear friend," said the attorney. "She really dedicated herself to this project and we miss her around here."

Dusty nodded. "I guess that explains why they think you and I are workin' together."

"Who are 'they'? Did you pick up any names?"

The pilot recounted his meeting with Joe, along with what had happened to him since arriving in Claremont. But he carefully hedged about his true relationship to Peg, accounting for the years of being out of touch with his family by explaining how he'd been working in Alaska.

For Westwood, this filled in some missing pieces. His instincts told him that Dusty was someone he could trust.

"What we have here amounts to a minor civil war," the lawyer began, "and this is what it's all about."

He reached behind his chair and produced a large drawing which he then unrolled on his desk.

What Dusty saw took him back many years. It was a finely detailed sketch, penned in color, of his old neighborhood - houses, trees and all.

"Some of these you got here no longer exist," he noted.

"We have the plans to reconstruct them, though," said Westwood. "A lot of people want to live in them."

"Why the sudden interest now?"

"The Old Town Project started out as a desire to retain something of the city's character," Westwood went on to explain. "But since then, it has emerged as a symbol for a lot of other issues - overbuilding, lack of proper planning, uncontrolled growth, inadequate affordable housing for the poor and elderly - just to name a few. Now that the developers have turned their eyes toward the Old Section, it has turned into a major rallying point."

Dusty rose to examine a watercolor on the wall of a Model T pickup parked in front of a 1920's cottage.

"How do you think it's gonna go," he asked.

"Not too good, I'm afraid. The conglomerate's got all the money and resources. They're planning to saturate the community with a media blitz we couldn't begin to match. We had our biggest asset in Peg. She provided the guiding spirit that gave our cause its life. Without her, well...," Westwood shook his head woefully, "I just don't know."

"You keep sayin' how close you and Peg were, yet not once have you been by to see her or reassure her of your support for her." He looked up at Westwood. "Have you been threatened too?"

"What makes you say that," the attorney asked warily.

"Seems to be the way these people work. When I saw Peg yesterday mornin', she was in good spirits. But when I stopped by later on she was very tired. I think that while I was gone something - or someone - upset her. I figure it was Joe.

"What I want to know," continued the pilot, "...is what have they got on you?"

"What do you mean?"

"What else could keep two friends apart like that?"

Westwood resented this intrusion into a part of his life which he had hoped to keep private. But then he realized that further silence would be pointless, and it would only be a matter of time before it all came out anyway.

The attorney heaved a sigh.

"Do you remember the fifties?" he began. "All those lofty ideals and expectations: work hard, strive to achieve your maximum potential and get ahead? Well... I swallowed it all, hook, line and sinker: straight A's in high school, class president, Yale undergraduate, Harvard Law. Joined a prestigious firm, got married, had a family and a nice two-story home in the suburbs. I made all the right moves and attained the pinnacle of success by the time I was thirty.

"Didn't pay much attention to the stomach pains at first. When they got worse I went to one doctor and then another. They all thought it was an ulcer. Then one morning I woke up and I couldn't get out of bed! It seemed like nothing mattered anymore. This time they diagnosed acute depression; I was having a nervous breakdown. My whole world was crumbling around me and there was nothing I could do about it. Well... eventually I lost everything. My wife left and took the kids with her, and I spent the next several months in a sanitarium.

"In a way, that proved to be a turning point for me. During the course of my stay there, I gradually came to realize that my entire life had been... well, a sham. I had never been truly honest with myself. I'd spent all that time and effort trying to live up to the expectations of others.

Then as I began to reexamine those values, I saw them for what they were. Those months turned me around like nothing ever did before, and yet the public seems more concerned with where I spent that time rather than what I gained from the experience."

Dusty listened respectfully.

"I think most folks deserve more credit for understanding than that," he said. "All you've told me is that you're human."

"It didn't help Eagleton."

"Who?"

"McGovern's running mate. Have you forgotten that already?"

"Oh yeah...," Dusty replied, faking his way through a part of history he had missed out on. "But I still think that in the long run, it'd be better to bring it out."

"Are you kidding? Look, Dusty... it's not for myself I'm afraid, but what happens to our cause when this gets out? All the trust and credibility we've worked so hard to earn will go right down the drain."

Dusty, however, didn't see it that way.

"Doesn't it take a bigger man to admit he had once embarked upon a course which turned out to be wrong than to continue sufferin' in silence for the sake of appearance? If this is what they're holdin' over you, I'd beat 'em to the punch."

"And how would you have me do that?"

"When you go public with it," Dusty smiled, "...tell 'em you used to be like *them*."

Mark came to dread those evenings when his father came home for dinner. In the tension-charged atmosphere, each sound was amplified to its largest volume, from a fork hitting a plate to the slurping of Joe's coffee. The boy's objective was to make it through the meal in silence, for he knew that the utterance of a single word could trigger a major argument.

Tonight he would not be successful. No sooner had the family sat down at the table when Joe started in.

"Mark, I think it's best if you don't visit your grandmother for awhile," he declared in a peremptory tone.

Mark looked up at his father.

"Why not?"

"Because she's not feeling well."

"Why wouldn't she tell *me* this?"

"Because she doesn't want to hurt your feelings," and with that, Joe picked up his fork and began to attack his salad.

Mark knew his father was lying. "This doesn't sound like her. If she felt that way, I'm sure she would have told me."

"Nevertheless, you are not to see her. End of discussion!"

Lynn could see that the conflict was rapidly spinning out of control.

"Mark... Joe...," she pleaded, "...let's eat before dinner gets cold."

"Is this another one of your dumb directives," Mark shot back.

Joe, thus confronted, resorted to his time worn tactic of shifting the attack to another front.

"No, it's that snotty attitude that got you kicked out of Claremont Academy."

"That dumb school was *your* idea, not mine!"

Lynn cried out, "Could we all please settle down and eat?"

But Joe, once committed to the offensive, was not about to let up.

"My idea? Yes... I suppose it was my idea to want the best education for you."

"It wasn't so bad before."

"Before what? You mean when you hung around with all those kids that turned you into a lazy good-for-nothing bum?"

"They were my *friends*! And they were a helluva lot better than those snotty assholes at Claremont."

"Do you ever stop to think that maybe it's not everyone else who's out of step, that maybe it just might be you? Those fellows you seem to have so much contempt for are a helluva lot farther up the ladder than you are."

"I don't give a damn about your stupid ladder," Mark fired back. "They're just the kids of people you're tryin' to suck up to!"

Lynn put her hands over her ears and screamed, "Please stop this arguing! I can't take it anymore!"

But Joe pressed on. "You will no longer visit her. Moreover, you will no longer have anything to do with that kook claiming to be your grandfather. Is that understood?"

"Dusty is not a kook! He *is* my grandfather and I'm gonna see both of them whenever I feel like it!"

Joe suddenly sprang forward to swing at Mark, but the boy ducked as his father missed his aim and knocked over a glass of water.

"GO TO YOUR ROOM, YOU LOUDMOUTHED BRAT!" he screamed. "AND YOU'LL DAMNED WELL STAY THERE UNTIL I SAY YOU CAN COME OUT! YOU'RE GONNA LEARN TO DO AS YOU'RE TOLD IF I HAVE TO BLOODY YOUR GODDAMNED BEHIND WITH A *STRAP*!"

Mark stormed upstairs. The slam of his bedroom door reverberated through the house like a gunshot.

Tears welled in Lynn's eyes as she glared angrily at her husband.

"We just can't do it anymore, can we! We can't even have a peaceful meal at the dinner table without it escalating into a major battle!"

"It's not my fault he's become like this," he shrugged.

"Oh *no*!" she shot back. "It's never your fault for *anything*! You're so damned wrapped up in your role as the town big shot, it's now extended to becoming the dictator at home too!"

"Somebody's got to discipline him. You seem too busy socializing at your tennis club."

"Oh, look who's talking about *clubs* now! *Clubs* have become such a way of life for you it's a wonder you even come home at all, and when you carry on like this, I'd just as soon you *didn't*!"

"I transact a lot of business at those 'clubs' as you put it. That's how I make all the money you love to spend!"

"Money?! You mean for all the trappings and fancy cars *you* need to enhance your image!"

"Oh sure," Joe said sarcastically. "Giving *your* ungrateful son the opportunity to get ahead... I suppose that was for my image too, huh?"

"There was nothing wrong with his friends. They just weren't good enough for *you!* Mark was right. You weren't doing this for him. You were doing it for yourself!"

"Alright!" Joe shouted, "That does it! I try to work out the best deal for your mother before she gets wiped out by the new zoning change. If that's the way you want it *you* go visit her and put up with the crap she dishes out! But let me warn you right now... I won't be responsible for what happens! And what's more," he said pointing his finger at her, "...you'd better steer clear of that jerk, too. You understand me!"

Lynn pressed her fingers to her temples and slowly shook her head.

"How can you pass judgment on a man you've never even *met*," she cried out. "My God! What kind of curse has come over us since we've moved into this house? I don't even know what's *happening* anymore! We don't see any of our old friends, I'm no longer on speaking terms with my mother, and we can't even have a decent conversation without it erupting into a full-scale war!"

"I don't need this shit!" Joe snapped as he jumped up shoving his chair aside and storming to the hall closet to grab his jacket.

"Where are you going?"

"Out!"

The front door slammed. She heard the car start, screech out the driveway and speed off. Then, slowly turning to gaze at the barely touched meal on the table, she slowly sank into her chair, buried her face in her hands and cried.

Chapter 13

To Peg, Dusty remained an enigma. He stood before her a young man, yet his eyes evoked the wistful dreams of a bygone time.

His visits brightened her spirits, and for a brief moment provided her a kind of escape. The magic of old memories would return with a clarity as though all of the many passing years had never taken place.

In the years following his disappearance she had come to remember him for his gentle qualities and deep inner strength.

But now she saw before her a vulnerable man, adrift in a vast sea which threatened to swallow him up. The signs were all too painfully apparent.

He would relate to her his experiences learning his way around, and they'd share a laugh or two over old times. But then as the conversation ebbed and his mind drifted off, his eyes would once again take on that faraway look, and she would know.

She loved this man who had come back to her, but now she also feared for him. How could he ever find his way in this modern world whose myriad complexities must make it seem like a cage? How long would it be before it overwhelmed him and crushed him?

And what hung heaviest upon her heart was that she could do nothing to protect him as he had once protected her.

In a kind of motherly way, Peg assumed the role as his advisor, bringing him up to date on a wide assortment of contemporary issues ranging from the current cost of food to the subtle pitfalls he had to be aware of when buying something on credit. And as Dusty took all this in, he could not help but marvel at how the years had transformed the young girl he had known into this wise and scholarly sage of the latter Twentieth Century.

From what Dusty had related to her, Peg had figured out what Johns and his group were up to; he was going to use the pilot's name to promote his own.

It was quite obvious. Since no one had ever returned from the dead before, Dusty's story - once it could be confirmed and made public - would have a stunning impact upon the world. He would be more that just another famous athlete or movie star - he would be a legend! And Johns would stop at nothing to gain control over the rights to it. He would force Dusty into a series of binding contracts controlling all aspects of his life: what he could say in public, when and where he could appear, and what products he could endorse. Ahead lay glittering prospects of fame and fortune far beyond anything he'd ever imagined. But these would all come at a heavy price in the restrictive constraints which came with life under the heel of a dictatorial man obsessed with his own power.

If this world seemed strange and hostile now, warned Peg, that which Johns had in mind for him would be far worse, for he would rob Dusty of the two things that mattered most - his independent spirit and his dignity.

This did not really come as a surprise to Dusty. He had already picked up on Johns and his motives, but Peg's perspective gave a welcome confirmation.

If Dusty was amazed at Peg's intuition, she was about to find that the pilot possessed a few insights of his own.

On this afternoon, Dusty once again seemed off in his own world as Peg caught him gazing out the window with that distant melancholy look.

"What is it, hon," she asked tenderly taking his hand.

"Oh, nothing," he shrugged.

"If you've come here to cheer me up," she said, "…you're not doing a very good job of it."

He gazed at the floor in deep concentration as if trying to put together the best way to explain some complex theory. Then he looked up at her.

"Peg…ever since I've come here, there's been somebody lurking in the background… the kind of guy you don't see too much in the spotlight… someone who seems more at home in smoke-filled rooms."

Her eyes narrowed on him curiously. "You mean Joe?"

He nodded. "I met him yesterday."

Peg's jaw dropped. It was the one thing she dreaded, seeing a loved one out of his element confronted by a bully very much in his own.

When he finished relating what happened, she lay back on the pillow and heaved a sigh.

"Dusty... I never meant for you to get mixed up in this."

"What?" he said. "And just stand by while he tries to force you into doing something you don't want to do?" Then he added, "Peg... I know about his visit the other day."

She remained silent for a minute or two.

"What do you think I should do," she said. "I don't have the strength to fight him anymore."

It was now Dusty's turn to buoy her spirits.

"Why... just continue to do what you've been doing," he said in an upbeat tone. "The way I see it, I think he's gettin' a little edgy."

"What do you mean?"

"I did a little checkin' around. For one thing the council meetin's not far off and he hasn't delivered on your houses. Could be his buddies are worried... maybe even threatenin' to pull out."

"He... told you this?" she said skeptically.

"Well... not in so many words. But hey, kitten... just because I've been out of circulation for awhile doesn't mean I can't follow a trail."

Dusty rose from the chair and looked out the window.

"Real honorable, isn't he. Systematically cuttin' you off from your friends, drivin' a wedge between you and Maddie... And all the while he spins this little web of his, he sets himself up as the great mediator."

He turned and looked at her. "Kinda sad when you think about it. We can fly across the country in a matter of hours, send a man to the moon, and cure diseases which were a virtual sentence of death in our day. And yet for all this progress, nobody's ever been able to come up with a cure for common greed!"

"Joe is certainly capable of this," she acknowledged. "But what can we do about it? We don't have anything on him we can prove."

"No... not yet maybe. But there's another angle to this which nobody else has ever considered."

"What's that?"

"The disappearance of my stuff."

Her eyes widened. "You suspect Joe had a hand in that?"

The pilot nodded.

"But how would he have known of their value? He didn't even know you'd been found then."

"He wouldn't have to. I think he was reached."

"By whom... Johns? How would he know that Joe would be the one to see?"

"Wouldn't be too hard to figure out given his resources," Dusty explained. "A greedy man is sittin' on top of this incredible story. So to keep it from gettin' away from him, he sets out to hedge his bet. He needs some kind of leverage - old pictures, letters - anything dated which could establish who I am and what happened to me. You with me so far?"

"Yes," she said. "Go on."

"Now let's say an honest man wants to do some research for a book he's gonna write. The first thing he'd most likely do would be to track down whatever descendants he could find and tell them of his intentions. All on the up and up, right? Most folks like you or

Maddie would probably jump at the chance of public recognition for one of your own. You'd show him some authentic documents, pictures and such, and when he saw somethin' he liked, a mutual agreement would be worked out. He might even settle for reproduction copies he could take with him. Then maybe some legal papers would be drawn up, and he'd be off on his way.

"But suppose this guy isn't satisfied with just half the loaf? He doesn't want just one or two pictures; he wants the whole shebang - everything you've got: negatives, old newspaper articles, the works. Even wants to check through your attic. Wouldn't that make you a little suspicious?"

"I'd throw his rear end to hell out," Peg said indignantly.

"Most people would, so ol' Johns takes a different approach. He does a little research of his own. He learns about all of you: Maddie, Mark, and especially Joe, the big-time promoter and wheeler-dealer. He even picks up on everybody's routines and habits. Then when he sees his chance, he hits Joe with a proposition."

"Suppose Joe had ideas of his own? Maybe he wanted part of the action himself?"

Dusty shook his head. "Not too likely. Johns was too quick for him. I think it was a simple matter of Joe simply succumbing to the smell of fast money dangled in front of his nose."

"But how would he explain it when Maddie or Mark went to look for the pictures and found them missing?"

"He wouldn't have to; all he'd have to do is maintain that it was an ordinary burglary. He probably figured it would be a month or so before the loss was discovered, by which time the trail would grow cold. And it almost worked except..."

"You showed up!" she interjected.

"That must've really unglued him! You see, it prompted Maddie to search the trunk earlier than he had counted on, and thus it narrowed the time frame when the theft could've taken place."

"It certainly makes sense," agreed Peg. "But again, what kind of case can we make of it? There's nothing illegal about a man selling his own family's belongings."

"I'm not up on the current bribe scale, but I'll bet that a lot of money changed hands. And what's more, I'm sure that neither Maddie nor Mark knew anything about it. I'd sure like to know where all that money wound up. I'll bet Joe's keepin' a private account somewhere, and who knows what else might be there?"

There was a tone of misgiving in what Peg said next.

"Suppose it turns out that Joe is indeed keeping a secret fund of some kind - what then?"

"It might well be the tip of the iceberg," Dusty replied. "Once we establish that, we can bring his whole house of cards down right on top of him!"

"And then do you know what'll happen," she argued. "The fallout from a scandal of this sort would cast a stain on Lynn and Mark! I don't want anything of this sort if it comes to them at a cost in public shame and humiliation."

"It shouldn't come to that," he said trying to reassure her. "But then you can't go on givin' in to people like that. They gotta be stopped, and yes... there's a chance things might get a little messy for awhile."

His tone turned solemn. "There's no guarantee, Peg. Sure there are always risks involved in anything. But in the end, what's gonna matter most is how you fought this thing to the finish."

He rose to put on his jacket. "One thing I can tell you for sure," he said with confidence. "When this is all over, I know of a certain young man who's gonna be real proud of his grandma."

"Where are you going?"

"To make sure Joe doesn't pay you any more visits. Besides there's a couple of loose ends I want to check out."

"Dusty?"

"Yes, kitten?"

"*Please* be careful," she pleaded. "There's no telling what those men will resort to. Honey... I beg you... stay out of it. I don't want you to get hurt."

"Gee," he grinned with a twinkle of mischief in his eye, "You wouldn't take this away from me now, just when it's gettin' good."

Peg bit her lip and turned away. Dusty sat down on her bed and took both of her hands in his. "Peggy, Peggy," he said softly. "We've come through a lot worse than this."

He searched in his mind for some way to reassure her, but somehow he sensed it best to just let her cry.

Joe was working late at the office on some last minute details he had to complete.

There was a knock at the door. He looked up and smiled, "Come in, honey."

His secretary, an attractive brunette in her early thirties entered.

"How's it coming," she asked.

"Oh I think we're just about finished here," he said confidently. "It's all downhill from here."

She slowly walked over to the window where she surveyed the panorama of city lights below. She turned to find him standing behind her. He reached up for the chord and closed the blinds. Then they embraced, kissing passionately, her hands running through his hair while his caressed up and down her body.

"I miss that," she whispered.

"It'll only be just a few more days."

"I know. I'm just worried, that's all."

"Well, you needn't be. All you have to do is look at those two airline tickets and the travel brochures. Before you know it, we'll be out of here."

After checking to make sure the door was locked, he turned out the lights, and then joined her on the couch where they proceeded to explore the wonders of each other.

"Joe?"

"Yes, sweetie."

"Is everything all right?"

"Of course it is, darling. You know that."

"You just seem so...preoccupied lately."

"Well don't worry. Everything'll be just fine."

"I know," she sighed. "I just wish it were all behind us."

"In a couple of days, it will be."

The stretch of back road was deserted that night. When Dusty saw the flashing red and blue lights in his mirror, he thought to himself, I've watched the speedometer. Wonder what I've done wrong this time?

Two men, one in uniform, emerged from the patrol car.

"Let me see your license," demanded the patrolman.

The pilot complied and the patrolman took it back to the plainclothes sergeant standing alongside. Presently both men returned.

"Get out of the vehicle," ordered the sergeant.

Dusty complied and was directed to lean against his car. He was then frisked.

"What's this all about," he asked.

"It seems you've outworn your welcome here," the senior officer remarked. "You never learn do you?" He nodded to his subordinate who then swung his nightstick into Dusty's back. The pilot winced in pain but did not cry out.

"I don't know what it takes to convince you," continued the sergeant.

A blow to the back of his knees dropped the pilot to the ground. The patrolman hoisted him up and slammed him against the hood of his car. From the corner of his eye, Dusty could see the patrolman raising his stick to hit him again when the lights of a passing car prompted him to jerk his arm down. No sooner had the car gone from sight when another appeared out of the darkness, followed by yet another. Then there were cars going in the opposite direction.

"I thought there wasn't supposed to be any goddamn traffic out here at this hour!" the sergeant snarled.

"There usually isn't," grumbled the patrolman. "Must be some kinda party somewhere."

"Oh *hell*! Well, let's get this bastard out of here!" They shoved him into the back of the patrol car and sped off.

The car screeched to a halt in front of the airport terminal. Dusty could feel the stares of curious onlookers as he was hustled past the ticket counter, then on through a security check. Like a criminal suspect, he was ordered to dump the contents of his pack onto an adjacent table, and then repack it. When they got to the departure gate, the sergeant shoved his face up to Dusty's, and punctuated his threats by repeatedly poking him in the chest.

"You're gettin' to hell on that plane back to Los Angeles! And if I ever see your ugly face in my town again, there won't be enough left of you to shovel in a dustpan!"

The sergeant's threats had no sooner left his mouth when a strobe light flashed off in his face.

"That should be a good shot," Foster Westwood declared as the photographer scurried off into the crowd. "Ought to make tomorrow's front page for sure, don't you think."

The sergeant, caught by surprise, quickly resumed his menacing snarl. "You've gone too far this time, Westwood - interfering with police business!"

"Interfering with a beating? Go ahead, Moray... put him on the plane. Then when he comes back to prefer assault charges for that little scene out there by the road, he'll have plenty of witnesses to back him up. Yes sir, I believe a new day is dawning on City Hall!"

"Just keep it up, you bastard," threatened Moray. "Your day's comin' soon enough. You can bet on it!"

"I'm looking forward to it. Gee, I haven't felt this much satisfaction in years, knowing our people can now take an active part in the council proceedings without fear of your bullies and Billy clubs. It ought to be a real memorable evening."

"C'mon Jenkins!" Moray snapped. Both officers shot back hateful looks at the two men as they stormed off.

Westwood turned to Dusty. "Don't get him wrong," he said. "He's really a swell guy once you get to know him."

"It's a good thing you showed up when you did," the pilot said gratefully.

Then it all suddenly dawned on him. "Those cars back there... you?"

"These days, we need all the friends we can get," Westwood smiled. "I had a nice chat with Peggy this afternoon. She told me to look out for you."

Peg could tell a lot from footsteps. Each doctor and nurse of the regular staff walked with a distinct style which she could recognize. But she usually paid no attention to them unless they slowed down, indicating that one of them was about to stop by.

It was the peculiar pattern of these footsteps which alerted her. She detected an uncertainty to them: a slow halting walk, then a hesitation, then the walk again. She peered over her reading glasses at the door.

Several seconds passed.

"It's all right," she said softly. "You can come in."

The door opened slowly and the visitor appeared. She stood still in the shadows.

Peg motioned her over and she took a couple of steps forward. Tears welled in her eyes and her lips trembled.

"M...mother?"

Chapter 14

It was a tearful reunion. As Lynn and her mother spoke for over two hours catching up, the wall of misunderstanding between them soon crumbled and a heavy burden was lifted away.

Once Lynn acknowledged the truth there could be no turning back. But Peggy now found herself with a new concern. Fearing Joe's reaction once he realized they were on to him, she insisted that her daughter and Mark move out of the house at once.

Lynn agreed, but first there was something she had to do. She wouldn't say what it was, for had Peg known what her daughter had in mind, she would never have gone along with it.

Financial matters had always been an area jealously guarded by Joe. Lynn, whose knowledge of these things had not gone beyond balancing her own checkbook, had heretofore been content to remain ignorant of them.

In the den, an eerie chill came over her as she turned the dial of the wall safe. The slightest sound made her heart skip, but whenever that happened she would pause for a moment, take a deep breath, and go on. With the final click of the tumblers, she gingerly opened the vault.

Inside were several stacks of bills. She reached in, pulled one out and examined it. It was twenty thousand dollars! From what she could estimate, there must be several hundred thousand dollars here - more money than she had ever seen in her life!

As she replaced the stack, she noticed a small ledger. She took it out and began to thumb through it. On each page there were two columns; one consisted of nicknames or initials, the other of numbers with four and five figures. She needed no accounting background to tell her that this was some kind of payoff list. One or two names she recalled hearing him mention on the phone, the rest she had not.

Her stomach tightened in fear as she realized that all this money here was probably illegal.

Carefully putting everything back as she found it, she was about to close the safe when the door to the study suddenly swung open. She turned to find Joe standing there.

His face reddened. His upper lip tightened and his eyes had a wild maniacal look.

"What are you doing in the safe?" he said in a tone of repressed rage.

Lynn stood there trembling in stark terror, unable to speak.

"WHAT ARE YOU DOING IN THE SAFE?" he yelled out as he shoved her aside, storming into the safe to check its contents. Seeing nothing missing he refocused his wrath upon her. "WHO PUT YOU UP TO IT?"

"Nobody, Joe."

He moved menacingly toward her. "DON'T GIVE ME THAT CRAP! YOU'RE TOO STUPID TO HAVE COME UP WITH THIS ON YOUR OWN! NOW ONCE AGAIN, WHO PUT YOU UP TO IT!?"

"I told you Joe… nobody!"

She slowly backed towards the door.

"IT WAS YOUR MOTHER, WASN'T IT! THAT GODDAMN MEDDLING OLD BITCH! THIS WAS HER IDEA!"

"Leave her out of this!" she cried. "She had nothing to do with it!"

"OF COURSE SHE DID! SHE JUST SENT YOU TO SPY ON ME! CONNIVING OLD BITCH!"

Her initial fear now gave way to a loathsome contempt.

"How *dare* you accuse her? How *dare* you! What were you planning to do? Run off with that *woman*?" She spat it out as though it were a dirty word. "Yes, I know all about her. Is *that* what this was all about? Why didn't you just *ask* me for your freedom, Joe? I would have given it to you on a silver platter!"

"Yeah… and taken me to the cleaners in the process! You make me *sick*! You, your mother, that goddamn kid! I've spent too many months setting this up to have you flush it down the toilet! Now I'm not gonna ask you again, WHO PUT YOU UP TO IT?"

Lynn started to bolt for the doorway when Joe grabbed her, spun her around and slapped her, knocking her to the floor. Her eyes widened in terror as he jerked her up and shook her. "NOW DAMMIT! I'M GONNA

GET THE TRUTH FROM YOU IF I HAVE TO BEAT IT OUT OF YOU!"

He raised his hand to hit her again when a voice from behind stopped him cold.

"She can't give you much of a fight, Joe," Dusty said with icy calm. "Why don't you try me?"

The eyes of the two adversaries riveted on each other as the pilot slowly entered the room. Lynn shakily got up and Dusty motioned her over to him.

"Go outside, hon," he said evenly.

"DUSTY, HE'LL KILL YOU!" she screamed.

But his immediate concern was for her safety.

"No he won't. Go on outside now," he repeated, his eyes riveted on Joe. "I'll be along shortly."

Her eyes fixed on them in stark terror as she backed out of the room.

Now alone, the two men began to slowly circle each other, one confronting a threat to his family, the other regarding his adversary as a piece of vermin to be exterminated.

The odds were not good. In addition to being several inches taller, Griffin had a fifty-pound advantage over the pilot, who was no longer confident in his own agility.

Suddenly Griffin snatched up a fireplace poker and began waving it menacingly. "You sonofabitch," he snarled, "...I've been waiting for this a long time!"

"Take your best shot, Joe."

Griffin began teasing at him with it, alternately feinting and swinging at the pilot who focused on just staying out of the way.

Joe rushed at him and he jumped aside. Griffin attacked again, this time savagely swinging the poker as Dusty leaped behind the desk.

The big man smashed the poker on the desk top, and Dusty darted to a large chair near the opposite wall. He picked up a wastebasket and hurled it at Griffin who quickly stove it in with one blow. Then the pilot pitched books, paperweights and anything else he could throw at his antagonist. Some hit home, one even bounced off Joe's forehead, but these futile shots only intensified the fury of this oncoming maniac.

Dusty was playing for time. He was rapidly growing winded, finding it increasingly difficult to stay clear of the deadly swings of his attacker. He pushed the chair in the path of Joe, who with sheer brute force simply flung it aside.

The pilot now found himself cornered. He focused on the vicious hate-filled look in Griffin's eyes as the latter closed in for the kill.

"Okay you bastard," Joe snarled through clenched teeth, "This is gonna be over real quick!"

Dusty dove past his attacker, who whacked him hard with the poker and sent him sprawling. A sharp, blinding pain shot through him like his entire back was on fire. The monster relentlessly pressed on, eager to dispatch the final blow. In desperation, Dusty's groping fingers felt an overturned desk lamp. Joe struck down hard again, delivering a glancing blow to the pilot's leg as he twisted to the side. Then, as Griffin raised the poker to strike again, Dusty lunged up, shoving the lamp's business end deep into Joe's groin, shattering the light bulb and sending him reeling back grabbing his crotch and screaming like a wounded banshee.

The pilot staggered to his feet, then with his last bit of strength, he swung the lamp like a baseball bat, dispatching his adversary with a well-placed blow to the head.

As he gradually caught his breath, he stood there gazing upon his fallen foe. Presently he heard a sobbing sound coming from the hallway.

It was Lynn sitting at the bottom of the stairs crying. A .38 revolver hung limply in her hands.

He went over, gently took it from her and set it aside.

"I don't think we'll need this now," he said softly.

He then realized what this terrified woman had come perilously close to doing. She had not left the house as he had told her to do; she had been outside the study all the time, for had Joe prevailed, Lynn had prepared herself to shoot him.

"It's okay now, honey...," he said tenderly cradling her. "It's okay. He won't be botherin' anybody anymore."

Joe began to stir. Dusty walked over to the shambled curtains where he yanked down the cord and proceeded to tie him up.

Then he looked up and smiled at Lynn. "Not bad for an old man in his seventies, would you say?"

He turned once more to look at Joe.

"I guess we'd better call the police," he said. As Lynn picked up the receiver her father added, "No... better make it the state boys. We don't know how high up the food chain this mess goes."

As Griffin regained consciousness, he began to moan.

But Dusty was far from being sympathetic.

"I'm sure he'll have a lot to tell them, but while we're waitin'...," he said pulling Joe's head back by the hair, "our friend here is gonna tell me about a couple of visitors he had!"

"What's taking him so long," Peg said testily as she looked at her watch. "Doesn't he know the meeting starts in ten minutes? We're late already!"

"He'll be here, Grandma," assured Mark. "He said something about some last minute alterations to his suit."

Peg appeared the personification of dignity in her navy dress outfit as she sat in her wheelchair in the lobby of the nursing home.

"I'll give him an *alteration* in a minute! He's doing this just to spite me for insisting he wear one!"

Just then Dusty's car pulled up to the front and he bounded to the door. "Sorry I'm late," he said sheepishly. "Got hung up in traffic."

"I'm sure that whatever it was, must've been really hard to tear yourself away from." Then, noticing the cuts and bruises on his face and hands, she asked with astonishment, "My *God*, Dusty! What *happened* to you?"

"Fell down some stairs," he said, then he looked at his watch. "Hey, we'd better get goin'!"

When they entered the foyer of Town Hall, Foster Westwood ran up to greet them. Then they all proceeded into the council meeting room.

Peg immediately noticed that something was different. There were police present, but only two officers, the minimum number required by law at any ordinary meeting. She had expected at least a dozen or more. Also conspicuous by their absence were three members of the Council Board, all of whom had been vigorous proponents of the Superblock.

"Where are all the big shots?" Peggy whispered to Westwood.

"Nobody knows," the latter replied.

"Who's that speaking now?"

"Oh, I've seen him around. Some second stringer they got." The man to whom they referred was delivering the expected standard party line of jobs, growth and prosperity. The audience, restless at his monotone, rudely shouted for him to sit down as the chairman pounded his gavel repeatedly to restore order.

After about twenty minutes, it was her turn. Mark kissed his grandmother and wished her luck, as did Westwood. A surge of pride came over Dusty as he wheeled her down the aisle.

Many who had known this frail woman sensed a deep urgency in her presence here.

She laid a few sheets of paper on the table and then put on her reading glasses. A respectful silence descended upon the room.

"I would like to thank all of you for letting me speak this evening," she began. "As I look out among you, I feel the presence of many other dear friends who are with us in spirit."

With moving eloquence she extolled the achievements of a generation who had seen this country through two world wars and a major depression, and who had made tremendous contributions in the struggle against disease. She spoke of them in loving terms and reminded all present of the debt which they were owed.

Then she began to weave the local issue before them into the larger fabric.

"In the wake of these tremendous accomplishments, however, something became lost. In our endeavors to make a better world, we were guided by the belief which equated growth with progress. We never questioned it. For many years we basked in the sunshine of prosperity as we enjoyed its blessings. But along the way, we became complacent. We went on building and growing, and as we did, we turned our backs to many of the basic virtues of common sense. Then one day we began to look around and found ourselves bisected by a freeway nobody wanted, a massive flight to the suburbs, and a new center of town two miles further west. The town we once knew became choked off, and had fallen into decay. We suddenly realized that in our pursuit of affluence, we had given up something along the way... something which we had always taken for granted - our sense of community. We no longer knew our neighbors. We no longer cared about one another. And worst of all, we no longer had any say in what was happening around us.

"You now have a chance to rectify some of these ills. The task which confronts you is as formidable as any generation has ever faced. We have poisoned our air and water. We have grown so dependent on our modern technology that, should a major catastrophe befall us, our very ability to recover has come into question.

"This neglect did not come about overnight, and it will not go away soon either. We have a long road ahead, one which will require a massive effort over many years. If we are to survive, we must recognize the limits to which modern technology can go before it no longer benefits the healthy human character but acts to its detriment. The current oil crisis is but a warning of what is to come. If we continue to put off the long-term decisions affecting our future, then before long the day will come when these decisions will be made for us."

Peg put her papers down. She removed her glasses and rubbed her eyes. A slight murmur ran through the audience. But after a few seconds, she looked up to them and gently smiled. Her next words were extemporaneous.

"The Old Town Restoration Project is but a symbol - a small piece of a larger dream. As you realize this dream, many people throughout the country will be looking to you for inspiration of how to stand up against an entrenched power of self-interests. Let us restore a sense of permanency to our world - a world in harmony with nature, which incorporates the best of yesterday and the wisdom and foresight of today toward a better tomorrow."

These words were no sooner spoken than the audience rose to their feet in a thunderous ovation which continued for several minutes. The chairman tried to restore order with the repeated pounding of his gavel, but seeing the futility of it, sat back and let it run its course.

Tears welled in Peg's eyes as she reached over her shoulder to squeeze Dusty's hand.

"That's some speech," he smiled.

The meeting went on for another half hour before the Superblock went to a vote. It was soundly defeated.

In the lobby they were rejoined by Mark and Westwood, who after the congratulatory hugs and kisses announced, "I've got a table reserved at the Villa."

"Fine," Peg smiled. "Listen, Foster... why don't you and Mark ride on ahead and we'll join you."

As they drove to the restaurant, she looked at Dusty.

"You tangled with Joe, didn't you?"

"Oh, we had ourselves a little meetin' of the minds," he said modestly.

"What happened?"

"Well, y'know, kitten,... I think he's gonna come around to see the error of his ways. Right now he's havin' a little chat with the authorities, and - oh yeah, the IRS wants to talk to him too. They're kinda curious about all that money Maddie turned up."

Peg opened her mouth to speak, but then decided not to push the matter any further.

The next few days found the newspapers ringing with a succession of angry headlines...*MAYOR INDICTED... COUNCILMEN NAMED IN LAND SCHEME... LARGE KICKBACKS DISCOVERED.* The investigation of one level of corruption unearthed others in their turn.

It was not long before the Old Town renovation proceeded with a rekindled spirit of hope and dedication. The din of hammers and saws could be heard as weeds and rubble accumulated through years of neglect were cleared away. Buckled sidewalks were ripped out and replaced. Old houses regained their lost charm as people, many of them young, set to work replacing rotted siding, sagging beams and shingles.

Foster Westwood's political star was on the rise. His election to the city council heralded the beginning of a series of sweeping reforms throughout the city government.

There wasn't room for all the flowers Peggy received, mostly from people she'd never met. She found herself the subject of a major feature story in the local paper, complete with a photograph taken twenty years earlier. She wasn't happy about it.

Dusty, Mark and Lynn were visiting her when the nurse brought in another vase of roses. "Where shall I put these, Peg," she asked.

"Why not put them on your desk," she said gruffly. "There's no more room for them here."

"Oh come on, Peg...," smiled the nurse. "You know I can't do that. How about this window sill?"

"Do you want to block out what little view I have left? Look...why don't you distribute them among the others... yes... that's an *excellent* idea! Shirley, get that pushcart and load up as many of these as you can... go on. They'll cheer them up. Give the red roses to Mrs. Puccini. She'll love them."

"Are you sure?"

"Yes, I'm sure. And don't forget to take some for yourself. As it is, I'll be up to here writing acknowledgments for the next six months!"

When the nurse had left, Dusty turned to Peg. "Better get used to it, kitten" he smiled. "It goes with the territory."

"If you don't quit with that," she said facetiously as she brandished a small vase, "I can find a more direct use for this one!"

"It's time you had your day in the Sun, Mother," Lynn added. "You most certainly have it coming to you."

Soon however, the mood turned more somber.

"I've long known Joe to be a complete jerk," Peg remarked, "But the depth to which he stooped, and what he almost did to you-." She shook her head. "I'll never get over that. And to think he almost got away with it!"

"He had just refinanced the house and converted all our joint assets into cash, explained Lynn. "He was going to run off with everything. I wasn't aware of any of this until now."

"There's no way you could have been, honey," Dusty explained. "Corruption is a strange disease. It's often hard to tell just where it begins and, once it takes hold, it can spread like an epidemic."

"What will happen to him now," asked Mark.

"It's too soon to tell, son," replied the pilot. "But my guess is that he'll try to make a deal with the authorities. I don't think he wants to take the fall all by himself."

"How were you able to untangle all this?" asked Lynn. "You had it all figured out way before anyone else did."

Dusty paused for a moment as he searched for the right words.

"Times may change, hon, but human nature doesn't. Someone who comes up with a scheme like this usually works out some kind of backup plan in case it falls through. When he realized the game was up, he knew he had to make a run for it."

"One thing still kinda puzzles me," said Mark. "If he didn't believe who you were, why did he consider you such a threat?"

"Didn't make sense to me either at first," said Dusty. "But the way I understand it is that, when I showed up, he thought that those men who took my stuff were part of some kind of a sinister plot Foster Westwood and your grandmother cooked up to trap him. And that spooked him because, real or not, he couldn't afford to have any kind of attention drawn on himself."

"It sounds like the imaginary plot he conceived in his mind led to the unraveling of the real one," the boy noted.

"That's about it, son. He was a victim of his own delusion."

Lynn suddenly reached into her purse for a handkerchief, and put it up to her nose. "Excuse me," she said as she got up from her chair and walked quickly out of the room.

Mark was getting used to seeing his mother cry a lot.

"Grandma, how are we going to get her to stop this?"

"We don't want to," she said gently.

He then left the room to comfort his mother.

Peg turned to Dusty and sighed. "I wish they'd get rid of all these flowers. They have no meaning for me."

"Oh, c'mon now, kitten. Y'know… you were an inspiration to a lot of people."

"Yeah… while our children stand unjustly disgraced by a scandal they had no part of. Their own hell is just beginning. Damn it, Dusty, it was just this kind of thing I wanted to avoid!"

"It couldn't be helped," he said solemnly. "Had this gone on, the consequences would have been much worse. I wouldn't worry too much though. It may take a little time, but they'll come through it okay. I just know it."

It turned quiet once again. Presently her eyes met his and her expression turned very serious.

"You're going back, aren't you?"

"Only for a little while," he said. "Just till we straighten out that mess back there."

"Why must you go, Dusty? You don't need them. Why can't you stay here and rebuild your life with us?"

She could not see how it was tearing him apart, for he had found the warmth of a home and family, and with them, a major part of himself.

"Do you think I want to go?" he cried. "My God, Peg, everything that's within me is fighting against it!"

"Then why must you? What do you hope to gain? Some dumb old pictures? Public recognition? Let me tell you something, Dusty. It won't be like you imagine. You'll never be able to go out for a walk without being hounded by curiosity seekers wherever you go. You'll be the target for every reporter out to milk this thing for all the cheap sensationalism they can get. You'll never again know a moment's peace for as long as you live. I've lived a lot longer than you, and believe me, I've seen this happen. Please listen to me, sweetheart. There's nothing in this life more precious than peace. Peace... and anonymity."

He walked slowly over to the window and gazed longingly out at the tranquil scene of trees and rolling lawns.

"If I do nothing," he said, "...won't just this sort of thing happen once Johns determines that I have no intentions of goin' along with his game? He's sure to open the floodgates himself if for no other reason than mere spite."

Peg had known this was coming, for she remembered Dusty and how determined he could be whenever he found himself obsessed with a sense of mission.

"How do you plan to stop him?"

"I don't know Peg. I haven't thought that far ahead."

"You mean you're going to charge in there like Custer and expect him to just capitulate?"

"Well, not exactly. I figure when I get there-"

"That somehow or other the answer will just come out of thin air, is that it? Dammit Dusty, it's not going to work. He's probably got himself surrounded with people who are expecting you to try exactly this sort of thing!"

She stared into his eyes for a moment, and then heaved a sigh.

"Come here," she said.

He came over to her bed and sat down upon it.

She reached across to her nightstand, opened the drawer and produced an envelope.

"Here," she said, "I want you to have this."

He gave her a puzzled look as he opened it.

Inside was a cashier's check made out to him for ten thousand dollars. Dusty bit his lower lip and turned away.

"Peg...," he said in a choked voice, "I can't accept this." He placed it back on the nightstand.

"Take it!" she insisted shoving it back into his hand. "You'll need it if you're going to fight him on anything like equal terms!" Then, in a softer tone she added, "It's yours too. If it weren't for you and what you did back then, I wouldn't have it in the first place."

"Kitten... I... I don't know what to say."

"When you get there, deposit this in a bank," she cautioned. "Take just what you need. Banks are safe now, and there are lots of kooks hanging around in the big cities out to rob you."

Then she reached up and touched his cheek.

"Be careful, hon," she cautioned. "You will be walking a long and lonely road in a world filled with subtle pitfalls. You will find yourself up against people who are in their own element. You have always been a man of courage. But that may not be enough to protect you from the many dangers which lie in wait.

"You are a legend, dear," she went on. "What you don't want to become is a *symbol*. Being a symbol has killed a lot of people. When this gets out, as it is surely bound to, you'll find yourself suddenly cast into a world that is artificial and unreal, for which nothing in your background has prepared you. If you think you're in a strange place now, what you will experience will be a hundred times worse. Millions of people will have high expectations of you that no one can ever possibly live up to. Then they will hate you and turn against you for disappointing them.

"The only advice I can give you is to always maintain your perspective. Don't ever allow yourself to become seduced by all the glitz and glamour, for once you give in to that, you will have lost everything."

For several minutes she remained silent. Then her mind began to reflect upon a more positive side.

"If you can make it through all this, you just might be able to do what those still left of our generation no longer can. Your eyes see the dreams of another time, Dusty - *our* time.

"The young don't listen to us," she went on to explain. "They see no further than what's directly in front of them, and they make the same mistakes we did in a world which has now become less forgiving."

"What can I do about that," Dusty asked bewilderingly. "I have no education. My skills are too out of date to earn a livin' with. I have nothin' of value they could possibly want."

"Oh but you *do*, sweetheart. You have your good name. And when they learn of it, many will want to hear what you have to say - the downhearted, the disillusioned - all those who for one reason or another have lost hope. You can restore their lost idealism and raise their spirits."

"What *I* have to say? What could I possibly tell them?"

"The truth, hon. Always stand by the truth. Many of our dreams have somehow gotten lost along the way. People will want to hear what you have to say about solving the problems of pollution, hunger, overpopulation… conservation of our wildlife and natural resources. Who has a better perspective of what we have gained and lost? Your words could go a long way towards influencing mankind to restore balance to the world if we can ever do it at all."

"But how can I tell others the truth when I'm not always sure what it is myself?"

"Tell them *your* truth dear. It's how you see it that they'll want to hear. Just be honest. Many vested groups will oppose you, and you may occasionally find yourself caught up in controversy. But if you stick by your principles, the majority of people will come to respect you in the long run."

She paused to gather her thoughts. "Of course, hon, it would be much better to make these decisions at a time when you felt a bit more sure of yourself. Do you understand what I'm saying?"

"I think so, kitten."

Once again the silence returned. The time had come when all that could be said had been said.

They tenderly hugged each other for several minutes.

Tears welled in her eyes and her voice began to choke.

"This... this thing you must do...you be careful now. Get it over with and come back to me ...you hear?"

"You know I always do."

"Yes... I know," she nodded. "Just... don't take so long this time."

Chapter 15

The stark concrete buildings loomed even more sinister than before. Where Dusty had formerly regarded the institute with a mixture of awe and disappointment, he now did so with a deep foreboding for there was treachery here.

He saw it as a symbol of greed, a monument to a man who had seized an opportunity for his own gain. Yet for all his duplicity, Johns had technically violated no law. He had legitimately purchased from a relative the papers of someone declared legally dead. And even if the true extent of his deceit came out, he would still be in the clear since no precedent of this kind had ever existed.

All Dusty had was his past and they had taken it away from him. With no means to verify his skills or experience, his total life amounted to little more than thirty years of blank pages.

His initial impulse was to charge into Johns' office and have it out with him on the spot. But as anger gave way to reason he came to see the folly of such a move, for he was not merely up against one man; he was up against a system.

They were not fools. Johns no doubt had anticipated the possibility of Dusty's figuring out what was going on. There would be no surprises here. In this complex web of intrigue, each step had to be carefully thought out, and the next move was now up to the general.

It was not long in coming. When Dusty got to his desk he found a message directing him to meet with Halleck and Reynolds at 0900.

He walked across the green to the auditorium where he found the others waiting. Standing by the doorway was an armed burly security guard, whose purpose ostensibly was to keep out unauthorized persons, but as Dusty guessed, more likely to add to the aura of intimidation Johns was trying to project.

Presently, the general entered the room and strode up to the podium.

In a style formal and correct, he extended a welcome to the pilot as if he were an explorer returning from a great journey. Then he promptly went into the main pitch.

"This is the moment we've been waiting for," he announced. "The time is near when the shroud of secrecy is about to be lifted". *[smile]* He then pushed a button and a large movie screen descended behind him.

"Space… the next frontier. Right now we are landing men on the Moon and sending forth satellite probes which are exploring the farthest reaches of our Solar System. Construction on a series of space shuttles is currently underway for regular manned flights. We stand at the threshold of the future!" *[smile]*

He switched off the lights and a projector hidden behind the rear wall came on. For the next half hour they watched a documentary film covering the past, present and future of the space effort, complete with stereophonic music and rocket blasts.

To Dusty these buzzwords had by now become familiar: countdown, liftoff, launch vehicle, orbit, and reentry. Ancient names from Greek mythology had been given new meaning: Mercury, Atlas, Gemini, and Apollo. He found the colorful animated simulations of future missions quite intriguing.

When the film was over, the lights came on and Johns returned to the podium.

"Impressive, isn't it? *[smile]*. As I've indicated earlier, we are totally committed to the space effort, to the tune of several billion dollars. A major part of our ongoing job is to convince the taxpayer that it's all worth it, and this is where you come in."

Dusty shifted on the armrest of his seat.

"We have assembled a package for you," the director went on. "Once you've had a chance to review it, we can set the wheels into motion. You will attain fame and glory beyond anything you've ever imagined. There will be major tours around the country, and even the world, involving travel, posh hotels, and meeting with famous influential people. Just as Lindbergh was a hero of his time, you can be a hero for ours! Your name will become a household word and your autobiography will be read by millions. Your unique circumstances will enable you to establish a fresh link between the glorious achievements of yesterday and the colossal challenges of today."

He handed Dusty a large manila envelope. "For the next couple of days, I want you to look this over. I'm sure you'll find the plan we have designed most agreeable. When we get together next time, I'll be glad to answer any questions you may have." *[smile]*

The general gave a curt nod to his associates, indicating that the briefing was over.

Ken Reynolds came forward to shake his hand. "Looks like all the hush-hush is finally behind us," he smiled. "It should be smooth sailing from here on."

But these words were no sooner uttered when Halleck suddenly came forward, brushed him aside and took the envelope away. "I'll have to hold onto this for the time being," he said. "When you want to review it, you can do so in my office."

The initial impact of all this was not lost on Dusty. To a country boy who had often found himself one step ahead of his creditors, the prospect of riches beyond his wildest imagination was not something he could easily dismiss. That afternoon when he returned to his apartment he put on a record on his victrola and cranked it up. Then he stretched out on his bed, closed his eyes, and once again drifted off to a distant time.

The following morning, he received a call from Dr. Verneer.

Their animosity was rooted in a basic personality conflict. The psychiatrist resented this independent, free-spirited man who did not play by the rules. Yet there was a certain quality about him the doctor envied, for, in the face of what must certainly be a cataclysmic upheaval in his life, the pilot displayed a certain self-assurance which Verneer, with all his education and professional standing, could never acquire.

The psychiatrist wanted the pilot's fresh impressions of his trip home. Dusty, who no longer trusted him, related only the broadest account, omitting any personal details.

Verneer peered over his glasses. "Is that it," he asked.

"That's it," the pilot replied.

The psychiatrist shook his head. "Come on now," he said with a hollow laugh. "You wouldn't have me *believe* that nothing significant happened in three weeks, would you? Tell me..." he inquired with the pressing tone of a prying reporter, "How did your family react when they finally realized who you were? Why, it must've really *shocked* them to be hit with all that at once!"

Dusty raised his eyebrows. "Do I get to go over your notes when you write everything up?"

The question was so preposterous to Verneer as to hardly merit a reply. "Of course not," he said dismissively.

Dusty leaned back in his chair, grinning slightly as he looked at the doctor.

"Okay then..." said the pilot, "Let me ask you this... What was your relationship with your mother like? How did your parents get along? How did it feel the first time you actually slept with a woman - uh... you *have*, haven't you? Y'know Ronald, honesty works both ways, and maybe if you start actin' like a man of medicine instead of one of those Hollywood ding dongs, you just might find me a little more cooperative."

Verneer stiffened at this effrontery. "Let's get one thing straight right now! *I'll ask* the questions, not you! What's more, *I'm* not the subject of this study; *you* are! And if you want to be *smart* about it, we can take it up with General Johns and see what *he* thinks!"

"Fine with me," Dusty shrugged, obviously pleased with himself at having gotten Verneer's goat.

Just then the telephone rang. Picking up the receiver, Verneer directed the operator to transfer the call to his other office. Before leaving, he followed the usual precaution of taking his notes and tape recorder with him.

A few minutes later he returned. "That will be all today," he said. "We can resume this later."

"Somethin' wrong?" Dusty asked.

"I said that will be all!"

As he went over the contents of the envelope in Halleck's office, Dusty found they amounted to a series of speeches extolling the space program. Echoing Johns' presentation, they stressed the program's objectives, where it was going, and why it was important to get there. He singled out one of them:

> It took a special courage to fly the mail across the stormy skies over the Alleghenies. Under the ever-present shadow of death, these brave men pushed back the frontier to do what had never been done before.

Today our astronauts, inheriting the mantle passed down from those intrepid fliers of half a century ago, face new challenges, carrying their mission beyond the giant step for mankind forward to maintain our position of leadership. The light of inspiration burns as brightly now as it did to the roar of the old Liberties, and no one feels more than I the immense pride and satisfaction from having come so far.

The others followed the same dry melodramatic monotone. "I'm not sure I understand this," Dusty said scratching his head. "There's nothin' here some other official couldn't say."

Halleck was accustomed to enforcing the policies of his chief, not explaining them.

"It seems pretty straightforward to me," he said bluntly. "What's the problem?"

"These viewpoints... Maybe I'm not gettin' this right. Does he want me to *correct* them, or maybe come up with some ideas of my own?"

"You don't correct *anything*!" Halleck snapped. "You will deliver them exactly the way they're given to you!"

"Okay, okay...don't get your dander up," Dusty said rising from his chair. He dropped the folder on Halleck's desk, and walked out.

Once back in the privacy of his apartment, his outward self-confidence gave way to loneliness and despair. He lived for the phone calls to Peg, his sole connection with the normal and familiar world he knew. When they spoke, the precious minutes flew by all too quickly. And when he hung up, he would lie on his bed, even more depressed than before, gazing endlessly at her picture.

He found an escape in a subject he would never have considered in the days of his boyhood - history. Initially kindled by a desire to trace the logical developments from his time to the present, he found that just merely reading about those years seemed to make them come alive again.

One late afternoon on his way to the college library, he heard someone calling his name. It was Donna, the hostess from the restaurant.

"Well *hi*," he smiled, uplifted at the sight of a friendly face. "What brings you here?"

"Just taking a couple of courses," she replied, "…and you?"

"Oh, just reading a little."

They continued their conversation in the cafeteria where he talked about his recent trip home, again leaving out the personal details. Donna revealed that one of her classes was American History, and it turned out that she was currently working on a term paper dealing with the twenties.

She showed him what she had written and he looked it over closely, nodding his head as he went. After several minutes he looked up.

"Very good," he said.

"Do you really like it?"

"Yes, I like it very much," he replied. "Lots of interesting stuff here."

But something in his tone, suggested to her that he detected something lacking.

"What is it, Dusty," she asked curiously.

"Well... it's good as far as it goes. But what you've got here is a series of facts: in 1919 there was a race riot in Chicago; in 1924 such and such happened...; in 1927 so and so did this. You've got down the specifics all right, but don't you think there might be a little more flow to it than just a chain of names and events?"

He described the popular picture of an America emerging from the disillusionment following World War One, and then he went on to depict another America, the more obscure Midwestern America, made up of small, isolated communities. She sat spellbound as he transformed a dull history lesson into a living narration.

"Gee that's beautiful, Dusty. You tell it in a way I've never heard before."

"It was a time and a world people lived in, just like the time and world people live in today. There's not too much you have to change," he noted. "Here... let me see your pencil a minute."

Chapter 16

As science reporter for the DAILY TRIBUNE, Dale Rudd covered the beat of local developments in high technology and research. He was thirty years old, cocky and abrasive; and his blond shoulder length hair and walrus mustache, along with his faded blue jeans and open shirt, suggested prior involvement in the protest movement of his college days.

He tapped his pencil on his note pad which had only three words written on it, little to show for the incredibly bizarre tale he'd been listening to for the better part of an hour.

"I've heard some pretty good ones in my time," he said shaking his head, "but this here's an all-time classic."

"You don't believe it," Dusty asked.

"Sure, along with Mickey Mouse and the tooth fairy."

"If you think I made it all up, why don't you go check out the names I mentioned?"

"I already know the names you mentioned. Johns is head of the agency and all the others report to him. Hell, anyone can drop names, but so far you've given me nothing I can substantiate."

"Why don't you ask around? That's what a reporter's supposed to do, isn't it?"

"What do you think we do all day?" scoffed Rudd. "Sit at our desks and dig up dirt when we're not peeking through windows and back alleys? I get *leads* through sources I've cultivated over the years. My effectiveness hinges on the rapport I've built up with these sources. Now you – whom I don't know from Adam - come in off the street with some crazy tale concerning the respected head of an established institution which has regularly provided me with feature stories over the years. Do you know what would happen if I went to my editor with this? I'd come out looking like a jerk! Doors would suddenly slam shut in my face, my sources would dry up, and I'd be out on my ass!"

Dusty was annoyed with Rudd's sarcasm. "Are you doubtin' my word," he asked.

"No... not at all," replied Rudd. "For all I know you may sincerely believe what you're telling me. I'll give you this, though; it certainly stands out from some of the ones I get." He glanced at his watch. "Look... it's been nice talking to you, but it's getting late and I've got deadlines to meet."

Dusty resented Rudd's abruptness. "Why would I possibly cook up somethin' like this," he argued.

"How do I know? Maybe you're a disgruntled employee, or you've got some kind of grudge against him for something that happened to you in the Air Force. Hey, I'm not saying the guy's a saint. Most people in charge of an outfit like that usually aren't. But I'd need a helluva lot more than what you've given me before I'd step into the middle of what sounds to me like a family squabble."

When he saw that Dusty had gone, Rudd picked up the telephone and buzzed the desk of his friend in Sports. "Hey Larry," he laughed, "I got one for you that'll knock your socks off!"

"I don't like it, General," said Halleck with concern. "Something about him bothers me."

"Anything specific," asked Johns.

"No... nothing I can put my finger on. It's just lots of little things that when you put 'em together just don't seem right."

"Go on."

"Well, sir... it's not so much what he does, but he *must* be aware by now of what we did. Yet so far, he hasn't alluded to it even slightly. Like, when he went over your speeches, he..."

"He *what*, Tom?"

"He wanted to *critique* them! He *asked* me if he could *correct* them! Well... when I jumped on him about it, he just sort of shrugged and walked out."

"What else did you expect him to do?"

"I expected him to be *angry*, General! Very angry! I was sure he'd have let fly at you the first chance he got, but so far he hasn't shown even the slightest indignation or hostility!"

"Maybe he had second thoughts when he saw Bruce," Johns smirked.

"That's possible. But he would have at least *raised* the matter. I don't like it, General. Those questions he asks. On the surface they seem innocent enough, but underneath," he added with a tone of caution, "…this guy is not stupid!"

Johns, however, was not about to concede the possibility of any error in his judgment.

He leaned back in his chair. "So you think our boy may be up to some sort of skullduggery. Tom, I think you've been watching too many movies. You're looking for something that isn't there. It's culture shock, pure and simple. Hell, his whole world's been turned upside down on him. He's disoriented and confused. And even if what you say is true, I think we've taken sufficient measures to preclude his going independent on us. Before long, he'll come to realize that ours is the only game in town. You know the old adage: *'when you got 'em by the balls, their hearts and minds quickly follow.'* [smile] I appreciate your concern, Tom, but I don't think we have anything to worry about here."

The night custodian had just completed his shift and was taking a shower while singing one of his favorite radio hits.

His coveralls hung over the open door of his locker.

Presently, an unseen hand reached into the right pocket and pulled out a key ring. Dusty then tiptoed down the hall where he sorted out the master key and unlocked the door to Verneer's office. He knew he couldn't get into the safe where the psychiatrist kept his notes, but he had something else in mind. He ran a piece of electrician's tape across the bolt and closed the door.

The riskiest part was returning the keys before the janitor discovered them missing. If he were caught, Dusty would have a hard time explaining his presence there. Also the weight of the many keys on the ring would be readily noticed when the coveralls were lifted and put back in the locker. But to the pilot's relief, he found the janitor still merrily singing away and he slipped the key ring back into the pocket.

One of the latter day inventions Dusty discovered was the replaceable typewriter cartridge. He found it particularly intriguing how the disposable one-time-only feature of the electric typewriter ribbon made it possible for him to reconstruct what was typed on it.

He also observed that all of the typewriters in the department were the same. To cover his tracks and reduce the chance Verneer might find something amiss, Dusty replaced the ribbon cartridge in his machine with that of one of the secretary's, and in turn switched hers with a fresh one which he found in the supply cabinet. Then, after determining that the coast was clear, he sneaked out the door and vanished into the darkness.

"Dusteee... Dusty!"

Donna's jubilant cries could be heard clear across the inner quad. She ran up to him, hugged him and kissed him in wild excitement. "I got an *A* on my term paper, Dusty! An *A*! The professor had me read it in front of the whole class! He said he'd never *seen* a paper before with such depth! Oh Dusty, thank you so much!"

It took him by complete surprise. "Gee Donna," he smiled modestly, "you did all the work. I didn't really do anything."

"You pointed the way. Do you know what he said? He said it had *soul*! That's what he called it. A quarter of my grade for the course depended on that paper. Do you know what it means to *achieve* something like that?"

"I have a pretty good idea. Gee, that's great, Donna. You deserve it."

"Well then, why don't you let a grateful girl treat you to dinner?"

As he looked at her across the table he saw a radiance which illuminated her eyes and imparted a certain warmth to her smile.

Suddenly his mind flashed back to Peg, and his eyes took on a sad faraway look.

"Is something wrong, Dusty," she asked curiously.

He was giving himself away again. "Oh, no," he smiled shaking his head. "No, everything's fine."

By the time the main course was served, his mind returned to the present.

Donna had already formed her own perceptions of him. She saw in him an honest openness she didn't find in other men she'd met with their smooth talk and not so subtle attempts to impress her with their own self worth. From time to time, she would also notice a troubled look she could not figure out. She made him for a man of about thirty, yet his eyes held a certain sadness suggesting that he had seen a lot more of life than he was letting on.

What Donna didn't know was that she was providing Dusty with a unique perspective into contemporary life. For example, television to him was a modern technological wonder. But Donna, having grown up with its developments, began to point out some of its subtleties and drawbacks.

"It may have brought the world closer together," she said, "but I'm not sure that it's been always for the good."

"How so?"

"It presents a distorted picture of the world, Dusty. Like, for example, violence solves everything. Car explosions have become a cliché. And on any given night you can witness at least a dozen murders."

"Don't you think it's meant to provide an escape from the ordinary everyday world like the movies do?"

"It has gone way beyond that," she explained. "In the name of capitalism and the almighty dollar, it preaches a phony value system which emphasizes youth and glamour over everything else. It tells us what to buy and how to think. Instead of stimulating our intellect and heightening our awareness, it plays down to the lowest common denominator. It paints a picture of an America which doesn't really exist, and holds up all sorts of contradicting unrealistic ideals which we can never possibly attain, all in the name of selling products. There's no longer even a clear distinction between news, drama and advertising. We've seen a president assassinated, bloody wars brought into our living rooms, and hundreds of thousands of people starving to death. And we've become so blasé about it because we've seen it all so many times, mixed together as part of this big media hype."

He looked up. "Media hype?"

"Yes... you know... newspapers, radio, television. It's now the primary tool used to push anything from refrigerators to politicians. Don't tell me you've never heard that term in Alaska?"

"No… not where I was," he replied.

They continued their evening at a popular disco spot. Dusty was hypnotized by the flashing lights and quadraphonic sound which made it seem as though the big band was surrounding them. He found the new dance steps a bit awkward and the music rather loud, but before long he managed to get the hang of it.

Following a series of swing numbers, the disc jockey took a break and the two sat down at a cocktail table.

"Gee," she said admiringly, "You've got that down pretty good."

"I have a good teacher," he smiled.

A cocktail waitress came by and took their order. Then Dusty returned to what they discussed earlier.

"This *media hype* you tell me about. I guess they use it a lot for the space effort."

"Oh yes," she nodded emphatically. "It's probably the biggest national endeavor the country's ever undertaken up to now, outside of a war."

"Then the people are pretty much behind it?"

She reflected for a moment. "Oh, I suppose so. When they launch a rocket, many cheer for it like they do their home team in a football game. Why do you ask, Dusty?"

"Well, it seems to me, if everybody's for it, why would they need to do such a big job tryin' to sell it?"

"Well…it's taken a lot of our tax money; I guess that's the main thing. And we've got to keep ahead of the Russians."

"I see," he nodded. "What would be some of the arguments against it?"

"Oh, many people feel that the money spent on it could be better used to alleviate poverty, clean up the environment, or speed up advances in medicine - like curing cancer." She looked at him curiously. "Dusty, what are you getting at?"

"Have you ever stopped to think, Donna, how certain notions have become so widely accepted that nobody ever questions them? They've been pushed for so long that they've come to be taken for granted as the natural course of things. It's as if a long time ago, we came to this fork in the road and we've traveled so far down the one path, we've forgotten that there ever was another one. Maybe it's time we backtracked a little."

This seemed a bit abstract for her and she was about to ask him to be more specific, but the mellowness of the wine caught up with her and she let the matter slide.

When the music resumed to a slower beat he asked her to dance. She felt relaxed and comfortable with him. As he held her, feelings long dormant began to surge within him, desire mixed with a need for intimate warmth. Donna, sensing this, looked up at him. She felt in his arms a slight tenseness and uncertainty. She slowly ran her hand up and down the back of his neck, and he gradually loosened up.

For the rest of the evening neither said very much. Her soft hands found comfort in his. When they came to her apartment she invited him in. Then they talked some more, and he sensed that she wanted him to stay. She gently touched his cheek as she searched his eyes.

"What is it, Dusty?" she whispered.

The words he wanted to say would not come.

Later on that night they made love. When they had exhausted themselves in joy and satisfaction, she snuggled securely against him, her head resting contentedly upon his chest. It would be awhile however before Dusty fell off to sleep. He just lay there, gazing out the window into the night sky.

Chapter 17

When Dusty walked into the conference room he once again found an atmosphere of rigid formality. Seated around the long table were Dr. Reardon - the physician he encountered when he had awakened from his coma - , Halleck, Reynolds, and, of course, Johns.

For Johns the payoff was at hand - the culmination of months of effort. Once the contractual agreements were signed, the elaborate program he had worked out could be set into motion.

The pilot appeared somewhat puzzled as though he still could not fully comprehend either what all the fuss was about or why he was at the center of it.

It was a scene reminiscent of a surrender signing. He was seated directly opposite Johns at the middle of the table. The general began by once again extolling the brilliant future which lay ahead. He then motioned to his deputy who produced a manila envelope from which he took out some typewritten legal papers and carefully spread them out before Dusty.

"Are there any questions," asked Johns.

"No," said the pilot shaking his head. "It all looks pretty clear to me."

"Well then let's get on with it, shall we," the director said handing Dusty the pen.

Dusty picked up the first page and read it through, then did likewise with the second, and the third. When he came to the bottom, he poised the pen over the signature line.

"Let me understand this," he said to the general. "You say that once I sign here, it's the end of all this secrecy?"

"That's right," Johns replied.

"And I get all my papers and personal effects back?"

"That's what we agreed upon."

Dusty paused to reflect for a moment.

"One thing I'm still a bit fuzzy on," he said. "These speeches... How do they fit into all this?"

"Why... they're what you'll be *delivering*," he answered in a sardonic tone.

The others chuckled nervously.

"You mean just as they are?"

"Just as they are."

Dusty scratched his head as he looked the papers over one more time. He sensed that Johns was growing impatient. Then following a brief moment of silence, he said, "I don't think I can do this."

One could have heard a pin drop in the room.

Johns looked at him with an incredulous stare. "What do you mean you *can't*?" he said.

"I just can't, General. There's a lot of stuff in here I simply don't agree with."

"You don't *agree*?" mocked Johns. "It's not your place to *agree* or *disagree*!"

"It is if I'm the one who's givin' 'em. You've depicted the pilots of my generation as little more than forerunners of your astronauts. They deserve a helluva lot more credit than that!"

"Come off it!" snapped the director. "You can't even *begin* to put those hicks and their old box kites in the same *league* with highly trained men who fly advanced jets beyond the speed of sound!"

"Of course not," Dusty shot back. "There are no comparisons here. They were a different breed of cat. They took an untried concept and pushed it to its limits without the benefit of your newfangled science and research. Many of these guys paid with their lives for the stuff you seem to take for granted. But I'll tell you this, General... without those fellas and the sacrifices they made, you would never have *gotten* to first base with your hi-speed jets and your rockets. And as for their place in history, they don't have to take a back seat to anybody!"

Indignant at this display of insubordination to his chief, Halleck sprang to his feet. "What the hell are you trying to pull, boy?" he snarled. "General, Bruce is outside and if you want we can -"

"That won't be necessary," said Johns, his eyes fixed on Dusty's. "I think Dervin here just needs a little more time to reconsider!"

"Not really," said Dusty. "You're askin' me to distort history to promote some space agenda of yours and I'm not gonna do it."

Johns made one last attempt at salvaging his plan.

"There's nothing wrong with promotions and ad campaigns, Dervin. Hell, they're used every day. Many famous people are paid to endorse products they don't even use and they make damn good money at it!"

"That's not what this is about, General, and you know it. You want to turn this into some kind of publicity campaign for yourself. What about all the other areas along which aviation developed? Air transport for instance - doesn't it deserve mention too? No, General, aviation can stand alone on its own merits."

"Those achievements are fine for museums!" Johns shot back contemptuously. "Not for the world of *today*! If our country is going to retain its position in world leadership, we've got to maintain our leading edge here. And as director of this institute which, by the way, is responsible for your being here, I determine the course for how these efforts are to be applied, and therefore I will decide what goes into the speeches and you will give them as *you* are directed! Is that understood?"

Dusty would not be intimidated.

"Let me get this straight," he replied. "What you're tellin' me is that technology has now reached the point where it's gotten beyond the grasp of most common folks, and so it's up to an elite class of specialists like you to decide what's good for them."

Johns now realized that he had underestimated his adversary and had foolishly allowed himself to be trapped in a game of words before his own staff. He hardened his resolve to put this upstart in his place.

"It's time you grow up and faced reality, *boy*!" he said, his face livid with rage. "And you'd better get that into your head right now! We've put a lot of money into this project and you're not gonna do anything else other than what you're *goddamn told!* Right now, you have a choice as to whether or not you're going to be part of it, and you're on the verge of losing *that!* We can present you in the media as a *freak* if we want to, and there won't be a *goddamn* thing you can do about it! We can proceed *with* or *without* your signature! It's all up to you. You can grandstand all you want, but you'd damn well better be aware of what the consequences of your obstinacy will be!"

Dusty calmly rose from his chair, his fingers rested on the conference table.

"You've really done your homework," he acknowledged. "I don't recall seein' anything so thoroughly worked out and planned like this. It looks like you're capable of doin' pretty much anything you set your mind to."

He then looked around the room. "Y'know, General, there's one thing I've known for a long time. You can always tell a lot from the finished product about the people who built it: their visions, their dreams and aspirations. My friends are all gone now, and I missed out on the best years of my life with my family, along with the chance to grow old with them. There is no greater loss than that.

"But you've lost sight of somethin' basic about us. You see… we knew how to fight with our backs to the wall. We had pride and dignity, and you can never take that away from us. So you see, General, I'm not impressed with your commercialism and I'm certainly not afraid of you!"

Johns slowly shook his head. "You damn fool," he fumed. "Do you have any idea what you're throwing away? Your life belongs to us, all bought and paid for! What's more, *you* won't get a damn thing out of it! No money. Not even privacy! Reporters will hound you like flies for the rest of your life. You want to fight us? Fine! Go hire a lawyer. He'll be up against a whole legal staff we've got on retainer! The law won't help you here because it doesn't even *exist*!"

Dusty remained unperturbed.

"It ought to be real interestin' how the public will react when they find out how you stood by while an old lady was about to be swindled out of her property!"

Johns refused to acknowledge any culpability in a matter he considered irrelevant.

"I'm not your goddamn nursemaid!" he said.

"Except when it suits your purposes. You can't just step in and out when it's convenient for you. Go ahead - tell 'em! The sword cuts both ways, y'know"

Johns' face reddened and his teeth were clenched in a vicious snarl. "I can do anything I damn well feel like. And before we're through with you, boy, your credibility will be so low you won't know what the hell the truth is!"

"Oh? And just what do you intend to use to blackmail me with... that phony psychiatrist's report?"

The shock barely registered on Johns. "What are you talking about?"

"Oh you know... the crock of bull that quack of yours cooked up. I take it if I don't cooperate, you're goin' to release that to the press, right?"

"Who gave you access to that report," interjected Halleck. "You have no business-"

"I just don't get it," Dusty said, shaking his head incredulously. "You have so much here. You've attained heights in your careers most folks never dream of. But with you guys it's never enough. You always want more and more, and you don't give a damn who gets hurt along the way... even if they're innocent folks who just want to be left alone!

"I'm not worried so much as to how *I* come out of all this, but I'll be *damned* if I'll stand by and let you put down a generation of people who mean a lot to me! You want to go public with it? Go ahead. I'm not afraid of an open fight, but if I were you, I'd think twice about it, because it's gonna blow up right back in your face!"

He picked up the contract papers, tore them in half, and threw them on the table. Then he turned and walked out of the room.

Halleck started after the pilot, but Johns touched his adjutant's arm in restraint.

"Let him go," muttered the general. "Before we're finished with him, he'll be *crawling* back!"

The die was now cast.

The precipitating issues were merely superfluous. Dusty was not inherently opposed to the Space Effort; it was just not part of his world. The only reason it had become the focal point was because Johns had made it so.

The underlying issue was as old as time itself: a struggle between a man who wanted to control his own destiny and someone who was determined to do it for him.

A feeling of pride came over him as he walked away from the institute. He was fighting for something he had helped Peg fight for, a set of ideals of which America, in this age of high technology, somehow seemed to be losing sight.

It wasn't over; these were just the opening volleys.

But the war was on.

When he was summoned to Johns' office, Verneer thought the general merely wanted a progress report, but upon entering the room, the ominous stares of Johns and Halleck sent through him an eerie chill.

"Your services with us are terminated," Johns said abruptly. "Your severance check is waiting at Payroll where you will be escorted."

Verneer's face turned pale. "W-what is this about, General Johns?" he stuttered. "What did I do wrong?"

"You allowed the subject access to classified material in direct violation of the agreement you signed."

"I… I did not!" he cried. "I've *always* observe the security precautions and I *always* lock the material in the safe whenever I'm not there! I swear, General, I never divulged *anything* to him. In fact, he *resented* me for it! He never saw anything pertaining to him or the project. He *couldn't* have!"

"Did you bother to observe the same precautions with the typewriter ribbons?" Halleck added coldly.

"Your negligence has compromised us," Johns went on. "You are no longer of any value to us here. The terms of the contract give us the option to terminate at will, and I am exercising that option. You will not be returning to your office. Any personal property you have there will be identified and returned to you. Meanwhile you are still bound by the secrecy terms of the contract you signed when you came aboard. You will not divulge any aspect of your work here. Should you violate these terms, I'll see to it that you'll never be able to find work as a dogcatcher!"

Johns pushed a button on his console and a tall, burly, bullet-headed security guard promptly appeared. "Bruce, escort this man to payroll and then out the gate!"

As he was led away, the psychiatrist continued to protest his innocence. Then suddenly his stammering turned to anger. "You...you fabricated this to deny me any credit for my work here! This is *your* doing!"

Then in one final gesture of defiance, he turned and shook his fist shouting, "I'll get you for this, you bastard! So help me! I'll get you!"

Chapter 18

As Donna grew to know Dusty better, something about him came to puzzle her. It was nothing specific she could put her finger on, just lots of little things.

His accounts of his early years were sketchy. When she asked him about them, he would offer generally vague descriptions about the small farming community he came from. He spoke very little about his family, his childhood, or any of the little things which fall under the realm of common knowledge, such as how the major sports teams did, the latest movies, current events, or all the various other elements of contemporary popular culture.

Donna attributed this to his many years of working in the isolated bush country of Alaska, although again he never made it exactly clear what he did there.

She was particularly curious about the dated photograph of Peg which Dusty prominently kept on his dresser. Who was this woman Dusty seemed to hold in such high esteem? When she asked him he said simply that she was someone he once knew. Donna sensed that he didn't really want to talk about it and this only piqued her curiosity.

He seemed to know a lot about the twenties and she could never figure out why that period of history held such special fascination for him. At first, she took him for a buff on that era. The furnishings in his apartment made it look like a time capsule. She noticed how he would speak from time to time with certain dated expressions she remembered her grandparents had used. She might have dismissed it as mere role playing, yet she found not the slightest pretension in his overall demeanor.

He would often seem distant, lost in a fog she could never penetrate. Whenever she brought this to his attention he would wake up from his daydream and just laugh it off, but that only served to intrigue her all the more, making her wonder what mysteries lay hidden beneath his gentleness and easygoing nature.

Dusty, however, was well aware of what was going on. With no opportunity to follow the social evolutionary changes and developments spanning several decades, he was very conscious of the fact that he did not possess a sufficient ready knowledge of all the many subtleties of the times in which he now found himself.

He could not tell her the truth, at least not yet. He feared that disclosing his secret would open a can of worms. She probably wouldn't believe him and would most likely consider him some kind of a kook. And even if she did believe him, the last thing he wanted was for her to regard him as some kind of freak or object of pity.

He remained on his guard against saying anything which might inadvertently reveal his true circumstances. Often, whenever a term came up with which he was not familiar, he found that most of the time if he just followed along with the overall context, its meaning would soon become apparent. Yet, as in the case of spies, there was always an ever-present danger that, in the course of casual conversation, he might say something which could give himself away.

That summer, one story dominated the headlines, the resignation of the President of the United States.

From the news, Dusty gathered that this was the culmination of a major series of events they called Watergate. As he understood it, some burglars got caught breaking into Democratic Party Headquarters in a place called the Watergate Hotel, and this had somehow mushroomed into a major scandal involving the president himself.

Since he had not been around to witness the political developments over the years, the pilot didn't quite know what to make of it. He had no opinion of the president, one way or another. As with all politicians, Nixon was liked by some and disliked by others. What else was new?

The reader must keep in mind that although the events of Watergate dominated the news, the story behind the disclosure of the break in and the roles of Woodward and Bernstein and the *Washington Post* in uncovering the scandal were still obscure at this point. To most people of the time who followed the developments and the Congressional hearings on television, it all sounded somewhat sketchy.

Dusty asked Donna for her take, and from what he gathered, she didn't seem to have much of a handle on it either.

"Politics have never really made any sense to me," she said. "There are people who are really into that stuff, but I've never been one of them."

"Was Nixon tryin' to get dirt on the opposition so he could get re-elected," Dusty asked.

"That seems to be the gist of it, but I guess he overdid it. You know he never really got over just barely losing to Kennedy back in '60, and he had this paranoid obsession with getting even with everybody he thought was against him."

Oh yeah, Kennedy, Dusty thought to himself, ... the president who was assassinated.

"It wasn't enough for him merely to win," she went on. "He wanted a larger mandate than he got in the last election, so he raised all this CREEP money in order to 'win big' as he put it."

"All for himself, huh?"

"Yep, all for himself."

Dusty's mind drifted back to the Teapot Dome Scandal of the twenties, during the course of which the president died, two officials committed suicide, and several others including the Secretary of the Interior wound up in prison. Now that was a scandal, he thought.

"What I don't get," he said, "is how a botched-up burglary managed to mushroom into something that led to the resignation of the president. Nobody died in it. There weren't any incidents of embezzlement or fraud. What did they get him on?"

"They say it was obstruction of justice," answered Donna. "The president withheld information from the investigating committee."

"So if he'd used some of this CREEP money to help more of his own party get elected to Congress," he reasoned, "the Democrats wouldn't have had enough votes to impeach him."

Donna's eyes widened at him in amazement, for that had never occurred to her.

"Yes," she said, "that's right. But he didn't; he was too greedy."

Dusty reflected for a moment as he recalled how Al Capone had been convicted for income tax evasion after getting away with all the murders and other crimes he committed.

"It's always the little things," he said.

At that point it suddenly dawned on him that he had managed to hold his own in a contemporary discussion, and he did it by juxtaposing a major current event onto the basic framework of government and politics, the fundamentals of which had not changed that much over the years.

The moment he spotted it, it was love at first sight. The Stearman stood resplendent in all its glory. Built some ten years after his disappearance, Dusty regarded it as the ultimate in aircraft design.

The biplane belonged to Newstead Aviation, an aircraft dealership and flight school at one of the outlying airports.

Everyone on the field knew about James Newstead. The big money was in aircraft sales and bulk time, he would tell his staff; the occasional renter with his piddling twenty-five bucks for an hour's flying time was not worth the bother. There were also rumblings of questionable business dealings such as soaking customers for excessive dual instruction, and discouraging potential competition by intimidating independent flight instructors or mechanics who wanted to advertise at the field. He had no legal right to do this, but these were mostly young men just getting started, with neither the money nor the inclination for prolonged litigation. And this, along with the large monthly rental he paid, induced the county airport commission to look the other way.

Newstead had no intention of letting the Stearman for solo. His real purpose was to use it as a bait-and-switch to lure people in the door. That way he could subsidize his own flying time at the expense of the suckers who wanted to say they'd been up in an old timer.

Dusty was not aware of this. He may have regarded it as odd that the instructors with their white shirts and ties had an apparent disdain for getting their hands dirty, but other than that, his mind was on little else as he went ahead with his appointment the following day.

The weather was clear and sunny with occasional puffs of cumulus dotting the sky.

When he climbed into the cockpit it was like old times. Newstead gave him the standard instructions about strapping in, then climbed aboard himself.

He yelled CONTACT, and turned on the switch. This Stearman was equipped with an electric starter, and when Newstead engaged it, the propeller labored through a couple of revolutions before the engine caught, belching forth a cloud of blue smoke from the exhaust.

Newstead radioed the tower which instructed him to proceed down the taxiway. When he got to the end, he ran up the engine to check the ignition and the carburetor heat. After this was done he gave the engine a little power and rolled up to the edge of the runway. The tower then cleared him for take-off.

As the Stearman gathered speed, its tail rose. Once again there was that exhilarating timeless majesty as it lifted off and gracefully ascended up to its intended element. When they got to about three thousand feet they headed out over the hills where there would be less traffic.

"FLOWN MUCH?" Newstead yelled through the intercom.

"SOME," Dusty hollered back.

"WE'LL TAKE HER OUT A WAYS AND DO A FEW TURNS."

When they got over an isolated spot on the edge of town, Newstead looked around for traffic, then entered into a left turn. That was followed with a right turn, then a series of standard basic maneuvers.

Now came the next part of Newstead's little con. Since he wanted to fly the plane himself, he discovered the best way to do this was to cause the passenger to lose interest by inducing airsickness.

For most novices unaccustomed to abrupt maneuvering, this usually achieved its desired effect. Newstead began with a few skids. Then he put the plane through a sequence of stalls and spins.

"WANNA TRY SOME?" he yelled expecting no reply.

"SURE!"

Dusty repeated the sequence of maneuvers, and then threw in a few of his own. Pushing the stick forward to gain some speed, he suddenly zoomed up into a loop.

"WHAT THE HELL ARE YOU DOING?" Newstead screamed as he fought to regain control of the stick.

"JUST GETTIN' TO KNOW HER A LITTLE. GEE, SHE REALLY HANDLES LIKE A CHARM!" Dusty shouted back.

For the better part of an hour, people in the vicinity were treated to a spontaneous display of aerobatics. Traffic was stopped for several blocks as curious folks got out of their cars to watch the biplane dance around in the sky like a specter from another age.

To Dusty it was like being reunited with an old friend. He went into a half-loop, followed by a series of barrel and snap rolls with an occasional Immelman and Cuban Eight thrown in. Then he entered into an extended loop zooming down to just above treetop level, breaking into a victory roll as he soared back up into the sky.

"I GOTTA HAND IT TO YOU, JIM," he yelled out. "YOU REALLY GOT SOMETHIN' HERE!"

After several more loops and split-S maneuvers he looked over at the fuel gauge and shouted, "I GUESS WE'D BETTER HEAD BACK TO THE FIELD."

He could almost hear the crowd cheering as he slipped down to the runway. An exhilarating triumph came over him as he taxied over to the tie-down area, shut down the engine and rolled to a stop.

As he put his leg over the side to get out, Dusty paused to observe Newstead slumped over in the after cockpit. A closer look revealed that he had lost his lunch.

Dusty no sooner climbed down when he noticed three police cruisers screeching to a halt on the other side of the cyclone fence. Five officers jumped out and ran through the gate in his direction. "That's him!" yelled one of Newstead's instructors.

Before Dusty realized that he was the object of all this attention, he was slammed up against the fuselage and handcuffed.

He was taken directly to the county jail where he was booked, fingerprinted and photographed. It was only then that he learned the nature of the formal charges drawn up against him, Disturbing the Peace and Reckless Operation of an Aircraft. His watch, wallet, and other personal effects were confiscated by two deputies and placed into a large manila envelope on which was crudely printed the name DERVIN in black crayon. He was then ordered to undress and undergo a strip search. Then his clothes were taken from him and he was given an orange prison gown.

They threw him into a holding cell, a small concrete enclosure with a window of bulletproof glass and a slot through which a food tray could be passed. There were three bunk beds with little room to walk around. The air smelled of urine.

His mind now became a mixture of shock, anger and bewilderment. Within the space of one hour he had descended from life's highest peak to its deepest pit. He climbed to the upper bunk and gazed at the blank ceiling.

Dusty shared his cell with a black man in his early twenties named Homer. When the initial shock of sudden captivity wore off, they began to get acquainted.

"They pulled my license six months ago," Homer explained, "...but my mama got sick and I had to get her medicine. This cop started flashin' his lights at me and I floored it. We went about fifteen miles before I spun out at the roadblock." Then he looked at Dusty and asked, "What're you in for?"

"I think it had to do with a little show I put on this afternoon," the pilot said modestly.

As Dusty recounted the events of the afternoon, his cell mate's eyes widened in shock.

"Man you must be crazy," Homer exclaimed. "Why'd you bring it back? If it'd been me, I'd of flown it off somewhere and ditched it."

They tried to make light of their situation by seeking humor in whatever they saw around them. In one incident a huge trustee came up and down the cell block delivering the food trays. They estimated his weight at over 300 pounds.

"I guess our dinner's comin' if Tiny there don't eat it first," noted Homer.

"He can have mine for all I care. I wonder what he's in for."

"I don't know, but it sure ain't no *B & E.*"

The following day Dusty was arraigned.

The courtroom may have been modern, but like all courtrooms, its overall oppressive atmosphere was still there. The colors of the flags seemed unusually vivid, and the bailiff in his tan uniform, immaculate and crisply pressed, lent a provocative air as if daring somebody to start something.

The session was well into its second hour before Dusty was brought before the judge. Since he had neither a lawyer nor the ability to raise bail he was given a continuance and remanded to custody.

When he learned what had happened, Johns could not have been more pleased. He regarded Dusty's arrest as an added stroke of fortune. Perhaps this would provide the final incentive to force this insubordinate into line. He was sure that his control leverage would be reinforced now that the legal system was about to do his work for him.

"It was only a matter of time," he remarked to Halleck with a smirk.

"He's had it coming for a long time," agreed the deputy director. "He got too damn big for his britches. What do you plan to do next?"

"Nothing yet. Not until he begs, and *then* we'll let him stew awhile longer. I'm sure that the atmosphere of confinement is hardly to his liking." [smile]

"Will we have to explain anything?"

"To whom? The judge? Dervin's got no friends, no job, and no money. He's a transient. Not likely to stick around for trial. Hell, with all that, the judge won't have any choice." [smile]

Later on that afternoon, Dusty met his public defender, a young woman recently out of law school.

He could present no real defense, she told him. When he explained to her how Newstead had challenged him to what he thought was a contest, she was not very encouraging. The law was quite specific as to reckless flying, she told him; it was all cut and dry. His best hope would be a guilty plea in exchange for reduction of the charges as a first offender.

A few days later Ken Reynolds came by. Of all the people Dusty encountered at the institute, Reynolds had been the most up front with him, but even so Dusty regarded his motives with suspicion, for when it came down to it, he was one of them.

Reynolds expressed deep concern and understanding for the pilot's plight, and then hinted at the possibility that the general might take steps to expedite his release, and even possibly use his influence to have the charges dropped if only Dusty would agree to the conditions previously discussed.

"I know where you're coming from, Dusty," he said. "I really do. But you've got to realize that it's his ball game and he's the one calling the shots. What good is it to keep this up when he's only going to get his way in the end?"

But Dusty still couldn't see trading one hell for another. "You speak of it like it's a matter of *choice*," he argued, "when there really isn't any choice at all!"

"How can you say that? It couldn't be any clearer. Can't you see it's the opportunity of a *lifetime*? If it were me, there wouldn't be the *slightest hesitation* what I'd do. Damn it Dusty, why do you choose to continue with this stubbornness?"

"Why should I make a deal for somethin' that's rightfully mine in the first place? Johns can't keep a lid on this forever. It's all bound to come out. You go tell him I can sit this out as long as he can!"

As the days passed, the depression brought on by prolonged confinement began to weigh on him. With neither access to a clock nor any view to the outside, he could not determine what time of the day it was. Other inmates could do so with some accuracy from the television programs emanating from the guards' station: morning talk shows, kiddie cartoons and soap operas in the afternoon, and prime time shows in the evening. But Dusty, still unfamiliar with the subtleties of modern culture, remained at a disadvantage. Only at mealtime could he determine whether it was morning, noon, or night.

Of course, none of this really made sense to him. The punishment did not fit the crime. The laws he was charged with breaking did not even exist in his day. If the truth were known, he was sure that everything could all be quickly cleared up. But the general was the only one in a position to do so, and Dusty knew that he was not about to give up his bargaining chip.

The legal system, designed for the protection of the individual, had evolved over the years into subtle intricacies obscuring its original intent. It was not simply a matter of right and wrong, or cause and effect, but was rather a complex web benefiting only those who were in a position to manipulate its rules.

"DERVIN," the guard's voice rang out down the corridor, "LET'S GO!"

"Where," Dusty asked.

"You're getting out of here." He unlocked the cell and led Dusty to a room where the property bags were kept containing the clothing and personal effects of the inmates. Checking the tag number, the deputy shoved the bag into his hand, and then ordered him into an adjoining room to change. When this was done, Dusty was escorted to the main lobby where two other guards waited.

The large manila envelope was produced which the deputies promptly tore open, and with military correctness, emptied and declared the contents on the counter. The money was once again counted and his other items verified. Following a warning not to miss his court appearance, he was released.

The clean fresh air of freedom was intoxicating. He wanted to put as much distance between himself and the ugly concrete edifice as possible, so he decided to walk the five miles back to his apartment. It had been a nightmare which was not yet over.

When he got home he threw his clothes in the laundry and took a long hot shower, but the stench of jail still lingered in his nostrils. What had seemed like an eternity had been in fact two days. He went through his mail. Among a stack of bills and solicitations he found a letter from Peg.

Before long, however, the initial joy of freedom began to give way to a deep melancholia. In jail he had experienced a deep fear of suddenly vanishing without a trace. The last time it happened, he had not been aware of it. He opened the letter, but when he tried to read it, found it hard to make out the words through his tears.

Then the phone rang; it was Donna. She wondered why she hadn't heard from him.

Dusty told her he needed to see her immediately. She would be right over.

From the sound in his voice over the phone, and the warm hug with which he greeted her, Donna sensed that he had been through some kind of ordeal.

When he related to her the chain of events which led to his arrest, her eyes widened in shock and disbelief.

"Why didn't you call me, Dusty?" she cried. "I went through hell wondering what happened to you!"

"I couldn't get to a phone," he explained. "Besides I didn't want you anywhere *near* that hole!"

"That was foolish and I never *will* forgive you for that," she said. "You didn't have any faith in me." Then in a more solicitous tone she asked, "What made you do it, Dusty? Weren't you even *aware* something like this would happen?"

"Actually I didn't think about it much at the time. I just got carried away, that's all."

"Can't you tell me what's behind all this?"

"No," he said slowly shaking his head, "...not yet." He gazed down at his coffee mesmerized by the rising pattern of steam. "They treat everybody like... *dirt*," he muttered clenching his fist on the table.

"Of course they do, Dusty. It's *jail*." She looked into his sad eyes and tenderly unrolled his fist as she pressed his hand in both of hers.

"Dusty, sometimes our society isn't as free as we're all led to believe. Justice for all really means *for all who can afford it*. It's not like a small town where everyone knows everyone else and a man is taken at his word."

"We've always had crime," said the pilot. "It's nothin' new."

"But it's on a much bigger scale now," she went on. "The gap between the rich and poor has widened. People have become more isolated from one another. Drugs have become so prevalent that they're even available to little kids. We used to look forward to the future; now we're afraid of it. If nuclear war and radiation don't get us, pollution will. These are uncertain times, Dusty. We live in a society at war with itself."

She could feel his hand trembling in hers. "Dusty...," she said softly, "What is it?"

He gazed down at the table. He wanted to tell her, but the words just wouldn't come. Then his eyes rose to meet hers.

"I don't expect that you'll understand this," he said. "You may think I'm crazy, and you're probably right. But all the while I was up there, it was like my whole life had come together for that one moment. The world down here seemed so small... so insignificant."

There was now a wistfulness in his voice, as if recalling a distant happier place.

"It was like being in harmony with the birds and the sky," he explained. "For the first time in many years, I felt like I was *alive*!"

Chapter 19

Retirement seemed to agree with Reuben Abrams. At last he had the time to catch up on those dreams he had put off for so long. When not busy cataloguing the mountain of slides he and Phyllis had taken on their recent trip to the Orient, he was immersed in his beloved woodworking projects, the current being an old highboy which he was painstakingly restoring to its former glory.

Yet as he embarked upon this new chapter in his life, he was never quite able to close the door on the old one.

The world of science had long ago lost its luster for him and in his eagerness to be free of the ICR and the pressures of its hostile political climate, the offer of an early retirement had been too good to resist.

It was all part of the game. In exchange for his freedom he had been forced to forego any recognition or benefits to which he was entitled for his role in the Recovery Project.

But as the months went by he came to increasingly regret this decision. Now he was left with little to show for all the years he had devoted to it. He could not alter what had been done and now he found himself bitterly reflecting on what he might have accomplished for himself and his group had he only held out a little longer, fought a little harder.

When he read about Dusty's predicament it didn't require much effort to read between the lines. It took him even less time to recognize an opportunity to at least partially rectify an injustice, if not settle a personal score.

He knew what the consequences of his actions would be and once again found himself walking down the long corridor to the director's office in response to an angry summons. But this time there was no sinking feeling in the pit of his stomach. In fact he rather enjoyed it.

"I don't like this," Johns fumed in his staccato voice. "I don't like this one bit!"

"I haven't the foggiest notion of what you're talking about," Abrams replied with mock innocence.

"You know *goddamn well what I'm talking about!*" the director yelled, pounding his fist on his desk. "*You* signed an agreement relinquishing *any* connections you had with the project and you *violated* that agreement!"

"I've done nothing of the kind," the scientist replied. "I haven't been involved with any part of the project since I left."

"No? That agreement included contact with *any* active participants in the project! It was very *explicit* on that point! Now wouldn't you consider that meddling where you're not supposed to falls *directly* under that category?"

A smugness came upon Abrams' face. "I take it all this is over my helping an innocent man caught in an unfortunate predicament," he smiled. "Surely you weren't going to just let him rot in jail, were you?"

"He breaks the law, he pays the consequences! Anyway that's no damned business of yours! You were to have no contact with him whatsoever!"

"Maybe he didn't know it was against the law."

"Ignorance of the law is no excuse!" snapped Johns. "By going bail for him you *deliberately* stuck your nose where it didn't belong!"

"No, Ed. You're trying to twist the law for your own purposes and I can't stand by and let you get away with it. This idiotic scheme of yours is just not going to work. He's not going to play along no matter what you do."

"Nevertheless, the fact remains that you have violated the conditions of your agreement. The legal staff has been notified and appropriate measures are now underway to reevaluate your retirement benefits! You're gonna have to go back to work boy, and it sure as hell isn't gonna be here!"

"I doubt that you could pull that off either," Abrams shrugged. "You don't have a leg to stand on."

"Oh *no?*"

"Uh-uh. If you did, we wouldn't be having this conversation. I'd have already been summoned to appear before a board of some sort and I don't think you really want that. You'd have to explain away all those insidious measures you've taken to keep it under wraps and you'd come out looking like an ass."

"Real smart, aren't you," Johns smirked, "using those tactics you people are so widely known for."

An old coded phrase, intended to push Abrams' button. But the scientist refused to rise to it, choosing instead to take this anti-Semitic slur as a nothing more than the reaction of a someone whose bluff had been called. Abrams' eyes remained fixed on his adversary as he rose from his chair.

"Like I said, go ahead. Call whomever you want. I'm not afraid to take my chances in the open. It ought to be interesting how it turns out!"

The scientist turned and walked out.

"DON'T BE SO GODDAM SURE OF YOURSELF!" Johns yelled out. "YOU HAVEN'T HEARD THE END OF THIS! NOT BY A LONG SHOT!"

The evening was not going well for Dusty and Donna. She had picked out a night spot where they played rock music. The pilot took an immediate dislike to it, finding the sounds loud, harsh, and monotonously repetitive. He took her hand and they left.

As they walked down the street she seemed oddly quiet. Dusty sensed there was more to it than just the bad music.

"Somethin' eatin' at you," he asked.

"No, nothing."

"Come on now, this isn't like you. You're usually the one cheering me up. Now what is it?"

She continued to gaze at the sidewalk.

"I don't know, Dusty," she replied with a sigh.

"Go ahead. You're doin' fine so far."

There was a pained look in her eyes as she turned to him.

"Dusty, relationships are built on mutual trust and understanding. But a lot of the time you seem so shut off. It's like you've built around yourself this... invisible wall!"

"Do two people always have to know *everything* about each other?"

"When it gets in the way of communication...yes! I sense a lot of anger pent up inside you, waiting to explode at any moment, and it makes me uncomfortable."

"I haven't been aware of this."

"Well it's true, Dusty. You go off into some private world of yours, and when you do, sometimes I feel like I don't even *know* you."

They continued in silence for several blocks until they came to a small coffeehouse. There were few customers at this hour and they went inside.

They proceeded to a booth over by the wall and sat down.

He told her his story.

Nothing had prepared her for this and when he finished, it turned out to be more than she could handle. She looked at him in shock and disbelief. She opened her mouth to speak, but the words would not come out.

"This can't be for real," she said slowly shaking her head. "No... this can't be for real."

Then she rose from the table, turned and hurried out the door. Dusty did not follow.

The following night, the pilot was home watching television when he heard a knock at the door. When he opened it his jaw dropped as though he was receiving a visitor from another world.

"Mark!" he exclaimed. "What brings you here fella?" They hugged. It was so good to see someone from home, especially now. Then his smile began to give way to concern.

"Your mama... she's all right, isn't she?"

"Yes," assured the lad. "She's fine."

"And Grandma?"

"Grandma's fine too."

Dusty took Mark's suitcase and laid it on the couch. "You were about to tell me... oh heck, it can wait. I know this ice cream place around the corner that's still open."

After they returned to his apartment and the initial excitement had subsided, Dusty listened solemnly as Mark recalled the events in the wake of the scandal which had enveloped him and his mother. Lynn filed for divorce, and the boy had no contact with his father, now somewhere in seclusion pending the upcoming hearings. The house had been sold and they had moved into a small apartment.

"Things have a way of workin' themselves out in time, son," explained the pilot. "It's not easy for your mama right now and she needs you back there with her."

"No she doesn't," he said dejectedly. "There's nothing for me back there anymore."

Dusty's looked into his eyes. "What do you mean by that? She knows you're here, doesn't she? Mark... she must be worried *sick* about you!" He got up from his chair and headed for the telephone.

"What are you doing," asked the boy.

"I'm gonna tell her you're all right, that's what! Then, in the mornin', I'm puttin' you on the first plane home."

"No, Dusty, you can't."

"Look son, I can't take care of you here. Your place is with your mom and your grandma. I'll be there to join you soon as I finish what I gotta do here."

"You don't understand, Dusty!" he cried. "It's not working out!"

Dusty noticed the tears welling in Mark's eyes and he now became aware that there was more to this than he had first thought.

"Mark... what are you tryin' to tell me?"

The lad described a dark world in which he and his mother now found themselves. Although they had neither participated in, nor had any knowledge of any of the events culminating in the scandal, the mantle of shame had fallen upon them. Once the initial shock had subsided, the aftermath and day-to-day uncertainties had set in. Maddie's friends had abandoned her, and with her life now in a shambles, she often vented her anger on her son, forgetting that he too was a victim in this. Meanwhile at school he faced an ostracism of his own, with fights, taunts and ridicule. It was just as Peg had warned.

Up to now Dusty had not realized the extent of emotional damage this had wrought. Mark had seemed to have taken it well at first, in fact considerably better than his mother. But apparently it had taken its toll on him as well. It was a sorrow equal in magnitude to death, yet in some ways worse, for with death there remained at least the good memories. Here even these had turned sour, and the set of values he had been taught all through his childhood seemed no longer relevant. It was a tremendous disillusionment to befall someone at any age, much less one so young.

In a way it seemed to parallel what Dusty himself was going through. Here was a boy groping about, trying to make sense out of a world which had suddenly turned upside down on him. In a desperate search for some thread of stability he had now reached out to his grandfather. Only his grandfather didn't have all the answers either.

Dusty put his hands upon the boy's shoulders.

"I guess we're both lookin' for the same thing," he said gently. "But we still gotta let your mama know where you are."

"And what about you?"

"I told you, son, I have somethin' I have to do here. And what I have to do, I have to do alone."

"You can't do it alone, Dusty. You're out of your league here." Then in a tone of optimism he added, "Maybe I can help."

The pilot looked at him quizzically. "And what do you think you can do?"

Mark took a deep breath. "Look… I may not be as old as you are and maybe I haven't done all the things you have done. But I know lots of things around here that you don't. You're just a fish out of water here. You may know a lot about the old days, but this here's a different time. There are lots of little ins and outs that you have no way of knowing about, and maybe I can help you avoid some of 'em. All this John Wayne stuff may have worked in your day, but it doesn't work here anymore. You'll never make it by yourself, Dusty. You need me."

The pilot remained silent for several minutes. Mark made sense, but Dusty was reluctant to concede to his grandson's logic.

"Well, okay," Dusty said. "You can stay here with me."

Mark's face brightened.

"But this isn't gonna be any field day," his grandfather warned. "For one thing, you're gonna keep up with your school work. And what's more... I don't want your grandma mad at me. First thing we're gonna do is call her and let her know where you are. If she says it's okay, then we'll take it from there."

"That won't be necessary," Mark said. He reached into his pocket and produced a note which he handed to Dusty. "She already has."

Chapter 20

"Would you like some more tea... uh, young man?" Phyllis Abrams asked Dusty. She was not really sure how to address someone who, although only half her apparent age, was in fact some thirty years her senior.

"No thank you Mrs. Abrams," he smiled. "This here's just fine."

"It seems we have an odd situation here," her husband noted with amusement. "We're not sure whether you should regard us as your elders or we should regard you as ours."

Thus set the tone for the amiable atmosphere as the scientist supplied Dusty with the remaining pieces of the puzzle - the story surrounding the discovery itself. Dusty liked his easygoing yet candid manner. No question however naïve seemed beneath him and the pilot felt an immediate kinship with this man who had brought him back into this world against such staggering odds.

"It began with a dream," Abrams recalled. "We felt sure that if the temperature of a frozen body could be uniformly controlled, the implications for modern science would be limitless: treating of the terminally ill, rescuing and reestablishing entire species of animals from the brink of extinction, just to name a few.

"After many years of frustration and perseverance the results began to look encouraging. First we tested and perfected our techniques on smaller animals. Then we moved up to larger ones like sheep, horses and cattle until we achieved results which were consistent. Finally it was time for our next step - testing on a human. But the many ethical, legal and moral issues raised brought us to a virtual dead end; we could go no further. Our only hope lay in a chance so remote, the odds were less than one in a million of finding what we were looking for.

"But that was only the beginning," Abrams went on. "First we not only had to *find* a body, but the circumstances by which it came to that condition had to be just right. It had to have frozen so quickly that oxygen starvation to the brain would have no chance to take place. And since the nature of such a search involved covering vast territory and requiring many years, we had to set up a network to alert us if and when one was ever found.

"Although our project was kept under wraps, we had the blessings of both the institute and the government itself. But when Johns took the helm, he immediately set about getting rid of those projects which had nothing to do with airplanes or space."

"How did a guy like Johns get control in the first place," Dusty asked.

"That, my friend, is a long story. A few years ago after we landed our first man on the moon, the government instituted a series of cutbacks, due mainly to the staggering costs incurred by the war in Vietnam. Among the agencies affected were the National Aeronautics and Space Administration. Many highly-trained and dedicated people were let go, but Johns, being one of their fair-haired boys, got a new assignment - and we drew the short straw.

"For some reason," Abrams went on, "Johns considered his transfer a demotion, so he took it out on us. He wanted to transform us into a miniature NASA as it were. Important projects in which years of money and research had been invested were arbitrarily scrapped, and a number of my friends and colleagues I'd known for years suddenly found themselves out the door.

"Of course, our group was number one on his hit list and he went after us almost immediately, but we posed a unique problem to him. You see, strictly speaking, we were under him - and yet not entirely - since we had received considerable recognition and funding from the outside.

"So we settled into a kind of siege mentality. He'd harass us with requirements for weekly progress reports and cost justifications, which he would then try to use against us. You see, Dusty," he explained, "...In the field of research we were in, constraints like that don't work very well. So for the last year or so we found ourselves deadlocked, that is until..."

"I turned up," interjected Dusty.

"That really blew him away," Abrams continued. "All along he was certain it would fail and adversely reflect upon him, so he shoved all the major responsibility onto me and my staff. Then when it turned successful beyond anyone's wildest imagination, he muscled himself in to take the credit. He took over with his own people, and in the blink of an eye we were no longer in the picture."

"I can see where he is capable of that," acknowledged the pilot. "But why, after all the effort you put into it, did you let him walk over you like that? Why didn't you fight back?"

The scientist shook his head ruefully. "That's a decision I have regretted since the day I left. I was just so damned tired of all the backbiting and the politics. A day never went by when Phyllis didn't plead with me to get out. So when Johns came up with his offer of early retirement at full pay, I was only too happy to take it. Besides, what else could I do? The project didn't belong to *me*; it was *theirs* now! I had no legal standing; I was nothing more than hired help. Why should I hang on... to gain personal recognition? It wasn't worth it. I just wanted out!"

"Wasn't there anyone you could report him to?" asked Dusty. "Surely he must be accountable to somebody."

"What could I report him for? He'd cut expenses, reduced personnel and carried out everything expected of him. That's all they were interested in. If he wanted to clamp a lid of secrecy on it, he had *carte blanche*! And what's more, if I had complained it would have brought a lot of additional trouble on us!"

"Like what?"

"Lots of things. Impromptu audits. Maybe they'd have found some kind of loophole they could use to terminate the project, and all of our careers as well. All they have to do is claim they made a mistake, and financially I'd have been out in left field. Sure I could have fought it, but lawyers are expensive and that kind of litigation could take years. And I don't have either the stomach or the resources for that kind of a protracted fight."

Dusty reflected for a moment.

"Suppose you had been in charge of this whole show," he asked. "How would you have run it?"

"Let me put it to you this way," answered Abrams. "Did they ever bother to tell you where your family was? Or who among them was even living? Did they even attempt to notify them or prepare them or you as to what to expect?

"No, they didn't. You went through this traumatic culture shock, yet they showed no concern for either you or your family whatsoever! It was all just a game for them. Hell, they weren't in it for the advancement of science; they were in it for themselves! And that psychiatric farce they pulled! I thought I'd seen everything but now they had stooped to a new low!"

"Please honey," begged his wife. "You promised me you wouldn't get worked up over this."

"I can't help it Phyllis," he fumed. "This crap has gone on long enough! It's long since time the whole world knew about it!

"We're dealing here with a man obsessed with power," Abrams concluded. "He can twist his own specious logic to his advantage. Since there are no laws to protect the rights of someone once declared legally dead, he has now been given what amounts to a license to *steal*! And what's more, he's got the whole damn system to back him up."

It was getting late.

As Dusty rose to leave, the scientist imparted to him a note of caution.

"Be careful, Dusty," he warned. "If they can discredit you, or even somehow get you out of the way, they'll have a free reign. You're wise to their game now and they know it. An awful lot's at stake here, and they will stop at nothing to get what they want!"

After Dusty had left, Phyllis turned to her husband.

"Aren't you putting yourself in jeopardy again, getting mixed up in all this?"

"When was I *not* mixed up in it," he replied. "I brought this whole thing into being. All the problems and uncertainties it may have brought upon us must surely pale in comparison with those that poor man must be facing every day."

Like other lads of his age, Mark held little interest in schoolwork. Dusty in his day had been no great student either, but their unusual circumstances now gave Mark's education a whole new meaning as the pilot took on the unusual role of mentor.

Dusty taught Mark the basics of piloting. Algebra took on a new meaning for the boy as he used it to figure out problems in navigation and fuel consumption.

The relevance of history, however, proved to be a bit more abstract. "To understand what *is*," his grandfather explained, "you have to understand what *was*. Most people don't see any further than what's in front of their noses. Newspapers miss the point because they're out to sell newspapers rather than inform or educate. They tell a story for its shocking effect, but after that there's usually little follow-through."

"Yeah, I suppose," said Mark, "but what's history got to do with flyin' an airplane?"

"In life, son, there are lots of times when you gotta be able to reason things out, and part of that is learnin' what mistakes have been made, so you don't repeat 'em. Times may change, but human nature doesn't. And there'll be lotsa times when a command of history can give one a little insight as to what the other fellow is up to."

Dusty could see he was still not quite getting through to his grandson, so he took it down to a more personal level.

"Your grandma Peg sees the world across a span of many years," he said. "You see it from only a few. Me... I'm kinda split in between. I was part of her world at the beginnin', but I got cut off. The only way I can make any sense out of it all is to find out what was goin' on durin' all those years in between.

"We can't experience what's gone on over several lifetimes because lifetimes have to be *lived*. But on the other hand we can't go on reinventin' the wheel, so we have to *read* about these experiences of those who have gone before us and make our own interpretations. The guy who knows his history has got a big edge over the guy who doesn't."

The buzzer sounded on Johns' telephone. He picked up the receiver.

"Yes?"

"Sir...," his secretary answered, "there's a long distance call from a Mr. Farnsworth."

"Farnsworth?" The name rang a bell but Johns couldn't place it. "I don't know anybody by that name."

"He's calling from Alaska, General... Yakutat, Alaska."

Now he made the connection. "Okay, put him on. Hello?... Yes, I remember... What can I do for you? No, Abrams is no longer with us. I'm in charge of the project now... what have you got?"

There was a long pause as Johns listened intently. "And how did you happen to stumble into this? ...I see ...I see. Okay Mr. Farnsworth, that's fine... no, no... don't send it by mail. Just hold onto it until I get up there... oh and Mr. Farnsworth... let's keep this between ourselves for the time being. That's right... we don't want anybody adding two and two and coming out with seven."

When Johns hung up he buzzed Halleck, who came in to find his boss looking somewhat perplexed.

"Yes, General?"

"Pack up some thermal underwear. We're going to Alaska."

"Alaska, General?"

"That's right. It seems they've turned up something else which belonged to our pilot friend... Something he neglected to tell us about."

Chapter 21

Dusty had not told Mark about Donna, whose unexpected appearance at the door had caught them both off guard. But a discrete nod from his grandfather gave the boy his cue, and he politely excused himself and went outside.

She was apologetic, yet still dumfounded. Dusty's disclosure had hit her like a bombshell and she had still not yet absorbed its full impact. She had heard of people who believed they were Napoleon - sincere even if perhaps a little off center - and she had considered more than once the possibility that perhaps he had fallen into that category.

Yet the realism and human warmth of his descriptions had lent certain credibility to his world in a way that made it seem somehow less distant. She delicately picked up the photograph of Peg and carefully studied the delicate features of this woman, a woman clearly from another era.

Was this lady a rival, she wondered.

"She's very beautiful, Dusty," Donna said respectfully. "Was she your wife?"

Dusty nodded. He didn't want to delve into the ambiguities of their marital status, nor did Donna ask him to.

"And the young man?"

"He's my grandson."

Donna put the picture back on the table and came over to sit beside him.

"I don't suppose it could be much different from pulling up stakes and moving to another part of the country," she said with empathy. "I know it's probably hard at first, but after awhile you make new friends and learn your way around. I've done that before."

"I know what you're sayin'," acknowledged the pilot. "But when you came out here, didn't you find a lot of familiar things that you had back home: the cars, all those big shoppin' centers... the McDonald's hamburger joints everywhere. They all look the same, one place just like another. But beneath it all, there's somethin' so vast... so all around you that I'll bet you're probably not even aware of it."

"What's that, Dusty?"

"The times themselves. From the moment you came into this world, you were exposed and conditioned to certain influences. As you grew, these influences changed and your perspective changed along with them. But by the time you reach adulthood they became pretty much fixed in your mind. And, no matter what later influences may occur in your life, it's the early conceptions which tend to stay with you. You can't see them - not at first anyway - but they're there just the same, and they date you in much the same way as a car or," he said, pointing to Peg's picture, "...a particular style of dress. We're all products of our times."

Donna quietly reflected for a moment. Then she pointed out his victrola. "What about this, Dusty? I like the music it plays. It sort of evokes the flavor of another time, don't you think?"

"Yes, I suppose so, although probably not the same way for you as it does for me. I think nowadays it's regarded more as a curiosity... a symbol of what folks like to think was a happier, simpler time. But we both know they would never trade in their high fidelity for somethin' that's old and scratchy. When I hear it, it brings back special memories for me. It can't do that for you because you weren't there. You didn't come of age then or go through any of the hardships and experiences."

"Are the generations really that different? You have your music; we have ours. And it must certainly evoke the same parallel of feelings and emotions for the people of my generation as yours does for you. I think what we're talking about amounts to little more than a matter of style."

"To some extent," he conceded. "But generations don't always lend themselves to mere one-to-one comparisons. Sure there may be parallels, but each era has its own character because the influences shaping it are so diverse and complex. Maybe someday I'll learn my way around in this world, but I don't think I'll ever feel truly at home in it. Now don't get me wrong... I'm not sayin' that mine was all that great. It wasn't. A lot of people suffered through some pretty awful times. But it was the world I knew and managed to get around in - at least for awhile anyway."

Once again, she could see the sad, wistful look in his eyes as he went on.

"I can't pretend to be somethin' I'm not, Donna. I can't just invent a place for myself in a world I don't really fit into. You see, all through each day I may see the sights and sounds you do. But at night I can still smell the hay in the fields, and hear the distant whistle of the steam locomotive. And Donna," he added taking her hands in his, "…it's probably never gonna be any different."

Several minutes went by before she could speak.

"Dusty," she said softly, "It has often been said that great people walk a lonely trail."

He looked at her curiously, for this was the same thing that Peg had told him.

"What do you mean?"

"What you say may be true. You may have indeed been cut off from the world you knew and the people you loved. And you may feel that you have no place in a world which has passed you by. But, Dusty, let me assure you… you're wrong. There is a definite place for you here, and it is an important one. That's what these greedy people are trying to control you over."

Her eyes now had a certain idealistic fire.

"This… this thing that happened to you… it may have taken something away from you but it's given you something in return."

"What're you talkin' about, Donna?"

"A perspective, Dusty. A very unique perspective. You have acquired a special ability to see the world in a way which the rest of us can't. From your vantage point, you may even be able to make us all take a fresh look at ourselves."

She then shifted to a different topic.

"Dusty... have you ever heard of the 'me-generation'?"

"The what?"

"The 'me-generation'. My generation. The one you would have been in had you come along with the rest of us. We're also known as the Postwar Baby-Boomers."

"Postwar? You mean World War Two?"

"That's right," she nodded. "There are a lot of us."

"Why do they call it the... 'me-generation'?"

Donna paused a moment to collect her thoughts. "There's never been a generation like ours," she said. "We grew up, for the most part, in suburbia outside the city... in look-a-like houses with white picket fences. We had two cars in every garage - one of which was usually a station wagon - and we were all instilled with the patriotic ideals of Mom, Apple Pie and Walt Disney. It was understood and reinforced that we were all going to get married and raise our 2.5 children and live happily ever after in this wonderful materialistic world our parents had built for us. That is, of course, if The Bomb didn't get us first."

"Sounds like it was a wonderful time," Dusty said, "...yet you speak of it with such cynicism. Where did it all turn sour?"

"That's not an easy question to answer. It's kind of difficult to describe to someone who wasn't there," she explained. "We saw a lot of hypocrisy in what was going on around us. Our parents would set standards as to how we should conduct ourselves, and then they would go and do just the opposite. Oh, I don't blame them completely. They grew up in the Depression and the War, and they wanted us to have all the things they didn't. But a lot of us couldn't see any meaningful fulfillment working the rest of our lives for material possessions in a cookie-cutter world like they did. We wanted to change the world and make things better.

"So we got into the Civil Rights Movement with all the sit-ins and marches. You see, the black people were making it clear that they were no longer going to put up with the 'separate but equal' restrictions which the white society had forced upon them for so many years. A lot of idealistic whites from the North came down to join in. Many were beaten, subjected to police dogs and fire hoses, and a few were even killed. Some progress has been made since then, but not nearly enough. There are still widespread slums and poverty. But at least you don't see 'white' and 'colored' signs posted over the water fountains and buses anymore."

"Tell me this, Donna... How did they manage to achieve the gains in recent years which they couldn't get before?"

"Television. That's been one of the *good* things about it. It has given us the ability to instantly focus our attention anywhere in the world. It showed those segregationists for the bullies they were. It's made us a lot more aware of what's going on - even if only on a superficial level. Now we can experience events *collectively*.

"But TV also promotes an image telling us what we *should* have. We are constantly bombarded with reminders that the shiny cars and expensive clothes are the key to the so-called 'good life'."

There was now a tone of cynicism in her voice.

"Make it big, make it early, and to hell with everybody else; that's the message," she went on. "Only now, the housing prices have gotten so high that the middle class is being squeezed out. The gap between the rich and poor has widened. They've got it all down to a science now. If you're a famous athlete, Madison Avenue will give you a contract to endorse products you don't use. You'll have your moment in the spotlight until the next jock superstar comes along. They've even got it figured out how long your impact on the public will generate the maximum profits for them before they consider you over the hill and cast you aside."

From what Donna was telling him, Dusty sensed that these attitudes must be widespread. Yet they were issues which were totally unforeseen in his time.

Their discussion then turned to something they had talked about before.

"Donna... do you remember the other day when we talked about the Space Effort?"

"Yes."

"Why would the ICR want me to promote it? There's nothing I know that would be of any value to them."

"It's all part of the media-hype I've been telling you about," she explained. "You'll become a major item once your story becomes public, just like all those athletes and movie stars. Only in this case you'd be even bigger. After all, how many airplane pilots get dug out of glaciers? Oh, I can see what a rich asset you would be for anyone connected with this stuff. That's why they're going to all this trouble to keep you under wraps."

The pilot rose, went over to the window and looked out.

"Suppose I don't play along?"

"And resist the big accolade, the recognition and all that money? Most people would give their eye teeth for something like that. Come on now, Dusty... greed and temptation will get to you sooner or later. You're just as corruptible as the rest of us mere mortals."

"What if I don't *want* to be in the spotlight? Maybe I don't like bein' led around with a ring through my nose like some kind of freak."

"I've certainly heard *that* before," Donna replied. "That's what they all say in the beginning."

"Maybe some folks, but not me."

"And what makes you so different?"

"I've heard all their offers," he said. "So far, they haven't come up with anything I want."

"Like I say, you're no different from anybody else. They'll find a way to meet your price."

"Don't bet on it."

Mark returned after she left. He was curious as to what exactly the nature of their relationship was, but from Dusty's moody silence he sensed that this was not the time to approach him about it.

Johns and Halleck looked on as Farnsworth opened the desk drawer and produced a small olive drab tin box which bore the dents and scratches of many years. Inside was a little black book, small enough to fit in the breast pocket of a shirt. The cover was worn and creased, and the pages had yellowed over the years. There was an old musty smell to it. Some pages were written in ink with a fountain pen; others contained penciled entries.

Johns could make no sense out of it. The first page contained four columns of data. The first was a list of initials: CC, B&W, DE, H&H, and several others. The next three consisted of numbers which, lined across the page, appeared to be small, medium and large values of whatever their respective initials signified. There were also indications of some pages having been ripped out.

"This looks like some sort of... price list," he noted.

"That's exactly what it is," said Farnsworth. "We think it's a listing of what were the current quotes for cases of liquor... see the first column of figures - that's for pints. The next is for fifths and the last one's for quarts. The abbreviations for the brand names should ring a bell: Canadian Club, Black & White, Double Eagle, and Haig & Haig. The pages that were torn out probably contained obsolete information."

"How do you know all this," Johns asked with a stab at humor. "Your career doesn't go back to Prohibition, does it?"

"No, not quite. But after twenty-five years in the Coast Guard I know smuggling when I see it. It's curious when you look at it. They've come up with more sophisticated techniques since then, but the basics are still there... look," Farnsworth noted as he turned a few more pages. "These are codes. I had a friend of mind break 'em down. Fairly simple compared to what they've got now, but there it is... consignments or number of cases brought in, times and locations of drops, even alternates. They had quite a system going for 'em. What we've got here is a bootlegger's handbook."

Johns, however, remained skeptical. He did not like surprises and regarded this latest discovery with suspicion.

He had been sure that he had acquired everything there was on Dusty, and there was the possibility that anything found subsequent to that could compromise his leverage. What else remained out there that he didn't know about?

"How did you come into this," the general asked. "And what led you to connect it with Dervin? I don't see his name mentioned anywhere. There must have been lots of pilots here then, smugglers too, for that matter."

"Just a hunch," Farnsworth replied. "After we turned the body over to you people we continued searching the area... you know, for wreckage of his plane or anything else that might be connected with him. We didn't find anything; it turned out to be just an isolated section of a long cold trail. But since we found him, the discovery has become big news up here. This whole region has built a legend around their great mystery pilot and he's turned into quite a folk hero. But other than the basic information you sent us, we had nothing else on him.

"Then about a couple of weeks ago, this kid came to the sheriff with this box here. He remembered seeing it among his grandmother's effects when she died. She was a prominent lady in these parts; owned the old Langtree Hotel up the street. They restored it a few years back, and when they tore out the wall in one of the rooms, one of the workmen discovered it behind the ventilator duct.

"It seems Dervin was staying there at the time he disappeared. Hiding it where he did... that would make sense. Be incriminating if it were found on him during a search, so he wouldn't likely carry it with him, but he'd want to keep it handy where he'd have ready access to it. My guess is he received a call to either pick up a delivery or make a drop. He got whatever information he needed and replaced it behind the vent before he took off. Most likely rented the room by the week and figured he'd be gone no more than two or three days tops."

"Only he never came back," concluded Johns. "Well, there's one sure way to find out for sure." He reached into his pocket and produced a copy of a letter in Dusty's handwriting which he then laid beside the code book.

"It's definitely a match," observed Farnsworth.

"So it would appear," said Johns.

"General, tell me this... did you guys find much money on him?"

Johns looked at him curiously. "No... not that I recall. Why?"

"Well, by itself it wouldn't matter much," Farnsworth surmised. "If he had, it would've indicated he'd just made a delivery. But even if he hadn't, it still wouldn't rule out that possibility. It's just as likely he went out to make a pickup, but we'll probably never know. No trace of the plane was ever found, so we have no way of finding out whether he completed the transaction or not."

"I think this just about wraps up our business here," Johns said. "Mind if we keep this?"

"Go ahead," replied Farnsworth. "We have no further use for it. As far as the sheriff here's concerned it's a closed case."

As they boarded their plane, Johns turned to Halleck with a look as though he may have stumbled onto something he could use to his advantage, but still wasn't quite sure.

"So far, this doesn't change anything," he said, "but I want to check into it a little further. If it's as Farnsworth claims, we may finally have that cocky little sonofabitch right where we want him."

"How, General?"

"If this little book here turns out to be genuine," he said shrewdly, "We won't need Dervin's cooperation. Oh we'll give him one final chance to play ball with us."

"And if he doesn't?"

"Then we'll lower the boom on him! We'll go public with our story - code book and all! I'm sure he won't relish the prospect of being exposed as a smuggler."

Farnsworth did not like Johns. He found him arrogant. Instead of showing any appreciation for the former Coast Guard commander's cooperation, Johns had dealt with him in a peremptory manner.

This was in stark contrast to the gratitude shown by Abrams. Farnsworth sensed that Johns had not been up front with him, yet he could not figure out why. Abrams had promised to keep him informed on the follow-up, but no information had come back. Why was it all so hush-hush? What was going on down there in California?

His curiosity now got the better of him. He shuffled through some papers in his upper drawer, then reached for the telephone.

"Los Angeles Information, please... Thank you... Hello? Could you please get me the number of a Dr. Reuben Abrams."

Chapter 22

For Johns, this discovery added a whole new dimension to the game. If authentic, the code book could provide the extra leverage he needed to finally bring Dusty to heel.

Surely the pilot would not want this shady side of his past revealed. His cooperation would be preferred but no longer necessary. Depending on how he played it, he could come out looking like either a hero or a bum; the choice would be up to him.

However the circumstances surrounding this latest find still left the general with some unresolved questions.

Johns did not like coincidences. Yet from the very beginning, this whole project had been just that, one bizarre twist after another. There were no definite contradictions or inconsistencies, just a disjointed collection of mementoes of a life which when pieced together seemed rather sketchy.

First, there were the photographs and letters. With the exception of a poster or two from his barnstorming days, these dealt mainly with the latter years of the pilot's life, up to his final flight.

Next, no trace of Dusty's plane was ever found. Yet the total disappearance of a flimsy stick-and-cloth aircraft over a fifty-year period would not be unusual, particularly in light of the nature of the country up there, given the harsh weather conditions or the probability of locals cannibalizing the wreck for whatever they could find.

And finally there was the little black book. It had not been found with either Dusty or his possessions, nor had it been referred or alluded to in any of his letters. It just seemed to pop up out of nowhere, supposedly discovered by a woman now dead, and brought to the attention of the authorities by a mysterious boy.

Yet this too was plausible. Smugglers and other criminals often led double lives and incriminating evidence of this kind would not likely be kept where it could be readily found or confiscated.

Could this code book be a forgery?

Before he could proceed any further along this track Johns would need to verify its authenticity.

From the telephone book he found a local gallery dealing in rare books and manuscripts.

The proprietor, a white-haired man in his seventies named Hendrix, took a cursory look at the code book and reached for his magnifying glass.

"Looks genuine enough," he nodded. "But then I'm not really a handwriting expert."

"Do you know anyone who is," asked Johns.

"Yes… yes, I do. Does some work for the police now and then. I could let him have a look at it."

"Fine, do it. When can I hear from you?"

"Oh, I'd say about a day or two. But there's something else you should consider."

"What?"

"Well in cases of this nature, handwriting is only one factor we need to consider. The others involve dating of the paper and ink."

"And how long would *that* take," Johns asked impatiently.

"Oh, maybe a week or two."

"That's too long. Can't you have it any sooner?"

"Sorry, it's the best I can do. He's got a heavy backlog and he's currently involved in verifying a medieval church manuscript for the University." Hendrix, now curious about this fuss over what seemed to him an ordinary notebook, looked up at his visitor. "Does this figure in some sort of crime?"

"Crime? Yes… you might say so," answered Johns. "However I can't go into that right now. Just tell your man that the Federal Government is concerned and it would be well worth his while to rearrange his priorities."

"I'll do what I can."

"Good. As soon as you come up with anything, let me know."

Dusty was puzzled by Mark's attitude over the last couple of days. The boy was quiet and sullen, and his grandfather's attempts to find out why met with little success.

The pilot knew that the events of the last few months had been a disillusioning time for Mark. The indictment of his father in a major scandal, his parents getting divorced, and the ensuing fallout could not help but take its toll on him. It was too much to put upon someone so young, and spells of moodiness were probably part of the picture.

He also knew that when Mark was ready to talk, he'd reveal what was eating at him.

A couple of days later at breakfast, Mark said, "I thought that the reason you came out here was to straighten out this Johns thing."

"It is," he said.

"Well how does your new girlfriend fit into it?"

Dusty looked up at Mark. So that's what this was about.

"And since when do I have to explain myself to you," he replied.

A prolonged moment of silence followed.

In Dusty, Mark thought that he had someone he could look up to and trust. He had believed that Dusty loved his grandmother, and that after this business here was finished and they went home, Dusty was going to try to make up for all those lost years.

Now, however, it turned out that his grandfather had revealed feet of clay.

"Donna provides a little escape, that's all," explained the pilot. "She has given me an insight into the world which I probably wouldn't find anywhere else.

"I didn't seek her out," he went on. "She came to me. It wasn't meant to wind up like this."

He was about to go into the *men-have-needs-and-when-you-get-older-you'll-understand* speech, but somehow that didn't seem appropriate at this time.

"You think you're still gonna return home when this is over," asked Mark.

"What has one got to do with the other?" replied Dusty. "Of course I am.

"But don't ever confuse my feelin's for Donna with those I have of your grandmother," Dusty went on. "She can never replace Peggy in my heart, and she knows that. The memories of the times your grandma and I shared together... they'll always be a part of me and no one can ever take them away."

Mark shook his head. There were tears in his eyes. "Nothing seems to make sense these days," he cried. "All the stuff I was taught to respect and value... it's all turned out to be a lot of crap!"

"No it isn't, son," said the pilot. "It's just that once in awhile some of the folks who teach us these values tend to lose sight of 'em themselves, that's all."

"How come?"

"Life isn't always black and white the way they teach you in school. It's often more like different shades of gray. And there are many times when circumstances don't conveniently fit into those neat little boxes of right and wrong."

"Does Grandma know this?"

"I'm sure she does, perhaps even more so than you or I do. But I think this is one of those things which we don't need to go into specifics about with her, if you know what I mean."

"Yeah, I getcha," the boy said with a wink.

Johns' call finally came through. The handwriting matched and the notebook, along with the paper and ink, were definitely determined to be of the post World War One period. The accepted criteria of authenticity had been met.

The general rubbed his hands in glee, for this was precisely the news he wanted.

"It's for you, Dusty," Mark said handing him the phone. The boy shrugged, indicating that he had no idea who it was.

However the sudden rise of tension in his grandfather's voice gave him a good guess.

Johns' initial tone was patronizing. He began by trying to relate to Dusty as a fellow pilot, reminding him of the recognition that he and his generation so richly deserved. All of his personal effects would be returned to him, and he would be free to go on with his life and bring pride to his family. All he had to do was come down and sign the contract papers already discussed. It was foolish to continue this stubbornness and there was no rational reason for it.

But Dusty still refused to go along.

"You still don't get it, do you," he fired back. "You think that you got the right to jump right in and walk all over people! Well, you're not going to do that with me!"

Johns' mask was off.

"You'd goddamn well better *believe* I can, *boy*," he said threateningly. "Are you really so stupid as to believe we would just walk away from this!? We own you lock, stock, and barrel and you'd better learn to accept that right now! Like it or not, your life is about to become a *feature story*! And *how* your story comes out will depend entirely on you!"

"I don't know what you're talkin' about," Dusty replied.

"Oh, I think you do," Johns snarled back. "It's the matter of a little *code book*."

"Code book? I don't know what you're - ". Dusty suddenly turned quiet. "Where'd you find it," he asked in a tone of repressed rage. "I told you before... I don't take to threats! You pull any crap like that and... You think I'm *kiddin'*... Go right ahead... *try it*! Like I said before, the sword cuts both ways... *Terms*? What kind of terms? That's mighty damn decent of you, especially when you *stole* 'em in the first place! Where? Tomorrow night? Yeah... you can *bet* on it!"

Dusty slammed down the receiver.

He then turned to his grandson. Presently his angry scowl faded, transforming into a wry mischievous grin as he said, "He went for it."

Chapter 23

Dusty had recently completed Thomas Wolfe's *You Can't Go Home Again*, a novel whose title suggested a plight distinctly similar to his own.

From his explorations into the history and pop culture of recent times, he had undertaken to educate himself as to how his own era had come to be perceived through contemporary eyes.

He found particularly amusing the stereotypical characters in reruns of *The Untouchables* television show, the recent film *The Sting*, and others shows purporting to depict events in his time but in reality portraying those times as they never were.

But for all that he read, and all the films that he saw, Dusty was constantly reminded that his world was long in the past. Like the old biplanes he had flown and the Model Ts he had driven, he too was a relic of another age. His scope of general knowledge was no longer relevant to the world in which he now lived, a world that had long ago passed him by.

He spotted it one day at an antique and collector's fair, while he was wandering among the many exhibition booths displaying a vast assortment of personal items from various estate sales. It was a small black pocket notebook. The cover was badly worn and cracked. Curiously he leafed through the yellowed pages. There was some writing on the first few, but the remaining ones were blank. It had appealed to him because Peg had once owned one exactly like it and it reminded him of her. He paid a dollar for it and went on his way.

One night an inspiration came to him.

Suppose he was somehow able to convince Johns that the latter had overlooked a key part of the pilot's lost past?

At first Dusty was not sure how he could accomplish this. For hours at a time he would mull over the notebook, but no bright flash of light came to him. Then in frustration he would lay it aside, realizing that he was trying too hard, focusing on it too much to see it in proper perspective.

But inspiration has a spirit of its own, borne aloft like a leaf in the wind and alighting in its own time. To be receptive to it, the mind must accordingly be open and free from its own pressures and constraints.

It happened one day as Dusty followed his daily routine of walking along the marina. Late that afternoon, as he was about to head for home, he saw a sight which stopped him dead in his tracks.

On the other side of the street was a 1929 Cadillac Sedan, immaculately restored with a black top and body of peacock blue. For a moment, Dusty just stood there, his eyes wide open and his mouth agape, staring at it as it pulled out from the curb.

It was like a ghost from his past. He had seen that car, or one just like it, somewhere before. An eerie chill shot through him when he recalled where.

It was the identical twin of the car the bootlegger McKittrick owned, the one in which Dusty found his bullet-riddled body at the lake, and it stood as a stark symbol of a horrible episode in his life he had wanted to forget.

The stratagem he had so earnestly been seeking now began to form in his mind. Before long it became clear to him what he was going to do.

Dusty never had the chance to examine any of his personal effects once they had fallen into the general's hands, but he could accurately recall the details of every letter and photograph. He knew all that Johns could possibly have on him because, after all, Dusty was still the foremost expert on Dusty.

Nothing in his writings implicated him in the smuggling business. That part of his life had been known only to Peg, and she had been too ashamed to talk about it to anyone else.

In the particular operation which the pilot was involved, a code book had been a necessary tool of the trade. He had destroyed it when he got out of the business.

Now from memory he was going to reconstruct it.

The plan was to convince Johns that he had overlooked something from Dusty's criminal past! And with this manufactured "evidence", the pilot hoped he could bluff Johns into breaking the stalemate.

Once Johns went public with the story, Dusty could turn the tables on him by exposing the codebook as a hoax. The director would come out looking stupid and the ensuing fallout would cast a stain on his credibility. A proper investigation would follow, hopefully exposing Johns for what he was, and ultimately restoring to Dusty all that was taken from him, leaving him free to go on with his life.

There would be one major drawback, however. Dusty would be in effect zeroing the full attention of the mass media in on himself, and he was well aware that the subsequent scrutiny and sensationalism could backfire on him.

Another concern was that, having been declared legally dead, Dusty had no defined rights protected by law. If and when the issue was brought before the courts, there was a good chance that they could rule in favor of Johns' *fait accompli*.

And finally, of course, there was the possibility that Johns might see through the deception, or for some other reason not buy into it at all.

Dusty had given it no more than a small chance of success. Yet he felt that, since anything would be better than the prolonged suspense under which he was living, the odds were worth the risks.

The forgery itself was easy. From memory he wrote the codes on scratch paper before transferring them to the code book. Aware that Johns might run tests on it of some kind or other, Dusty then copied these entries with an ordinary pencil; there would be no way to tell how old it was. And it was child's play to reconstruct the authentic prices of the various brands of liquor he had carried; again this was something he could do from memory. Some of the pages containing previous writing he ripped out. This too would add credibility as it would suggest frequently updated price changes.

Planting it, however, would be another matter.

It had to be done in a way that would allay suspicion as to why it had been previously overlooked. It was not enough merely to have it show up; it had to logically merge with the overall context of what was already known. Into this web of historic fact, he had to weave a thread of fiction.

1931

Dusty had made a clean breast of everything with the authorities. From the information he had provided them, the rival gang responsible for the massacre at the lake had been identified, apprehended and convicted. He also made a solemn promise to the authorities and to Peg that he would never again engage in this kind of business.

It all went well for awhile. The prospect of imminent financial ruin had eased for the time being. Bills were paid, repairs were made on the Stinson, and unbeknownst to Peg, Dusty had paid up the insurance premiums two years in advance.

But as the months passed, and it became apparent that the economic outlook was not likely to turn around in the foreseeable future, the money began to run short and once again they found themselves falling behind.

Then in the summer of 1931, Dusty received a letter from one of his old barnstorming buddies who had found work in Alaska, hauling supplies. Although practically on the other side of the world, it was honest work, and he would send for Peg and Maddie once he was settled. It would not be long he assured them, perhaps a month or two.

This good-bye was no less painful than the others. Maddie knew her father was going away again and Peg once again began to experience that feeling of anxiety in the pit of her stomach.

The trip was relatively uneventful if any such trip could be in those days. He waited out a thunderstorm outside of Butte, then the engine overheated near Boise, where he had to put down to repair the oil pump. He flew on to Seattle, then Vancouver, and up along the Coast Mountains of British Columbia, touching down at Ocean Falls and Prince Rupert, before reaching Juneau.

It was here he rested an extra day and mailed his final letter to Peg.

He had planned to reach Cordova before nightfall and everything was going well until three hours into the flight when, just past Mount St. Elias, he spotted an approaching storm. He would have to turn back.

But the blizzard closed in on him with a rapidity he had never experienced before. As he tried to push on to Yakutat, visibility quickly deteriorated.

Suddenly the engine began to cough and sputter. Dusty reached for the carburetor heat, but it was already pulled back as far as it would go. He was losing power and going down. Hastily scanning the terrain he spotted what looked like a plain of snow stretched along the vast ice sheet.

He picked out a landing spot and slipped his plane toward it, then lining up his approach, waited until the last possible second and pulled the steering yoke back into his chest. The plane stalled, mushed onto the snow mass, and nosed over.

When Dusty came to he saw nothing but white. He reached up and felt a painfully swollen lump on his forehead, caked in frozen blood.

With considerable effort, he managed to pull himself out by squeezing through where the twisted windshield had separated from the cockpit. Then when he was able to regain his sense of direction, he set out across the glacier for Yakutat.

He never made it. The last thing he could remember was fighting his way through the snow and the intense wind. He was never aware of either falling into the crevasse, or of the mass of ice and snow that had caved in on him.

1974

Now he was about to complete that journey.

He would have to reconstruct the past, a logical and plausible explanation of events filling the gap left by his letters.

Dusty recalled that in his last letter to Peg, he had made no mention of any cargo because he simply had not carried any. On the other hand, the same would have been true had there actually been contraband.

He decided to "reconstruct" a fictional smuggling trip from Vancouver to - let's see... it couldn't be Ketchikan or Juneau. They were too big. There would be too great a risk of finding evidence, such as preserved newspapers of the time, which could refute his story. It would be better to use a smaller isolated town or village. Memories and histories tended to be sketchier there because there would be less likelihood that accurate records would have been kept.

Such a place would be Yakutat.

At the library, Dusty did a little research. From what he could determine it fit the bill perfectly. There was even an old hotel, recently restored, which could easily fit into his story.

It turned out that the old Langtree Hotel had been completely renovated some ten years earlier by a previous owner, one Lucille Webb, who had since died. By examining old newspaper files and making a few discrete inquiries, Dusty found that she had been survived by several children and grandchildren scattered about the Lower Forty-Eight. From among these, he selected the name of a grandson now living in Albuquerque, New Mexico.

To accurately "retrace" his footsteps, it was necessary to make his way up there in secrecy. In the event that he was being watched, Dusty had to take extreme precautions so Johns wouldn't figure what he was up to; one wrong slip could give him away.

In the middle of the night, he and Mark began a series of hops. Not until they were in mid journey did Dusty disclose the plan to his grandson.

When they arrived in Yakutat, they found out that around the local bars, the recovery of a body from the glacier had become the hot topic of speculative gossip. However nobody knew anything about the "mystery pilot" who had disappeared years before. In that part of the county countless people went missing, particularly in airplanes; in fact, a plane carrying a prominent United States Senator had vanished without a trace just two years before. And since Dusty had never set foot in Yakutat before now, no one there knew that he had ever existed. Therefore his disappearance would have gone completely unnoticed.

Had the local authorities been aware of what was going on, they would have noted how closely Mrs. Webb's grandson, who had "found" the notebook and brought it to their attention, bore a striking resemblance to Mark.

Johns bought the story. It was ironic in a way because for all his suspicion and the precautions he had taken, he was fooled by the one factor he had never considered; in his contempt for someone whom he considered a backcountry hick, he had underestimated the pilot's resourcefulness and ingenuity.

And had neither Farnsworth nor Johns bought the story at all, a puzzled teenager in Albuquerque would have been left wondering how he came to receive in the mail a strange black notebook containing gibberish.

Back in Los Angeles, Mark turned to his grandfather with misgiving.

"You sure you want to go through with this?"

"We have to," Dusty replied as he put on his jacket. If I don't play this out, he's bound to get suspicious."

"Well at least let me go with you," insisted the boy.

The pilot put his hand on the lad's shoulder. "Thanks," he smiled, "...but I think this'll work better if I go alone."

Dusty, however, was far from confident as the hour drew near, for he wanted this meeting to be over and done with.

As Johns' house came into view, he could feel his stomach tightening with apprehension. Dealing with the general at the ICR was bad enough, but who knew what sort of countermeasures this cunning intriguer was devising against him.

He got out of his car and walked slowly up the driveway. The porch light was not on, although the inside lights were, indicating that the director was home.

When Dusty got to the front door he found it ajar. He rang the bell. There was no reply. Then he rapped on the door.

When there was still no response, his curiosity got the better of him. He cautiously pushed the door open and entered, then turned toward the study. When he got to the entryway he suddenly stopped short.

The room bore signs of a struggle. The general lay face down on the floor, dead.

Chapter 24

Mark was up all night waiting for his grandfather to return. As the hours slowly ticked by his worries intensified. Why didn't he insist on going with him, he kept asking himself. Didn't he realize that Dusty was too much out of his element to be wandering around a big city at midnight? He was tempted to call the police, but something told him to hold off a little longer.

It was not until around six in the morning that he heard his grandfather's footsteps coming up the walkway.

"Dusty, where you been man...," he exclaimed as he dragged him inside. "Are you all right?"

"Yeah, yeah," the pilot sighed wearily as he slumped down on the couch.

Mark sensed that something must have gone very wrong.

"Dusty, what is it? What happened?"

"Johns is dead," answered the pilot.

"WHAT!" Mark cried out. He stared at his grandfather in disbelief. Then to confirm what he'd just heard he went over and switched on the television.

The story seemed to scream out: *PROMINENT AEROSPACE DIRECTOR SLAIN!!*

A formal portrait of Johns, taken in uniform some years earlier, was flashed on the screen as the news anchor went on:

> *"Police arrived at the scene at ten PM last night where the general was found in his study. Details remain sketchy at this time. However the ransacked condition of the room leads investigators to believe that a violent struggle took place."*

There followed a glowing biographical account covering Johns' career tracing back to his service in World War Two and Korea, and highlighting his involvement in the space program.

"Turn it off," Dusty said.

Mark, still in shock, was not aware of what he said.

"I said, '*Turn it off!*'" the pilot yelled out as he leaped over and yanked the plug from the wall.

Mark drew back. He had never seen his grandfather blow up like this before.

The silence continued for what seemed like an eternity. Dusty sat there stunned, unable to understand how something which had begun as a childish prank could mushroom into something that had gone terribly wrong.

Searching for the right words Dusty tried to piece together the chain of events over the last several hours, but all he could do was to shake his head in bewilderment.

Finally he cried out in frustration, "Has the world become so tightly wound up in itself that the mere toss of a snowball can set off an avalanche?"

He looked at Mark, who continued to stare at him in disbelief.

"No... I didn't kill him," he said. "He was already dead when I got there."

He then related to Mark how he had gone to a nearby public pay phone where he anonymously called it in to the police, and then drove aimlessly around town the rest of the night.

A sigh of relief came over the lad's face.

"If you didn't do it," he said, "...then you got nothin' to worry about. Just tell 'em the truth."

"The truth?" Dusty said cynically. "Oh *sure*. They're not gonna believe the truth. Hell, I might as well just turn myself in and plead guilty. Besides a long drawn-out trial in court, there's gonna be an even *longer* one in the damned *press*! Boy, I've *really* made a mess of things now!"

The pilot buried his face in his hands. It was as if his entire world had collapsed upon him. Several minutes passed before he had sufficiently calmed down to a point where he could find the right words to say.

Dusty shook his head in despair. "I didn't want him dead... he was supposed to be my ticket outta this mess! Boy, all hell's gonna break loose now... the papers'll make a big carnival out of it, and when they find that damned notebook," his voice trailed off, " ...they're gonna hang me!"

Albert B. Folsum, inspector and twenty year veteran of the LAPD, had not slept that night either.

It was the kind of case senior investigating officers dreaded. High profile murder cases brought added pressure from both the media and his superiors with all the accompanying political overtones.

For him it would pose an added problem; Folsum was black.

A highly methodical and dedicated police officer, his rise up the ladder had been marked by a constant uphill battle against the prevailing racial tides of the times with the old pressure of having to "prove himself twice as good."

Now, once again, his reputation was on the line. He was expected to quickly apprehend the suspect with the eyes of the nation closely watching his every step. If he succeeded he would get nothing more than a pat on the back, but should he fail or be perceived as dragging his feet, he would be a convenient scapegoat. His career would be ruined, and his detractors "proved justified" in their prejudice.

One such detractor was waiting outside. His name was Charles Witt, and he was an agent of the FBI.

"This is *all* I need," Folsum grumbled to his sergeant, a stocky middle-aged man named Vinny, "...a damned jurisdictional dispute. *Hell*, it's not enough I've got the whole damned world looking over my shoulder. Oh well," he sighed with resignation, "...send him in."

Folsum's dealings with the FBI over the years had been less than amiable. He found them to be cocky, know-it-all types who always thought they knew more than the locals. His first glimpse of Witt through the pane glass window of his office indicated that the latter was no more than about 32. Adding insult to injury, they sent in a greenhorn.

The contrast between the tall, younger Witt and the older seasoned inspector could not have been more profound. Folsum wasted no time with formal amenities.

Photos of the crime scene were spread out on a nearby table.

"The ransacked condition of the room," Folsum pointed out, "...suggests that the killer may have been after something specific. It was not an ordinary robbery, nothing of any value seems to be missing. What's more, the lack of evidence of forced entry indicates that Johns probably knew his killer, and I'll wager a guess that whoever it was did not find what he was looking for."

"What was the weapon," asked Witt.

"Desk paperweight. Forensics found traces of blood and consistency with the fatal head wound, but no prints."

"Any idea as to motive?"

"No, not yet."

"All this conjecture and no motive?"

"We haven't questioned anybody yet," Folsum said irritably.

"Good," said Witt in a tone indicating that he was ready to take charge. "We'll start at the institute."

The territorial dispute was now underway.

"This is on *our* turf and *I'll* decide who we see and when!" Folsum declared.

"This is a federal matter," argued Witt, "...and we intend to remain on top of this case until the killer is brought in!"

"Then for christsake, let us do our job! Frankly, if it were up to me you could *have* the damn thing! Only it didn't happen on federal property; it happened in *our* jurisdiction! Now I don't give a damn if he was chairman of the Joint Chiefs of Staff! Media attention or not, we're gonna conduct this case the same as any other homicide investigation!"

"Hey look," said Witt defensively, "I'm under the gun too! Now we're not going anywhere on this case unless we work together. And since he was involved in classified work, you may need my help getting past some of the security hurdles."

"I guess we're all a little edgy," admitted Folsum. "You're probably right. The most logical place to start is the ICR. Let's start with the projects he was involved in ... you know... maybe there was a lot of pressure, or one of them wasn't going right."

At the ICR, Halleck, assumed the mantle of acting director, and began by issuing a tersely worded memo to all employees:

> *We are all shocked and saddened at this tragic loss. In accordance with the policies set forth by General Johns, all standing directives will remain in effect until further notice.*
>
> *No statements reflecting upon either matters of policy or the nature of our work here shall be released other than through the the Administrative Office and Public Affairs.*

To further drive home the point he called a meeting of all personnel.

"All of you remain bound by the agreement you all signed upon coming aboard," he warned. "No statement shall be issued to either the news media or the police, unless approved by either myself or whomever Washington appoints as succeeding director. Neither the ongoing investigation nor possible changes in management mitigates our obligation to follow the policies in place not to compromise what is entrusted to us. Anyone failing to comply with these directives will be summarily terminated."

This speech was met with the usual silence. But no sooner had Halleck left the room when several of those present commented among themselves how quickly he was stepping into the shoes of a man not yet buried.

The initial phase of questioning began that afternoon and continued over the next two days. At their request, Halleck provided the investigators with organizational staff charts, both at the overall and department levels. The acting director was a model of official correctness and formality as he described a loyal working relationship with General Johns going back over two decades. All ongoing projects, he maintained, were proceeding on schedule. And while the general may have had his share of detractors, this was not unusual for a man of his stature.

When Witt asked of possible candidates with motives, Halleck provided the names of several individuals who had left under less than friendly circumstances. Prominent among these were Abrams, Verneer, and Dusty.

The office staff, department heads, and others listed on the org chart, when questioned separately, followed Halleck's lead. All were polite and formal, but volunteered nothing. Everyone seemed to agree that General Johns was respected, if perhaps not universally liked, and he always got things done. So far as anyone knew, no one stood to gain from Johns' death.

As they drove back to headquarters, Witt commented to Folsum, "Did you notice how everybody seemed to adhere to the party line? 'It was a good place to work', 'the general was a nice guy who was a true leader...' It sounds as if they'd all been coached."

"They probably were," said Folsum, as he handed Witt a copy of Halleck's memo. "However, I also detected an overall undercurrent of relief. They're certainly not sorry that he's gone, but they're all nervous. Nobody's sure of their own futures right now. In the wake of what's happened, I suppose that's to be expected."

"Yeah, but did you notice the guys in the Life Sciences Branch? They were the edgiest of all."

Folsum shot a curious look at the agent. "Why should they stand out anymore than the others?"

"I'm not sure," Witt replied as he rubbed the back of his neck. "It just doesn't seem to fit in with the main structure. Look... this particular project falls under the domain of their Department of Life Sciences. Now as a rule, they don't normally get involved in defense related projects that require such stringent security measures. On the contrary, they tend to be quite open about what they're doing because their work is usually seen to directly benefit the public interest."

"Interesting point," Folsum concurred, "But don't forget we're still in the preliminary stages here. We have to look a little deeper into the complexities of the organization before we can determine what questions to ask.

"I'm interested in the *enemies* angle. Can you get me access to Personnel? I want to look at their files, particularly those who've been terminated within the last year or so. Added to the ones we've talked to already, this should give us a list of those who in some way or other may have felt that they got a raw deal."

On the third day, Dusty awakened from a short nap. He was by no means fully rested; his eyes were still bloodshot and his rumpled unkempt look suggested more that of a hangover. He rose from his cot, walked to the window and gazed out.

"Mark," he said in a somber voice, "...I think you'd better go home."

The boy gave Dusty a strange look as if he was not sure he had understood him correctly.

"What're you talking about?"

Dusty turned and looked at him. "It's too dangerous here for you to get mixed up in this. We need to pack your things and catch the next flight out of here. I'll drive you to the airport."

"I don't believe this," Mark said indignantly. "You're tryin' to get rid of me!"

"Listen, son," explained the pilot, "...this whole mess is likely to blow up at any time now, and I don't want you anywhere around here when it does."

"And you're just gonna stay here and face it all by yourself, huh?"

"You think I want to? Believe me, Mark, there's nothin' messier than a murder... especially one like this. They're just lookin' for somebody to pin it on, and most likely it'll be me 'cause they'll think I had the best motive for it! The taint of a murder is somethin' that'll *never* wash off - guilty *or* innocent! And the sooner you get away from here the better!"

Mark mulled over his grandfather's logic for a moment. "I see," he said. "And then what're you gonna do?"

"I don't know," replied Dusty shaking his head. "I gotta work this out somehow!"

In a tone of resolve, Mark declared, "Then I'm stayin' with you."

"Damn it Mark... you haven't heard a word I've said!"

"I heard you," said Mark. Dusty was about to press his point when the boy raised his hand indicating that he hadn't finished.

"No... now let *me* speak, will you! As far back as I can remember, Grandma was always tellin' me what a *hero* you were... how you helped all those people out. I used to wonder if I could've ever done any of those things, but I never had a chance to find out. My folks made all the decisions for me. It was always what *they* wanted, depending on whatever their latest whim or group of friends happened to be at the moment. It was always for my own good, they'd say. But it was never really about me, it was about *them*! Well, now I *have* that chance! I'm gonna ride out this thing with you, no matter what happens! And I'll be damned if you or anybody else is goin' to take this away from me!"

Dusty saw the firm resolve in his grandson's eyes and was deeply moved.

"You crazy kid," he said.

"Yeah," Mark replied. "It must run in the family."

Dusty's tone turned solemn once more.

"What we've got here is a case of greed gone out of control," he said gravely, "...and it has now turned on the man who set this crazy stuff in motion. I don't know... maybe it was one of his cronies... maybe some or even all of 'em actin' together. I can't really say at this point.

"But whoever did it knows he's got to get me out of the way, most likely by havin' me arrested or discredited — or even killed. Once they succeed in that they'll have a free reign, because even if I'm vindicated, things'll never be put right again. The newspapers and scandal sheets'll turn this into a carnival like a big fire feedin' on itself."

Then Dusty looked up at Mark.

"Is *this* what you want to be part of?"

"No," Mark replied. "No, I don't. But when it comes down to it, what choice do we have? Running out on my grandfather is *not* an option."

Dusty, deeply touched by this display of loyalty, managed a smile and mussed his grandson's hair. Then the clouds of gloom returned as his mind once again wandered off into that faraway world.

"I've faced some scary things in my time," he said, "...but what lies ahead may be the scariest of all."

"What's that," asked Mark.

"The waitin'."

Chapter 25

While the two investigators focused their attention on the ICR, they also backtracked into Johns' private life.

His two ex-wives were located, along with half a dozen other women associated with Johns in recent years. These leads turned out to be dead ends. All had alibis as to their whereabouts that night, and none seemed to have sufficient motive. When pieced together the picture emerged of an ambitious man full of ego, but who in his personal relationships turned out to be something of a bore.

Halleck was not very cooperative. He resented Folsum and Witt intruding into his private domain, but the Federal search warrant they produced left him no choice but to comply.

The investigators divided the personnel files into three categories: direct and contract employees who had left during the two year period before Johns took over, those who had left over the course of the four years Johns was in charge and those who had left within the past year.

From this information a curious pattern emerged. In the late sixties, the number of employees at the institute began to decline as the Viet Nam War led to massive cutbacks in available funding for research.

When Johns took over, the attrition rate began to skyrocket. Where most of the earlier terminations had been voluntary, there were now a considerable number of two-week notices and sudden terminations.

Folsum compiled his own organization chart of the ICR. The data from the files was compiled onto little flags, on each of which was written a former employee's name and his department. These flags were of three colors: those representing persons who had left before Johns took over were white, those who had left during the first three years, green, and those over the last year, red.

Once the flags were pinned in their proper positions on the chart, Folsum noticed that red ones predominated over the others, clustering chiefly in one department.

"It looks like he was really out to get Life Sciences," he observed.

Further examination of the dates revealed that many of the terminations took place in clusters, the most prominent of which was that of one department head whose exit was promptly followed by twenty of his staff.

"Come in, gentlemen," Reuben Abrams smiled affably. "I've been expecting you."

With candor the scientist answered their initial questions, and before long the discussion turned to the

Recovery Project. As Abrams went on to relate what had happened, Folsum and Witt sat spellbound as if they were listening to an incredible tale.

Abrams next took them downstairs to his basement which he had converted into a study. Adjacent to an old roll-top desk stood a pair of identical oak filing cabinets. He opened the drawer of one and produced a role of microfiche. Then from the bottom drawer of the desk, he pulled out a projector.

"What's all this," asked Witt as Abrams loaded the slide tray onto the projector.

"To fully appreciate the significance of the project," explained the scientist, "You have to understand the device which brought it about." He then went on to describe the development of the Heat Induction Coil and the role it played in the events which followed.

When he had finished, Abrams' presentation left the detectives with more questions than answers.

"Why did you maintain a separate set of these plans away from the facility," Folsum asked curiously. "Wasn't that in violation of their security procedures?"

"It wasn't classified at first," said Abrams. "In fact, up to the time Dusty was recovered, Johns had considered the Induction Coil a white elephant. I did a lot of my work down here where I had some privacy, so I kept a set of my own plans and other documentation. Later on, however, once I came to realize what Johns was up to, I put them on microfiche to protect myself."

"Against what," asked Witt.

"Liability. I knew that Johns wanted to hang me out on a limb. This idiotic secrecy business was his idea, a farce initially intended to give the project low visibility so he could dump it at the first opportunity. Later on, when the Recovery began to bear fruit, he decided to continue this policy until he had all his ducks lined up."

"Now that he's dead," suggested Witt, "that's no longer a problem for you, is it?"

The scientist looked up at him curiously. "I'm not sure I understand."

"Well, with him out of the picture, nothing stands in the way of your own claim to recognition."

Abrams slowly nodded with a faint smile. "I see. You know, I suppose that thought *may* have crossed my mind a time or two."

"A time or two? A major scientific breakthrough like that? This could have been your ticket to fame and immortality. Perhaps even a *Nobel Prize!* Johns may have been in charge, but surely he wasn't the only one with dreams of glory!"

"What person aspiring to a career in science *doesn't* entertain those dreams at one time or another," Abrams answered frankly. "Surely that doesn't make him a murderer. Hell, if it weren't for the idealistic inspirations of youth, there wouldn't be any scientific advancement at all.

"I'll admit," continued the scientist, "that those embers might have still flickered in me from time to time. After all, I devoted a major part of my life to it. But all the years of swimming upstream, and the back stabbing and the political intrigue took their toll, not only on me, but on the others who worked on it as well. Sure, I'd like to see everyone get the credit and recognition they deserve. We achieved a major breakthrough and the people who brought it about deserve a lot better than what they got!"

Abrams leaned against his desk and folded his arms.

"No... I'm not sorry the bastard's dead," he said candidly. "Whoever pulled it off did us all a big favor. If you're looking for a suspect, I suppose you can put me at the top of the list."

"Be assured you are," said Witt. "Now tell me... where were you that night?"

"My wife and I were at the symphony."

"Can anyone verify that?"

"Several people if need be," Abrams replied. "We're season ticket holders and went with a group of friends. I can give you their names if you want."

After jotting down the list of names, Folsum remarked, "I guess we've taken this as far as we can for time being." He turned to Witt. "Have you got anything else?"

"Not at present," answered the agent. "Just keep yourself available."

On their way back to headquarters Witt remarked, "I've seen my share of murders, and they've always been for the usual motives: drugs, money, power, women. But this is the first time I've ever heard of one over recognition for a scientific discovery."

"Isn't that just another version of power?" replied Folsum. "That's one of the oldest motives in the world."

"It still puzzles me though... the development of a machine, the resurrection of a frozen body. How could anyone *possibly* expect to keep a lid on something like that?"

"That's what we've got to find out."

"I don't know," said Witt. "This whole thing sounds so bizarre, it has all the earmarks of a hoax."

"The murder sure isn't."

"No," Witt agreed, "Definitely not." He then turned to Folsum with a look of serious misgiving. "You know, Al, we don't need this."

"Need what?"

"All these screw ups... a project arbitrarily classified secret, a corrupt high-level official, a conspiracy to cover it up and further his own self-interests. Christ Al, this has all the makings of a mini-Watergate. If there's one thing the government doesn't need right now, it's the embarrassment of another scandal."

Folsum looked at him suspiciously, "What are you getting at, Chuck?"

"I think we'd better watch what we say to the press until we've had a chance to look deeper into it, that's all. Hell, at this point we don't know where this is going to lead."

"You don't think I'm concerned about that? I'm just as anxious to keep this quiet as you are, but we can't let that cloud our objectivity."

"And what if we stumble onto something which could be... well... misconstrued?"

"We're not the court," Folsum replied. "The investigation must be allowed to take its course. Evidence needs to be examined and witnesses need to be questioned, and if they're innocent, nobody's gonna get hurt. But we can't bias ourselves trying to protect some fair-haired boys who may have gotten their hands dirty."

"So what's next?"

"We continue along our original tack. Let's see who else may have had their fingers in the pie."

Whereas Abrams had been candid, Ronald Veneer was defensive. From the moment he learned of the murder, the psychiatrist knew he would be considered a prime suspect. He regarded Folsum and Witt with almost total paranoia, nervously glancing from one to the other as if expecting each question to be a potential trap.

He had no kind words for anybody. Johns had been a tyrant who had surrounded himself with ingratiating ass-kissers. Halleck was his hatchet man at the ICR, and everybody who worked there lived under a reign of terror. His words sounded bitter and vindictive as he related his own role in the project up to and including his termination.

He had never been to Johns' home, he insisted; in fact he had no idea where Johns lived. Their relationship had been strictly business, and was confined to the institute.

When asked about his own plans now that Johns was dead, Verneer at first denied having any. But when Folsum pressed further, he grudgingly admitted that he was reconstructing the notes of his psychoanalysis on Dusty for a book he was undertaking.

"This was my study as much as it was Johns," he said defensively. "He had no right to pull the rug out from under me."

"Perhaps," Folsum acknowledged, "But wasn't that part of the agreement with him you signed?"

"No, not at all. We were *all* supposed to share in the recognition."

"What about Dervin?"

Verneer cocked his head in a questioning look. "Dervin? What about Dervin?"

"What was to be *his* share in all this?"

Verneer considered the question obviously absurd.

"*Share?*" he said. "Why... we gave him his *life!*"

"I see," Folsum nodded.

When asked of his whereabouts that night, Verneer said he had gone to a movie. He gave the theatre and the particular film, nothing however that could be verified.

"We'll check these out and get back to you," assured the detective.

Realizing they had gone as far as they could for now, the investigators got up to leave, giving Verneer the customary suggestion to keep himself available.

As the two men began to walk out the door, Folsum turned to Verneer and delivered a word of caution.

"Oh, one more thing. I'm not quite sure how the law works in these matters, but if I were you, before you go ahead with that book of yours, I'd check out all the possible legal ramifications first. If you're not careful you just might give this Dervin fellow some legitimate grounds for a lawsuit."

On their way to car, Witt noted ironically, "A real man of trust isn't he... truly dedicated to helping the troubled."

"The world is full of these so-called experts who are willing to prostitute their ethics at the first opportunity," replied Folsum. "The only principle he's dedicated to is his fee for signing the commitment papers of some unfortunate senior citizen at the hands of a greedy relative."

Ken Reynolds provided the officers with the most objective and comprehensive picture. Of all those thus far questioned, he was the only one with no apparent axe to grind. His answers pretty much fell in line with those of the other possible suspects; Johns ran a tight ship with no tolerance for dissent, and his policies had a negative effect on the overall atmosphere and morale.

Presently the discussion turned to Dusty.

"We all tried to do what we could to ease the transitional pains and culture shock he was going through," Reynolds explained. "But he always turned away. He wouldn't go along with anything we offered him… I don't know… maybe he *couldn't* go along. He was never a team player; he seemed more of a loner."

"Do you think he could have killed Johns," asked Witt.

"He didn't like him, but then who really did? You see… Dusty came from a world where he was accustomed to doing everything for himself - you know- where he was his own man. To him Johns brought on a world of restrictions. But whether that constitutes motive or not, I really can't say."

Folsum asked Reynolds of his whereabouts on the night of the murder.

"I was attending a management class I'm taking," he replied. "After that I spent a couple hours at the office catching up on some paperwork."

When Folsum and Witt rose to leave, Reynolds accompanied them to the door.

"He was a man of another time," said Reynolds. "He seemed to feel out of place here and had this tendency to mentally wander back to that other world he could never return to. But you've got to hand it to him though."

"In what way," asked Folsum.

"He has his own way of looking at things. Whatever else may be said about him, he always seems to follow his own convictions."

Dusty had encountered much danger in his life. It was usually the kind requiring some sort of immediate action where the outcome would be decided quickly. In the air, when a thunderstorm threatened or the engine quit, it was always clear what action he had to take.

But now he experienced a constant state of tension, for it seemed as if the world was slowly closing in on him.

The worst part was the suspense. At times it grew so unbearable that he often thought of turning himself in and coming clean with what he knew. But whenever he considered that option, the question always loomed in his mind; would he be dealt with fairly or subjected to political expediency?

How would the axe fall? He would lie awake at night, visualizing the most likely scenario: an army of police, guns drawn, surrounding his apartment in the middle of the night, busting in and dragging him off. Then he would be humiliatingly paraded before peering news cameras and curiosity seekers as he was whisked off to jail.

The prospect of prolonged confinement was what he dreaded most: that, and a long trial of scandal and sensationalism in which everything would come out but the truth.

It was Mark who first spotted them coming up the walkway, and in spite of their plain clothes, Dusty quickly recognized them for who they were.

They looked peaceful enough.

The pilot felt a slight relief when he saw them without their army. He waited for their knock and then calmly opened the door.

"Come in," he said.

Chapter 26

Although Folsum and Witt had by this time put together a fairly comprehensive picture of Dusty, their preconceived image turned out to be quite different from the man sitting across from them.

They had in mind someone more along the lines of a back country hick. Instead they found a down-to-earth, intelligent Midwesterner of whom nothing seemed out of the ordinary.

Dusty regarded Folsum with a curiosity of his own, for in his day, no black could have possibly risen to this kind of position and authority. Dusty was not prejudiced. It was just that from his particular vantage point, the police detective represented major advances in civil rights and the black cause, which to him seemed to have taken place overnight.

But this was no time for reflecting on social issues. He was about to enter into the fight of his life.

They asked him a few questions but let him tell his story in his own way. After all, who else had ever experienced half a century of change by closing his eyes in one world and waking up in another?

Incredible as it sounded, it all made sense. Everything he said appeared to dovetail with what the investigation thus far had turned up, and despite a lack of corroborating evidence, his account seemed to stand on its own merit.

Dusty's candid unpretentious manner had a lot to do with it. He never claimed to know all the answers, and this too added to his credibility. To the two investigators, his image evoked more the world of Sinclair Lewis than that of F. Scott Fitzgerald, and when asked about those icons traditionally associated with that era, such as flappers and speakeasies, Dusty admitted a lack of familiarity with what had been more prevalent in the larger cities and towns.

He described his return to the world with a mixture of bewilderment and awe. The staff at the ICR seemed kind enough at first, but before long, he began to sense a climate of fear and distrust. He came to dislike their presumptuous attitudes. He could not understand why his papers had been withheld from him. Then there was the buildup of tensions beginning with Johns' anger over Dusty's article in the aviation magazine. When he was able to return to his hometown and subsequently discover the full extent of the theft of all his personal effects, the break was complete.

The pilot went on to explain how, with no skills relevant to today's world and no means to earn a livelihood, he had found himself locked in a kind of stalemate. Yet despite all this, he could never have accepted Johns' terms. His pride would never allow it; it would have amounted to a humiliating servitude, totally against his grain.

"Had he been more up front with me," Dusty told them, "I would have cooperated anyway I could. But why did he feel he needed to resort to subterfuge to force me into line?"

"You tell us," prompted Witt.

Dusty slowly shook his head. "He was only comfortable when he was in total control. Now maybe *technically* it might not have been against the law to do what he did, but it should've been obvious to anyone with a sense of decency that it was just plain *stealin'* just the same."

Folsum and Witt looked at each other, somewhat amused at Dusty's apparent naïveté. But his account shed a revealing light on the most intriguing motive of all.

Folsum turned to Dusty.

"Tell me more about this stalemate," he said. "How did you plan to force his hand?"

"I didn't," answered the pilot, "…at least not directly anyway. I warned him that if he went public, I was ready to come forward with my own side of it, which would've put him in a bad light. You see, I didn't want all that publicity and sensationalism, but I tried to make him understand that it wouldn't be in his best interests either."

"So what then… you figured it was only a matter of time before he came around," Folsum asked.

"In a manner of speakin'."

"And with no money coming in," asked Witt, "how did you plan to support yourself during this prolonged state of siege?"

"Peg," Dusty said. "She's been helpin' me out."

"Can you tell us where you were that night," asked Folsum.

Dusty paused for a moment to collect his thoughts.

"Yes. I had an appointment with him," he admitted.

Mark froze. He was shocked at this potentially damaging disclosure and thought that perhaps his grandfather should have a lawyer with him before saying anything further, but the lad remained silent.

Folsum and Witt were astonished at this revelation.

"You had an appointment?" questioned the inspector. "At what time?"

"Eight-thirty," the pilot replied.

"For what purpose?"

"I don't know. He wouldn't tell me on the phone."

"Did you keep it?"

"No."

"Why not?"

"Because when I got there he was dead."

Folsum and Witt leaned forward, their eyes rigidly fixed on the pilot's.

"Let me get this straight," Folsum pressed on. "*You* found the body?"

"That's right," Dusty admitted.

"And you called it in?"

Dusty nodded.

"Why didn't you stay there and wait for us," inquired Witt.

"I... I don't know," the pilot said hesitatingly. "I guess I just spooked."

Mark could no longer remain silent as his grandfather was digging himself in deeper.

"Excuse me," he interjected, "but it isn't every day you go to a house and find a dead body lying there."

"It's okay son," Dusty reassured him. "I can handle it here." He then turned to the two men and explained, "He's spooked by all this too. I'm sure you can understand that."

Folsum nodded and then continued. "This business you had with him, what was the nature of it?"

"What do you mean?"

"What prompted him to call this meeting?"

"I don't know. On the phone, he said he had somethin' real important to talk about. Like this time he was sure we would - this was how he put it — 'come to terms'."

"And you had no idea what he meant by this?"

"No, he wouldn't say. But there's somethin' I think you should know," the pilot went on. "I had nothin' at all to gain from his death. When he was alive, I knew who I was dealin' with. It was only a matter of time before we worked things out. Now it's gotten way out of control. All hell's gonna break loose and there isn't a damn thing I can do about it!"

There was now anger in his voice. "For all this talk about fame and fortune, nobody ever bothered to ask me how I felt about all this! My world is gone and I'm just tryin' to pick up the pieces! So before you set about hangin' this rap on me, I think you ought to take a real good look at who else might've stood to gain from his death, because from where I stand, I lose either way!"

"Look," said Folsum trying to calm him down. "This is not an inquisition. We don't *make* people guilty. We go by evidence, not public opinion! Right now you're only one of several persons of interest to us, and we're checking all of them out too. We've got a lot of sifting to do through all this, and if you're innocent you've got nothing to worry about."

"Oh *sure*," Dusty said cynically. "That's really gonna stop the press from havin' a field day, isn't it. Once they smell blood, they're gonna descend on me and my family like a swarm of locusts! Hell, they won't want the truth! They'll want *sensationalism* to sell *magazines*! They're gonna turn this into a carnival!"

Folsum looked at Witt, who indicated he had nothing to add, and then the two men rose to leave.

"I think this'll do it for now," Folsum said to Dusty. "We'll be back soon, so keep us informed of your whereabouts and don't take any trips out of town."

Other than his initial outburst, Mark had not uttered a word. He had worried about saying anything that might have gotten Dusty into deeper trouble. But once Folsum and Witt had gone, Mark could no longer hold back his concern.

"Dusty, you almost incriminated yourself."

"How," replied the pilot. "I only told 'em what I knew."

"You were makin' their case for 'em."

"Makin' their case? How?"

"By makin' it easier for them to hang it on you. You should've had a lawyer with you."

"And what makes you such an expert in these things," Dusty asked quizzically.

"Geez Dusty, they've always got this stuff on television. Don't tell me you've never seen those lawyer shows before."

"Nope. It never occurred to me I'd ever need to. Besides... the more we show 'em that we're cooperatin' with 'em, the sooner they'll get the one that did it."

Mark couldn't believe his grandfather's naïveté.

"You don't get it, Dusty. They're *lookin'* for somebody to nail it on, and you're makin' it way too easy for 'em! You admitted to 'em that you don't have an alibi for that night. You even put yourself at the scene. By admitting that you found Johns, they think they're just a step away from arresting you! Hell Dusty, you might just as well have blabbed to 'em about the code book!"

Dusty walked to the front window and gazed out. "Funny they didn't ask about that," he said.

"What do you mean they didn't ask? It was that friggin' book that prompted Johns to call you in the first place. He may have been killed over it!"

"He probably was," acknowledged the pilot.

"Doesn't that make it evidence? When they find out about it, it'll direct even more suspicion on you."

Dusty turned around and leaned against the wall, his eyes focused on the floor.

"From the gist of what they said," he explained to Mark, "I don't think they even know about it. Otherwise they would've sprung it on me."

"How do you figure?"

"Johns must've had the book with him to confront me with. It seems to have disappeared. Could be that whoever killed him took it."

Mark did not follow Dusty's logic.

"Why would the killer take the book," he asked.

"I don't know," replied the pilot.

Mark's worries intensified. "Maybe you *should've* told the police about it," he said. "It might put them on the right track."

"No, I don't think so. With everybody goin' off half-cocked, it might add fuel to their fire. I could never convince 'em of the truth. You know that old sayin' about a little knowledge bein' a dangerous thing? They'd arrest me for sure, then everybody'll come out of the woodwork with all their suppositions, and there won't be a thing I can do about it, not from behind bars anyway."

Dusty turned to Mark.

"Maybe if we can let this thing play itself out," he explained, "there might be a slim chance that we can forestall doomsday."

Mark suddenly saw a ray of hope in Dusty's eyes.

"How?" the boy asked.

"By lettin' 'em continue to believe the book is genuine. I have this feelin' that sooner or later it's gonna surface again. Maybe the killer will try a little game of his own."

"What's that?"

"Blackmail. That little scheme we cooked up for Johns is about to take a new twist. This time, instead of usin' the book to set up somebody we knew, we're gonna use it to flush out somebody we don't."

"But what if it backfires," argued Mark. "It's already gotten one person killed. The next one might be *you*."

Dusty's face turned grim.

"Nothin' is without risk," he said.

Mark still did not fully comprehend his grandfather's reasoning. All he could see was a man waging a war of wits by setting himself up as the target.

And all he could do was to stand by and hope that his grandfather knew what he was doing.

Chapter 27

From the statements and other evidence they had gathered, Folsum and Witt drew up a list of suspects, chief among whom were Halleck, Abrams, Verneer, and Dusty. Of all those questioned, these men stood the most to gain. Their alibis had been gone over, and at this point all but Dusty's seemed to check out.

Yet there were too many pieces missing. All they had collected amounted to little more than four separate threads leading nowhere. Before they could focus more clearly on any one particular suspect, several discrepancies remained to be addressed: What was the killer looking for? Why was the house ransacked when nothing appeared to have been taken? Was there someone else with a motive of which they were not aware? Or were there two or more suspects acting together in some sort of conspiracy?

If the high-profile nature of this case was not giving him enough headaches, Folsum was saddled with yet another — Witt. From the outset, the personality conflict which had developed between the two men was pulling them in opposite directions. The detective knew his type only too well - young, ambitious and overzealous, all too anxious to make a name for himself. To the inspector, one thing didn't make sense; for all the FBI's concern over the potential political ramifications of this case, why had they sent in someone so young and inexperienced.

The many puzzling angles of concern to Folsum, however, did not seem to register on Witt.

"I already know who it is," insisted the agent. "It's Dervin."

Folsum peered up at him above his glasses. "And you arrived at that, how?"

"It's plain for anyone to see," replied Witt. "One, he certainly had motive. He was hamstrung by Johns and couldn't figure any way out of the bind Johns put him in. Two, he admits being there. Johns calls him over for a meeting. He lords it over Dervin that he hasn't a snowball's chance in hell unless he plays ball. Dervin blows up, they have a fight and he kills him. And finally, three, I think Dervin's holding out on us. Johns must've had something on him which made him panic.

"And there's another thing," the agent went on. "Other than the sketchy information he gave us, what else do we really know about him?"

"Have you attempted to verify any of his information," asked Folsum.

"Yeah, I did some checking into that small farming town he claims to have come from. It's still there; population's about 2400. Only nobody seems to remember him, and their city hall had a fire there several years back destroying all the records up to that time. Convenient, isn't it?"

"A sketchy man from a sketchy place," mused the detective. "But that in and of itself doesn't really prove much. If I recall my history correctly, very little is known about Columbus' early years either. That didn't make him a criminal. If Dervin had something to hide, why would he stick his neck out by admitting he was even at the scene at all?"

"To divert suspicion from himself. Did it ever occur to you that maybe he might've been there a little earlier?"

"That would be just pure speculation," Folsum shrugged. "We can't arrest him on that; there are still too many loose ends here. If we tried to build any kind of case on what we've got so far, we'd get laughed right out of court. No, we've still got plenty of trees to shake before we're ready to zero in on anyone in particular."

"And I say we'll save ourselves a lot of time if we just shake his tree a little harder," countered Witt.

Blessed are the ignorant, Folsum said to himself, for they think they know everything. "When I've got something more to question him on," he said testily, "I'll bring him in!"

"Well if you won't do it, I'll do it myself."

Folsum's eyes shot up at him. "Like hell you will!"

"Well pardon me," Witt said impertinently, "...but so far you don't seem to be making much headway."

For Folsum this was the last straw.

"Now get this straight," he firmly declared. "This is still my case and I intend to solve it through accepted police procedures! The day my professional judgment begins to take a back seat to the press, political expediency, or your own personal agenda, then I'll hang it up right then and there! And if you even *think* of end-runnin' me on this, so help me I'll do everything in my power to see to it that you take the fall for it all by yourself!"

Chastised and humiliated, Witt turned and stormed out the door.

As the days passed, Mark grew increasingly concerned about his grandfather.

Dusty would be gone most of the day, and when he finally did return his grandson would ask what was troubling him. However the pilot would merely shrug off these questions and retire to his room.

Mark noticed that these moody periods were becoming increasingly frequent. He tried to dismiss them as mere private escapes his grandfather needed in order to sort things out. But these earlier bouts had never lasted more than a few hours.

Dusty would wander aimlessly around town. One journey took him to the airport. He gazed across the field at the endless procession of great jetliners taking off and landing, while reflecting upon how his own life might have turned out had fortune taken a different turn. And as he did so, he found himself breathing the air of freedom a little deeper as if he might be tasting it for the last time.

On the evening of the third day, Dusty came home to find Mark in the middle of dinner. The boy got up to offer him some, but the pilot shook his head and motioned him to go on with his meal. Then he pulled out the other chair and sat down.

Mark sensed that some grave decision had been reached and looked up at Dusty. In a somber eloquence, the older man spoke as one who had at last come to terms with his fate.

"Y'know, son...," he began, "each of us is a product of his time. The way we come to look at the world, the people we know... all our basic perspectives are shaped by the peculiar set of conditions under which we come of age, and these influences remain with us all our lives. A man given the opportunity to live out his normal life span is supposed to grow old along with his generation. It's all part of the natural order of things.

"But if he should be suddenly taken out of his time and placed into the middle of another, well... it's like takin' an animal out of its environment. It's not really livin' anymore; it's just an existence.

"All I ever wanted was to live out my life with your grandma, and watch my family all grow and sprout wings of their own.

"Unfortunately, it was not to be. I took a gamble and I lost. Had it not been for this thing, I would have been a forgotten name resting in an ice-packed grave in a remote corner of the earth. And it would have been better that way. Now somethin' terrible is about to swoop down on us. And it's gonna hurt some innocent people who matter an awful lot to me."

Mark sensed where Dusty was going with this and was not willing to accept his grandfather's foreboding.

"Why are you talking like that," he said. "Have you gone out of your mind? Are you going to just give up and let 'em win?"

"It's just a matter of time, son. There's no way we can fight it. When you're up against a group of big powerful people like this, someone's bound to lose and it's usually the outsider."

"You don't know for sure that's gonna happen."

"It's inevitable. Don't you see? They're holdin' all the cards. To tell you the truth, I don't even know what's taken them so long, except maybe they're just gatherin' even more rope to hang me with."

Mark remained unconvinced. "You're wrong, Dusty. They wouldn't dare pull anything like that. Not with the news media and everything."

"That's just the sort of thing I don't want," Dusty said emphatically. "Right or wrong, our privacy will be invaded by hordes of curiosity seekers. Innocence or guilt won't count for much here, and for that matter neither will the truth."

"What made you sour on your original idea? You seemed pretty confident in it the other day."

"Maybe I've just been just kiddin' myself. I don't really know what makes people tick. I guess maybe I never did."

"I'd say you got a pretty good grip on it. Better than most folks I know."

"I sure missed the mark here," Dusty said dejectedly. "I was sure the killer would have shown his hand by now. He should've made contact already."

"Maybe we haven't given him enough time," Mark replied hopefully. "At least we know the police haven't found it either, or else *they* would have been here by now."

The pilot rose, pulled open a drawer and picked up a screwdriver, then reached up to the grate of the ventilator duct over the door. He loosened the screws, removed the grate and took out a large manila envelope which he handed to Mark.

"This here's the full story - my version of what happened, the code book, everything. If something happens to me, or I disappear where you can't contact me, you take this back with you to Foster Westwood. Hand it to him in person. He'll know what to do, but be real careful. I don't want this fallin' into the hands of the cops. God only knows how they'll twist it around. Do you understand?"

"If it ever comes to that," said Mark.

"What do you mean *if?* There are no *ifs.* You just promise me you'll do it!"

"Yes... I'll do it. But I still say these suppositions of yours are just that. You're assuming it's all going to turn out for the worst."

"And you still think it won't," Dusty said cynically. "We all gotta prepare for these things."

"I'm not so sure we're at that point just yet. I'll go along with what you say, but I still think your logic is full of holes. Hell! I can point out one minor assumption you've got completely wrong!"

"What's that?"

"You're assuming that the moment the police close in, I'm gonna turn tail and run. That's not gonna happen! I told you from the very beginning that we're in this fight to the finish. We're either gonna go home together or we're not going home at all!"

"You'll still have to get out with that story," insisted Dusty. "That's our only chance to save what little face we've got left."

"No, not yet! There's a lot we can do before it ever comes to that."

"Like what?"

"Catch the killer."

"And how do you figure on doin' that?"

"The more I think about it, the more you're original idea makes sense. But yes... we gotta wait until he makes his move. Wasn't it you who told me about patience being a virtue?"

Dusty shook his head. "I don't know," he sighed. "One moment an idea looks like it'll fly and the next moment it doesn't. Right now I can't seem to tell what's up or down anymore."

Mark went over to his grandfather and looked into his eyes.

"Your hunches have proven pretty good so far," he said. "There's no question about that. The big stuff hasn't changed all that much. Just a few little things, that's all. But nobody can do it by himself, no matter how smart he is. Even the best of us needs some help now and then... that's what I'm here for."

With a triumphant grin, Witt bounded into Folsum's office.

"Well Al," he cheerfully proclaimed, "...it looks like we've finally broken the case!"

The detective gave him that skeptical look again. "What have you got now?"

Witt could not resist the opportunity to rub it in.

"It just so happens that about an hour ago, our friend Halleck dropped in to see me. It turns out that there was some kind of little black book - a bootlegger's code book! Brands of liquor, prices, everything! It seems our old buddy had a little action going on in his previous life during Prohibition!"

Folsum's curiosity was piqued. "Code book, huh? How did Halleck find out about it?"

"He was with Johns when he came into possession of it."

"Hmmmph," Folsum grunted as he pondered over this sudden revelation. "...And you think maybe Johns was killed over this book?"

"It makes sense, doesn't it? Turns out that our buddy Dervin's got something in his past and this missing piece suddenly turns up! Johns finally has the leverage he can use over Dervin. Then he calls Dervin over for a little chat to inform him that the stalemate's broken - that he'd better get with the program if he knows what's good for him. It's blackmail, pure and simple. Dervin gets upset and kills him."

"This codebook... do they have it?"

"No," Witt replied. "It's gone now. No doubt he took it with him after the murder and probably destroyed it. But that won't matter because we've got photostats of a couple of pages Johns had made for handwriting comparisons while he was verifying it."

Folsum was disappointed at this disclosure. Why hadn't Dusty mentioned the book to him before? Up to now he had believed in the possibility of the pilot's innocence. But this new evidence of a possible criminal past made that position less tenable. Now, confronted with this latest bombshell, he now found himself with no choice but to follow the direction to where this new lead now pointed. This meant issuing a warrant for Dusty's arrest.

However some doubt still remained in Folsum's mind. "If Dervin had taken it after a struggle," Folsum said, "...how come we saw no marks on him when we talked to him? Also, like most murderers, he would have been frightened and panicky, and therefore not thinking clearly. Yet in spite of all this, he had the presence of mind not to leave any fingerprints?"

"I don't know," Witt replied. "We'll have to find that out when we bring him in."

"One other thing," Folsum added. "What's Halleck's angle in this? If he had possession or knowledge of this codebook, why did he wait until now to come forward with it?"

"Why don't you ask him yourself," Witt replied. "He's waiting out in the hall."

Peg had always been Dusty's guiding light. The mark of the passing years had not dimmed his love for her. He longed for her now more than ever, for it was she who provided the slender thread which connected him to the world he once knew.

To steel himself from the pain and sorrow, he had tried to build a protective wall around his heart. Yet the mere thought of her, the sight of her picture, or the sound of her voice was enough to cause that wall to crumble and bring on another bout of depression.

Whenever he would talk to her on the phone, he would always play down the gravity of the situation, trying to reassure her that everything was falling into place and that it was only a matter of time until he and Mark returned home.

Peg, for her part, had always been able to read between the lines. Yet she would do her best to hide her own inner misgivings from him.

On this night when she called, however, she would not be successful.

"Are you all right," she asked.

"Yes I am," he replied good-naturedly. "Why wouldn't I be?"

"Don't you think we get news out here too? We heard about the murder. Maddie and I have been worried sick and I haven't heard from you." She paused. "They haven't implicated you in it, have they?"

"No, they haven't, hon. A couple of men stopped by the other day to ask me a few questions, but they're questioning several others too. Seems a lot of people had it in for him."

"It's not the others I'm concerned about," Peg replied. "How's Mark doing? Is he helping you much?"

"Just fine, hon. Yes, he's been a big help to me. Don't know what I'd do without him."

"Dusty... are you a suspect in this?"

"No, kitten... I'm not," he replied. Then to change the subject, he asked, "How's Maddie?"

"How do you think? She's worried too. She's wants to drop everything and hop on the next plane."

That was the last thing Dusty wanted.

"No... no," he said. "She won't have to do that. We'll have this whole thing wrapped up in a few days."

He detected a hesitation at the other end. Her choked voice indicated that she was crying.

"Peggy...," he said gently. "This isn't like you. We've been through worse'n this."

"I know...," she said. "I know. It's just sometimes I don't think you're..."

"You don't think I'm what...? Levelin' with you? You know me better than that... this is nothin'. We're gonna lick this thing and then we'll be back before you know it."

"It's always been an uphill battle for you. Even in the old days, you had to fight twice as hard for things most people generally take for granted. It's not fair, Dusty. I wish there was something I could do to help you."

"Peg... this is something I've gotta take care of myself. Just... keep me in your thoughts. Be there for me when I need you, little girl. That's what I need right now. Huh? ...just a minute, kitten... somebody here wants to talk to you."

He put Mark on and the boy maintained his grandfather's tone of confidence.

Sadly, the time came too soon when all that they could say to each other had been said. When the conversation ended and they hung up, Dusty and Mark watched silently as the telephone cord swung to a stop.

Dusty rose from his chair and opened the refrigerator.

"We seem to be short of milk," he said. "I'll be back in a few minutes."

He put on his jacket and went out. He no sooner left the apartment when he bit his lip and rubbed his eyes with his handkerchief. He wandered through the park, then up one street and down another.

It wasn't so much for himself he was concerned. Now his family far away were worried. How much stress was this whole thing putting Peg through? Once again an overpowering guilt came over him.

He looked at his watch. Those fifteen minutes had turned into hours! His grandson must be having a conniption by now.

As he neared his apartment he sensed something was wrong. Then his eyes transfixed on the police cruiser parked in front.

His mind quickly kicked into high gear as he slipped back into the darkness.

Chapter 28

An all points bulletin was issued for Dusty's arrest. A chill came over Mark as he faced the grim reality of his grandfather being a hunted man.

They took the boy down to the police station. As he looked around at the uniformed officers and the overall surroundings, he could relate now more than ever to how restrictive the world must look through his grandfather's eyes.

Agent Witt in particular reminded him of an oppressive teacher with whom he had once clashed, and Mark had come to see him as the personification of this hostile system.

He was taken to an interrogation room. Folsum momentarily stepped down the hall to deliver some papers, leaving Witt alone with him.

The agent jumped right into the attack.

"Do you know where Dervin is?"

"No," Mark said sullenly.

"Do you have any idea where he went?"

"It wasn't my turn to watch him."

"We don't need the smart mouth here," snapped Witt. "This is a *murder* investigation, and we can make this just as easy or as hard as you want it. It's up to you."

"What's the matter," Mark shot back defiantly. "Can't you find the real killer, or are you just trying to cover your own butt!"

"You'd better watch your mouth, boy!" Witt threatened, pointing a finger in Mark's face. "I'm not fooling around here. If you know what's good for you, you'd better change your attitude damned *quick*!"

"Go to hell!"

Witt grabbed him by the shirt collar and jerked him out of the chair. "Look, you dumb little bastard …!"

Just then Folsum opened the door and what he saw infuriated him.

"Witt… Come out here!" he demanded, pointing the way to his office.

"I'm busy," growled the agent, locking eyes with the boy.

"I said, '*Come out here!*' *Now!*"

"You stay put!" warned Witt as Mark tore himself loose.

Folsum led him into his office and closed the door. "Just what the hell are you trying to pull," he asked.

"I'm trying to find out where his grandfather is," Witt replied. "What do you think I'm doing?"

"Do you think *browbeating* him is going to get him to tell us? Maybe you'd prefer to use a rubber hose."

"What would you have me do? Offer him an ice cream cone?"

"This is not the way we do things here," Folsum said in an exasperated tone to someone he regarded as having the mental age of three. "In case it hasn't dawned on you, the boy is our only hope of contacting Dervin, and now you've totally botched that. As I've tried to tell you fifty times, we're not after Dervin for murder; we're only after him for *suspicion*! And our best hope of clearing this up is by *convincing* the boy that it's in his best interest to cooperate, and you can't do that by coercion!"

Witt stood there sulking for a moment. "So what do *you* think we should do?"

"Release him. We don't have anything to hold him on. Besides, we've already got a tap on his phone. Dervin's bound to contact him sooner or later, and when he does we'll be ready, so all we need to do right now is wait."

"You know Al, they're making us look like fools here."

"No," replied Folsum, "I'd say you're doing a pretty good job of that all by yourself."

The detective sent for a female officer to drive Mark home, then returned to his office, sat down at his desk and buried his face in his hands.

There were now two different interpretations of the evidence, and at this moment Witt's seemed to be prevailing.

It wasn't only the clash of egos that disturbed him. While it was true that Folsum, an experienced senior investigator, resented being challenged by a brash upstart, there was more to it than that.

Folsum still maintained an inner gut feeling that Dusty was being set up. There were too many people who stood to gain with the pilot conveniently out of the way.

The fears Dusty had expressed to him were not without substance. In jail he would be unable to fight the resulting tide of publicity and sensationalism. Others involved in the project would emerge with their shirt sleeves clean, free to exploit the situation for their own personal gain while the pilot, guilty or innocent, would come out the ultimate loser.

However Folsum had no choice but to pursue the leads as they came in; and at this moment, these leads now pointed to a man who had taken flight.

The following morning he was visited by Reuben Abrams, his wife Phyllis, and another man who introduced himself as James Harris, their attorney. Phyllis seemed quite ill at ease.

"Lieutenant," Harris began, "In light of certain developments, my client wishes to clear the air over a matter which may or may not have direct bearing upon your case. In either event he wishes it understood that what he is about to say was not deliberately withheld but was simply overlooked during your visit."

"Go on," Folsum said curiously.

Harris nodded to Abrams who then recounted how he went bail for Dusty after the aerobatics incident.

Folsum recalled reading about it. "So you immediately connected Dervin with this when you saw it in the paper?"

"That's right," said Abrams.

"Tell me," inquired Folsum. "What made you decide to spring him?"

"Oh, I suppose *spite* as much as anything else," replied the scientist. "I knew it would upset Johns, and man, you should have seen him hit the roof! You see, Lieutenant,... Johns thought he had finally trapped Dervin into a corner where he could force him to come to his terms by letting him rot in jail. I didn't want him to have that satisfaction."

"I see," Folsum said. "Why didn't you come forward with this before?"

"You didn't ask me, and to tell the truth, it didn't seem relevant at the time. I was in enough hot water as it was without adding fuel to the fire." He shot a concerned look at his attorney, who nodded approvingly, and then looked back at Folsum. "Is this significant?"

Folsum pondered over this latest revelation.

"I don't know," he said. "It might be." He looked up at Abrams. "Could be that with him out of jail, it would be more convenient for you."

"How's that?" Abrams replied.

"One more suspect to muddy the water. If you planned to kill Johns, it would be a lot more convenient to have Dervin out loose. In jail, he would've had an alibi."

Harris jumped out of his chair. "Look," protested the attorney. "My client is telling the truth. He's the only one who even *bothered* to help Dervin through all this and then came here of his own free will, and now you're casting aspersions on his character."

"Relax. Don't get your dander up," Folsum said. "Nobody's casting aspersions on anybody. I have to consider all the possible angles here, that's all. If Dr. Abrams here is telling the truth, then he's got nothing to worry about." Folsum added, "Now is there anything else I should know?"

"No, Lieutenant," Abrams replied.

The detective rose to indicate that, as far as he was concerned, the meeting was over.

"Oh, one more thing," he added. "Keep handy and, uh... next time, let *me* decide what's relevant and what isn't."

When they left Folsum picked up the telephone receiver and pushed a button. "Lois, could you please get me the arrest record on a Dusty Dervin. City or County probably has it."

Just then a sergeant ushered in another visitor; it was the reporter Dale Rudd.

Rudd recounted how Dervin's visit to him with what he had considered a cock-and-bull story about Johns and the ICR. "I'm a science reporter," he explained, "...and the folks at the ICR give us some pretty good stories from time to time. In light of our relationship, I saw no reason to risk upsetting the apple cart with what seemed little more than the ranting of a disgruntled employee with an axe to grind."

"Did you make any attempt to check out his story?"

"Yeah, I made a couple of calls, but nobody I talked to had ever heard of him so I dropped it."

"And it didn't strike you as odd...," inquired Folsum, "that they might be covering something up?"

"The guy *himself* struck me as odd," replied Rudd. "In any case though, the last thing I ever expected was some kind of cloak-and-dagger stuff going on at the institute."

After Rudd left, Folsum shook his head as he leaned back in his chair. To him, it seemed out of character for a reporter who, by the very nature of his profession, was usually poking and sniffing under rocks in search of a story, often when there wasn't one. It was ironic how they'd always yell "fire" at the first hint of smoke, and yet now, on the verge of what could be one of the biggest news stories of all time, this guy sits back and allows it to go by because he doesn't want to rock the boat.

For Folsum, the disclosures of Abrams and Rudd added a few more pieces to the puzzle, but they also raised further questions.

It was Abrams who had connected Dusty with the aerobatics incident. Prior to that, Folsum had dismissed it as the act of a reckless fool who'd had too much to drink.

Now he was left wondering whether it was sheer foolhardiness or manifestation of culture shock. Dervin may have broken the law, the detective conceded, but it had probably never occurred to him since that law had not existed in his time, or if it had was probably not rigidly enforced.

It stood to reason that Johns would not want any premature publicity which would surely have resulted from a court hearing. After all, this would have forced his hand. Perhaps this aerobatic stunt had been Dervin's attempt to do exactly that, and the general had resorted to using his clout to suppress it.

But for all these theories and speculations, Folsum still had his job to do. He picked up the telephone and dialed Forensics, where the receptionist transferred him to a police sketch artist.

"Susan, can you come over," he asked. "It seems we've committed a minor oversight. In all our zeal to make Dervin the prime suspect in the Crime of the Century, nobody ever bothered to take his picture."

It was only after dark that Dusty felt it safest to venture out into the street. Moving in the shadows whenever he could, he was careful not to follow any pattern. One night he went into a 24-hour convenience store and bought a can of chili and a loaf of bread. The following night he had take-out Chinese. His heart froze whenever he heard the wail of a passing siren, but he would always manage to look straight ahead, betraying no sign of fear or nervousness. It was not until he reached the relative sanctuary of his dingy hotel room that he could let down his guard and spread out the newspaper on the bed.

SUSPECT SOUGHT IN DIRECTOR'S SLAYING! the headlines rang out. From what he could gather, Dusty figured that they had not found the code book. There followed a general description of the pilot, along with a recap of the overall developments - and, of course, the police sketch which really didn't look like him at all.

But, like Folsum, he too was plagued with questions. Had they found anything new, or were they keeping it all under wraps? Were they playing some kind of game, perhaps hoping to flush him out?

Dusty knew he was playing for time. Although his confidence in his original plan had waned, he had no choice but to stick with it. The longer he managed to evade capture, he hoped the edgier the killer would be to the point where he would make a slip. Dusty wasn't sure when it would happen, or what form it would take. But he had a gut feeling that when it came, he would spot it.

While the search for his grandfather went on, Mark suffered through the anxiety of endless waiting, while enduring the frustration of knowing there was nothing he could do. With the full weight of the law enforcement and the media brought to bear, the boy knew it was only a matter of time before Dusty was hunted down.

But Dusty's standing instructions to Mark were clear; under no circumstances was he to reveal either the truth about the code book or the contents of the envelope entrusted to him.

Mark spent most of his time by the phone waiting for the call which never came. One afternoon when the confinement in the apartment became too much to bear, he decided to take a walk out to the park.

As he watched a group of other boys his age playing football, he regretted that he was not one of them, and now felt that somehow his own youth was passing him by.

Just then, he became aware of someone standing next to him. He looked up to see it was Folsum.

"Mind if I join you," asked the detective.

"Free bench," Mark muttered as he rose to leave.

"Just a minute, son...," said Folsum as he searched for the right words. "I don't want to - hey look... I only want to talk... we may be on the same side."

"I doubt it," Mark said curtly.

"Look, Mark," he pleaded, "I'm not asking you to betray Dusty. I need your help to get a message to him."

Mark looked at him.

"*Help?*" he said bitterly. "You hunt him down like an animal and you want *my help?!*"

"I think he may be innocent," Folsum said.

Mark gave the detective a hard, suspicious look.

"*Sure* you do."

"Look," Folsum went on, "...Witt and I may not see eye to eye on this. But if your grandfather contacts you, you've got to convince him to turn himself in, if nothing else than for his own safety."

"*Safety?* He's probably a lot safer wherever he is than he would be with you guys."

"What's he trying to prove? He can't hold out forever. If he comes in on his own accord, I might be able to help him."

"Oh yeah, I can see the choices he'll have with your kind of help - life in prison or being shot dead in the street."

"Is that what you think we are? A bunch of vigilantes?"

"What do *you* think? You don't care whether he's guilty or not. You just want to close your case. Then you can turn loose all the news media and everybody else who want to turn this into a circus. He may be nailed either way, but I'm not gonna help you do it!"

"Where did you pick up this kind of talk," inquired the detective. "Television?"

"No, I've seen enough of it in real life! Everything's stacked in favor of the rich people, and everybody else gets screwed. Oh yeah, they used to tell us all about patriotism and freedom and equal justice under the law, but it's all a bunch of crap!"

Folsum did not like to see this hardened cynicism in a boy so young.

"Don't say that, son," he said with gentle reproach. "I don't know what they teach you fellas in school nowadays, but a lot of people have died for the very freedom you seem to take for granted. Our system may not be perfect, and maybe lots of times it may not even seem fair. But nobody's ever come up with anything better. And remarkable as our Constitution is, without dedicated people to make it work, it's little more than a mere scrap of paper. We may fall short of the mark now and then, but liberty is not something to be taken for granted. It has to be fought for, again and again."

Mark gave him a puzzled look. This was odd talk coming from a cop.

"Don't you think that's what my grandfather is trying to do," he countered. "Why is it considered right for people to fight in a war they don't believe in, and wrong for a man to fight for his own principles?"

"That," acknowledged Folsum, "...is an unfortunate byproduct of our legal system. To enable a vast complex government to work at all, there have to be certain institutions; most folks call them bureaucracies. Perhaps the people who created them may have started out with the best of intentions, but as time passed and these institutions grew larger and more complex, they often tended to coast along on their own inertia, concerned with perpetuating their own survival as much as serving the purposes which originally brought them about.

"When someone, maybe even through no fault of his own, gives these people cause to smell blood, they'll go after him like a shark. And once their momentum gets going, it's very hard to stop. It can leave many victims in its wake. What makes it even worse is that, when it's all over and the damage is done, there's usually no one particular individual on whom you can pinpoint blame. It's like a lynch mob. You can still wind up in trouble with the *technicalities* of the legal system, even if you've broken no law or have already been cleared of the charges which brought you to its attention in the first place."

Then Folsum returned to the matter at hand.

"I may be able to see that he gets a fair trial in court," he said. "But I can't protect him from the one he'll get in the press. I can say *this* for certain, though; the longer he remains at large, the fewer his options will be."

Mark was silent and pensive. "Look... I don't know where Dusty is," he said. "He didn't even tell me he was gonna split."

"I know, son," Folsum said. "But sooner or later he's going to make contact with you, and when he does I want you to call me."

"What makes you so sure he's gonna call?"

"He's got to. He figures that if he waits long enough, the real killer is going to somehow show himself. And it's just that kind of thinking that's liable to get your grandfather killed."

Mark looked at him curiously. "You think he's innocent too, don't you?"

"There's a good chance of it. But we can't do a thing for him unless he turns himself in."

"If he does call I'll tell him what you said, but somehow I don't think he's gonna go along with it."

"He damned well better. Don't you understand? Every minute he's out there, his life's in danger. Witt has declared open season on him!"

"You don't know my grandfather. He can be pretty resourceful. He comes from a different world than we do, and he sees things different. He can be real stubborn and determined once he makes up his mind. And whatever he does, he's gonna do it in his own time and in his own way."

For the time being, one set of circumstances was working in Dusty's favor; the conspiracy of silence was still being maintained.

Although the murder was getting the expected publicity for a crime of this nature, nothing was mentioned about the discovery or the project which brought it about.

This also worked to Folsum's advantage in that, by reducing the element of sensationalism, it was also buying a little time for him as well.

Playing upon the various political factions involved made it easier for the detective to convince all parties that it was in their best interests to hold off on any premature disclosures. A little discretion now, he reminded them, could be of greater benefit to them down the line.

Halleck and the others at the ICR having direct knowledge of Dusty and the Recovery Project were reminded that any advanced leak could prove politically embarrassing to the government and gravely detrimental to their own careers.

Convincing Dale Rudd was not as much trouble as anticipated. The reporter had been skeptical of Dusty's claims from the very outset and Folsum said nothing to change his preconceptions.

It was a delicate balancing act. Folsum still had to satisfy the press and the public that progress was being made. But he carefully limited any released information to that directly concerning the murder of a prominent official - nothing more.

Meanwhile in a dark room in a dingy skid row hotel, Dusty stretched out on a rusty cot staring blankly at the ceiling. Once again the clouds of self-doubt had gathered and the walls seemed to be caving in around him.

Nothing had worked. All of his instinctive hunches had proven wrong. Perhaps he did not know human nature at all.

He now gave serious thought to throwing in the towel. He had risked everything to buy himself a little time and now that time had run out. All he had to do was just walk on down to the nearest police vehicle and give himself up.

But each time he took a step in that direction, he would hesitate. There was more at stake here than just himself. There was his family to consider. Their lives too would be affected by the fallout from all this. He yearned to talk to Peggy. She could help him make the right choice.

He agonized over this painful dilemma until his mind began to hallucinate and spin around in utter exhaustion. He was unaware that he had drifted off to sleep.

Chapter 29

"Come in, detective," James Newstead smiled as he offered him a chair.

"Very nice setup you've got here," Folsum noted as he studied over the photographs and award plaques on the wall.

"Oh, we like it," boasted the airplane dealer. "We're number one in the area. Now… what can I do for you?"

Folsum reached in his pocket and handed Newstead a photograph of Johns. "Have you seen this man before?"

Newstead turned down the corners of his mouth. "Hmm… He's that guy in the papers… the one that was killed, right?"

"That's right," nodded the detective. "But what I'm talking about happened about a month ago."

"Nope," Newstead said shaking his head. "Can't say I remember him."

"Didn't he pay you a visit?"

"I can't say for sure. *Lots* of people have come in and out of here since then. Hell, I can't remember one face over another after a *week*."

"Try a little harder," Folsum pressed on. "It was just after that little escapade in the Stearman out there."

Newstead's smile now faded.

"What are you getting at?" he said.

"You could've pressed reckless endangerment charges against the man you took up that day, but you didn't, or if you did, you later dropped them. Did Johns persuade you to do that?"

"No, he didn't persuade me to do anything. I never met the guy."

"My pilot friends tell me that you're something of a legend around here," commented the detective. "You discourage competition by denying small independent operators and flight instructors the right to advertise on the field. You inflate your costs by sticking your students for more hours of dual instruction than they need."

"Are you a pilot?"

"No," Folsum replied.

"Well just take a look at the sky!" Newstead argued. "It's crowded up there! I'm not going to send *anyone* up there alone in one of my planes until I'm *absolutely* sure he's safe! And if it takes *eight* or *eighty* hours before I'm satisfied… well, then I guess that's my judgment to make!

"Second thing," he added, "I don't own this airport! The county does, and I pay them *plenty* for this lease! That includes the right to advertise! If some fly-by-night who lives out of his car wants to operate here, let him make his own arrangements with 'em like I do!"

"I'm sure that these *fly-by-nights* as you call them might be able to successfully contest that claim if they could afford a lawyer," Folsum replied.

Newstead rose from his chair. "I don't know what you're getting at, but I think any further discussion should be done with *my* lawyer present!"

"That's fine," assured Folsum. "I have a feeling that the county and the district attorney will be interested in the fine print of your lease agreement. Also, the Better Business Bureau, the IRS and - oh yes, the Veteran's Administration. They'll want to know why so many of their students on the GI Bill were padded with extra dual instruction time when it can be readily shown they could've soloed for just a fraction of that amount."

There was a momentary pause as Newstead gazed down at the floor. "All right," he said. "What do you want?"

"How much did Johns pay you to drop the charges?"

Newstead hesitated.

"I didn't hear you," said Folsum.

"Five thousand!"

"How did he pay you?"

"I don't understand."

"Did he pay you in cash? Did you set up some kind of a bank account? Did you go to his home?"

"No!" Newstead snapped. "He paid in cash, alright? Only it wasn't him; it was this other guy. He paid me out of a briefcase."

"What guy?"

"I don't know. He didn't give me his name."

"What did he look like?"

"Oh... middle aged and heavyset."

"And that was all there was to it?"

"Yeah, that was all there was to it! What else could there be?"

"A motive for murder perhaps."

"Hey!" he yelled out. "What reason would I have to kill him?"

"Where were you that night?"

"Givin' a guy a check ride in an airplane! The record's right here in my account ledger if you want to see it."

"That doesn't pinpoint the *hour*," noted the detective.

Then having gone as far as he could go for now, Folsum rose to leave.

"It's really quite funny when you think about it," he quipped. "You set out to take him for a ride and he wound up taking you for one."

Later on at headquarters, the detective admitted to Witt, "It wasn't too hard to figure out. From what we know of Johns and how he worked, his approach to Newstead was probably pretty straightforward. Halleck handled the payoff. I paid a little visit to him this afternoon and he confirmed everything Newstead told me."

"He *did*?" Witt replied. "You mean the loyal watchdog actually *ratted* on his master?"

"Why not? He figures with Johns gone it doesn't matter anymore. He's just looking out for himself now, like the rest of 'em."

Witt mulled for a moment over this latest revelation. Once again Folsum had trumped him with yet another suspect with a possible motive.

But the agent still stubbornly clung to his conviction that Dusty was guilty.

"I'm sure we've overlooked something," he maintained, "...and it's only a matter of time until we find it."

"You're really out to get him, aren't you," said Folsum.

"Yes, because I'm sure he did it, and I can't understand why you won't admit it."

Folsum looked at Witt for a moment and then heaved a sigh. Explaining anything to him was like trying to teach Einstein's Theory of Relativity to a monkey.

"In case you've forgotten," he said in a patronizing tone, "this is a murder investigation which will be handled in the same manner as any other murder investigation. Every shred of evidence must be thoroughly considered and the facts properly weighed before any arrest is made."

"He ran, didn't he," argued Witt. "I'd say under the circumstances, that's an admission of guilt!"

"He's scared, dammit! How would you feel if you were out of your element and everybody was out hunting you down like a mad dog? And suppose this man turns out to be innocent? *I* sure don't want to be remembered as the one who threw him to the wolves."

"Look," Witt said angrily. "I've had it with you and your plodding along. You handle it your way and I'll handle it in mine!"

With that, the agent stormed out of Folsum's office and slammed the door.

Folsum reflected momentarily over the folly of trying to reason with an idiot, then he shook his head, heaved a shrug, and went back to work.

It was now six days since Dusty had gone into hiding. Any shred of hope he held had long since gone down the drain. There had been no new developments, only the growing intensity of the search for him. He knew that in the eyes of the world, he was already guilty.

The strain had taken its toll. Every passing siren gave him the jitters. It was just a matter of time now; any further attempts to delay the inevitable would be for nothing.

He decided that the time had come for him to simply walk out the door, go to the police station and turn himself in.

He waited until late at night when there would be relatively few people about.

He passed a newsstand. Knowing it would probably be his last chance to look at the outside world, he dropped two dimes into the slot. With his newspaper in hand he set about finding a secluded spot to read it.

Dusty decided to indulge himself in one last meal in freedom. He came upon a small Italian restaurant. The lighting inside was fairly dim. There were only a couple of customers, so he went in and sat down at a corner booth.

"I'll be with you in a moment, sir," the waiter said and walked away.

Dusty picked up the paper and began to look it over. What he saw made his heart jump.

On the front page was a photograph of himself, taken almost fifty years before!

Less than a half minute elapsed before the waiter returned to Dusty's table, but when he got there the pilot was gone.

Chapter 30

The split between Folsum and Witt was now complete. It had become a scandal of its own, adding fuel to the already mounting accusations of foot dragging and overall incompetence.

When Folsum saw Dusty's picture in the paper he hit the ceiling. Apparently behind the detective's back, Witt had taken matters into his own hands. Folsum suspected that Witt had obtained the photo from one of Johns' associates.

With this single find, the agent had managed to both end-run Folsum and take over the lead in the investigation.

It was exactly what the detective had dreaded. With his case snatched from under him, his methodical approach had been pushed aside by the very politics and sensationalism he had sought to avoid. To make matters worse, earlier that morning, he received a directive from his chief to place himself, his men and his resources at the disposal of the FBI.

Like the others, Witt found his purposes best served by maintaining secrecy over the Recovery Project, at least for the time being. His objective was to apprehend a murder suspect as quickly as possible, and he did not want any secondary issues getting in the way. If others did not see things his way, he was certain that they would come around once Dervin was caught.

By now the pilot's picture was displayed at Post Offices and airports throughout the entire country. Border Patrol agents were put on alert should he attempt to cross into Mexico or Canada. Reported sightings were coming in with increased frequency, all thus far to no avail.

Mark rose to answer a knock on the door. It was Donna.

"May I come in," she asked nervously.

The teenager, wary of the possible presence of eavesdropping bugs, put his finger to his lips. "Let's go outside," he whispered.

They didn't talk much as they walked through the shopping mall. After lunch, they stopped before the window of an art store, where they looked at a poster of a jet pilot standing before his supersonic fighter. There was no face or other identifying features. Just the flight suit and helmet with the goggles pulled down.

"That's the way our heroes are today," she noted. "Faceless and mass-produced like something out of a cookie cutter. It says something really pathetic about our society, don't you think?"

"Yeah, I suppose," concurred Mark.

"There's no originality anymore," she went on. "No spontaneity. It's all so predictable now. What's news today is old hat tomorrow. People all seem preoccupied with just one thing - making money. They don't plan for the long term anymore. All they seem to be concerned with is what matters *today*.

"And then they wonder what's wrong with the young people. I'll tell you what's wrong. They don't have any real heroes to look up to anymore, people whose courage serves as an inspiration for them to follow."

Turning to Mark, she said, "Your grandfather is such a man."

Mark looked at her curiously.

"Who has gone through what he has," she continued. "Who else has seen fifty years of change spring up seemingly overnight? He's real."

But the young man gazed dejectedly at the floor. "What does everybody want from him," he asked rhetorically. "All he wants to do is get on with his life. Damn it, you'd think most people would show him some understanding and consideration, and maybe give him the space he needs, but no - they're all tryin' to make a *criminal* out of him!"

"Mark," she said gently, "...people are inherently blind. It's basic human nature. It takes a long time to make them see their own follies. We fight wars, and sometimes innocent people are persecuted and killed. Animals have been hunted to the brink of extinction, and the environment upon which our very survival depends is in grave danger.

"The war against ignorance is an ongoing struggle. And no matter how hard you try...," she said extending her thumb and forefinger, "you're lucky if you can only change things this much.

"Some of us help by writing letters, or raising money. A select few, because of special talents they have, are able to reach out to millions. Dusty is one of these people, Mark. He may be able to do what no one has ever done before. He could become the spokesman of one generation to another, and when the world is ready to listen, I think he will have his own message to give to them."

"What do you think he would say, Donna?"

There was a kind of dreaminess in her voice. "I don't know... I can't speak for him. But from what he's told me, I'd like to imagine he'd be concerned with the betterment of life on this earth. Perhaps he can teach young people about perseverance and determination and lead them away from the destructive effects of social alienation and drugs. Maybe he can show us that true progress is not always measured by what's bigger, or flies higher, or goes faster... that perhaps real progress must come from within ourselves, understanding where we've come from and where we are going... and what is good for us all in the long run."

Mark reflected for a moment over what she had said. "That sounds noble enough," he acknowledged, "but he'll never get a chance to say those things. They want to put their own words in his mouth... to make him say what *they* want him to say."

"That's what this struggle is all about, Mark. I don't know of anyone who's ever accomplished anything worthwhile without encountering some kind of hostility or prejudice. And overcoming it has often come at tremendous cost... even of their very lives."

Presently Donna looked at her watch. "I've got a class in about an hour," she said. "Will you be okay here?"

"I'll be fine," Mark smiled.

She took his hand in both of hers. "When you see him... please tell him there are a lot of us rooting for him. Tell him-." Tears welled up in her eyes and her voice choked, "Tell him to hang in there."

She kissed his cheek, then turned and disappeared into the crowd.

The following morning the telephone jarred Mark awake.

"Hello, Mark."

The boy jumped up out of bed. "Dusty! Are you all right?"

The weariness and fatigue in the pilot's voice were all too apparent.

"Yeah, I'm okay."

Mark's initial excitement suddenly turned to grave concern. "You know... they're looking for you everywhere!"

"I know, son... I know," he said. "I'm gonna turn myself in, but first we gotta meet someplace."

Aware that his phone was tapped, Mark warned his grandfather of the possibility of the call being traced should he stay on the line too long, then added dutifully, "Just tell me what you want me to do."

"He's made contact," Witt declared to his agents. Parked the next block over, they were gathered in a van, specially equipped with state-of-the-art telecommunications and eavesdropping devices. "This is what we've been waiting for," he added as he jammed a clip into his .45 automatic.

Folsum, aware it would fall on deaf ears, nonetheless made one last plea for restraint.

"Is that gun really necessary," he asked.

"It's standard procedure with a murder suspect who's resorted to flight," Witt shot back. He then walked over to the whiteboard on which was placed a map of Los Angeles.

"Our task will be to follow the kid from the moment he sets foot out the door," he announced. "He's real clever. He knows we're on to him and most likely he'll try to give us the slip, so keep on your toes. Tom's already positioned in front of Dervin's apartment so he'll signal us when he's ready to roll. Joe, you'll stay here to monitor the reports as they come in."

Folsum had done all he could, but now relegated to a subordinate role, he could only stand by and watch a bunch of misguided men filing out like self-righteous idiots on a crusade.

The bus pulled up and Mark got aboard. He took a circuitous route through the various blocks and boulevards, finally arriving at a predetermined phone booth across from the Beverly Hilton. He waited there several minutes, then the phone rang and his grandfather gave him a new set of instructions. He then took another bus and proceeded to the next contact point - a service station down the street from the Metropolitan Art Museum - where the entire procedure was repeated.

Mark was nervous. He knew he was being tailed. The length of time each leg took varied from ten to thirty minutes.

He now found himself in the crowded terminal area of the L.A. International Airport in front of the TWA check-in. After another twenty minutes a yellow cab drew up and he got in.

"Holiday Inn, please," Mark instructed the driver.

"That sounds reasonable," replied the cabbie in a familiar voice.

"Dusty!"

"Shhh. Not so loud," cautioned the pilot as he pulled out into traffic. "We don't want to draw attention to ourselves."

Mark's initial joy soon turned to concern as he saw his grandfather's grubby disheveled appearance.

"Dusty - you look terrible! Are you all right?"

"It's not easy to maintain one's appearance after several days on the lam," said the pilot.

"You mean you -"

"Son," Dusty cut in, "...we can go into all that later. Right now there's somethin' real important I gotta ask you."

Mark's eyes were wide open. "Sure, Dusty... anything! What is it?"

"Your mama told me you were the family historian."

"I never thought of it that way, but — yeah, I guess you could say so."

"Those old pictures, y'know... the ones you catalogued. How did you go about doin' that?"

"Oh, mostly dated 'em and put 'em into albums. My father turned them all over to Johns," he added. "The negatives too."

"Yeah, yeah... I know about all that. But right now what can you tell me about the photograph they put in the paper? As I recollect, that was part of a larger one your grandma and I had taken together."

"That's right," Mark said. "I remember that one."

"Those were happier days," Dusty wistfully recalled. "She didn't care much for how she looked, so she had the cut-out of me made from it."

Just then a small pickup truck cut in front of him, forcing him to slam on his brakes. "Damn jerk! Who the hell taught that moron to drive! Anyway, what I want to know is... did you have a negative made from that one?"

"Yes I did, Dusty. I had negatives made from all the pictures as backup just in case anything happened to the originals."

"Where did you keep it?"

"On a small table in the front room." He looked curiously at his grandfather in the mirror. "Why, Dusty... what are you getting at?"

"You may have helped trap the killer," said the pilot.

Mark's jaw dropped. "Me? Who is it?"

"I can't go into that right now," said the pilot, "but I think up to now everybody has been barkin' up the wrong tree."

"How?"

"I don't think it was the codebook Johns was killed for after all. He was killed over the picture."

Mark was dumbfounded. "The picture?"

"It's the only way it makes sense… the messed up room, the blackmail call that never came. And that's why it took so long to put the picture in the paper - that particular one and none of the others. How come with all the hubbub and everybody lookin' for me, this here's the only picture they've managed to come up with? Because it wasn't with the others, that's why."

The young man shook his head puzzledly. "I'm not sure I follow you, Dusty," he said.

"Just take my word for it. I think we're on the right track this time, and I'm willin' to stake my life on it."

There was a resurgent optimism in his grandfather's voice.

"I'd better let you off here," Dusty said, once again checking the rear view mirror. "It might look suspicious, you and me ridin' around so long."

Just then Mark heard a series of odd thumping sounds emanating from the trunk. "What's that," he asked.

"The driver," Dusty said nonchalantly. "Only way I could be sure of his cooperation."

"Why didn't you just hotwire an empty taxi instead of going to all that trouble?"

"Because if I'd done that, it would've been reported stolen almost immediately. The cops would have had a citywide alert out for it. This way nobody knows it's missin', and it buys me a little more time. Don't worry. I'll pay him double his fare when I let him out." Noticing Mark's look of concern he winked, "After all, he's on a secret mission for the government."

They pulled up to a crowded bus depot. "It's probably best for you to hail another cab," advised the pilot. "We'll lead 'em around a little bit longer. Right now, I got a couple things to take care of. You understand what you're to do?"

Mark nodded. His face bore a grave look as he made the appearance of paying the cab fair.

"Dusty, be careful."

"I always am," he smiled. "Don't you worry; this thing'll be over real soon."

It was just past midnight when Ken Reynolds unlocked the door to his apartment. He turned on the front light and hung his coat in the hall closet. He then went into his living room where he suddenly jumped back in shock.

"Dusty," he exclaimed. "Wha- what are you doing here? My *God* man - you look *terrible!*"

The disheveled pilot sat slumped in the stuffed chair. His eyes were bloodshot and he wore the expression of a hunted fox at the end of the trail.

"I hope you'll forgive the intrusion," he said, "but I've got nowhere else to go."

"They're looking all over for you... you know that?"

"Yeah, yeah, I know…," he said staring blankly at the floor. "I'm gonna turn myself in. I just need a little while to get my head together, that's all."

"That's a good idea," said Reynolds recovering from the initial shock. "Want me to come along with you?"

"Nah, that's okay. All things considered, it's probably best they come here."

"Sure Dusty… sure. Whatever you say. Shall I make the call for you?"

"No… I'll do that. Just let me sit here a moment and rest while I get my courage up." There was a sad look in his eyes as he slowly shook his head. "This… this *thing*, Ken… it's gotten way out of hand. It didn't have to, y'know. Too bad Johns had to go ruin it for everybody."

"He certainly did that, old chum," Reynolds agreed.

"The irony of it all," Dusty went on, "…was that whatever recognition might come out of all this, there would've been enough to go around for everybody. But for the general, y'see, that wasn't good enough for him. He wanted it all for himself."

"He sure did, ol' buddy."

"You gotta hand it to him though, the way he carefully planned everything on down to the last detail. Managed to get his hands on anything I might use to prove my identity. He tracked down my wife and my family, and it didn't stop there. Y'know he even figured out who was the best person to reach. … the weak link in the chain. Even made sure Ol' Joe didn't get any second thoughts.

"Curiously though… all the while this was goin' on, nobody bothered to let me in on it. I suppose that the real reason they tried to discourage me from goin' home was to buy themselves some more time. And instead of lettin' me know what he found, Johns thought it best to keep me in the dark about it. I guess he figured he'd have some more material for his story - maybe add to the pleasure he got watchin' me stumble my way around."

"He was something else all right," concurred Reynolds. "Almost from the very day he assumed control at the institute."

The pilot got up from his chair and began pacing back and forth across the room.

"Kinda makes you wonder how he consolidated his power, y'know like the way those dictators do, except on a smaller scale, of course.

"Y'see, Ken, guys like that don't trust anybody, and once he embarks on somethin' devious and complex, he's got himself two problems. First, he's got to make sure that the others in his little scheme don't get similar ideas and conspire against him. So he plays one against the other to keep 'em off balance. He has to convince 'em that he's the only game in town and they'd better play by his rules or else.

"And second, he's gotta make sure that nobody's got a handle on the whole picture. So he gives each person a specific task, all the while lookin' over their shoulders. Like whenever he had to go out of town he would take somebody along to lend it kind of an official air of sorts, and do whatever dirty work was necessary. He took Halleck with him when he went up to Alaska to get the code book. And earlier, when he visited my hometown, he took you."

Reynolds was astonished. "Who told you that?"

"I had a little chat with Joe before they took him away. He didn't want to tell me at first until I . . . well, *persuaded* him. He described the two men who came to visit him. One was Johns, of course. He didn't name the other but said he was a tall younger man in his early forties. That could only have been you."

"All right. . . so it *was* me," he admitted, "So what?"

"While Johns went into the study with Joe to close the deal, he needed a lookout in case Lynn or Mark suddenly came in the front door. He knew they might well take a dim view of what was goin' on and cause trouble for him.

"Only while you waited and wandered around the front room, you spotted a picture of me on the table. You couldn't resist temptation, so you decided to take a little souvenir for yourself. Only Johns found out about it later on. He was goin' to fire you. That's why you killed him."

Reynolds gave out a hollow laugh. "You are crazy," he said. "You don't know what you're talking about! Go ahead! Search this place if you want. You won't find a picture because there isn't any!"

"No," Dusty said. "I'm sure it's not here. With Johns dead you wouldn't dare risk having it connected with you, so you planted it with the FBI when you were afraid they were takin' too long to find me."

Reynolds reached for the phone. "I'm calling the police!"

"Go ahead. It'll be real interestin' to see how they react when they hear how Johns confronted you with it. You thought he'd never find out. After all, he didn't see it when he came in; his mind was focused on other matters. And besides, you had the only copy. You didn't know about the negative."

Reynolds looked Dusty over like he was some kind of lunatic.

"Negative? What negative?"

"The one my grandson had made when he reproduced the enlargement of me. You see, that was part of a larger portrait Peggy and I had taken. It turns out that my grandson had negatives made of everything. Unfortunately, he was too trusting. He kept everything all together in one place because he didn't figure on his own father betrayin' him by sellin' his family heritage to the general.

"Anyway, like I was sayin', one night while Johns was goin' through his little collection, he took it upon himself to match each of the prints with their corresponding negatives, y'know, to see what he had. And guess what? Instead of findin' a print without a negative, he came up with a negative without a print!

"So he says to himself, 'I'm supposed to have all the prints *and* all the negatives, but the print for this one is missin'!' He reasons that there indeed *was* a print. Then he asks himself what happened to it. When he thinks back as to who *else* had access to it, it didn't take him long to figure out.

"We have here what amounts to a fallin' out between thieves," Dusty went on. "Someone stole somethin' from him which he had in turn stolen from someone else, but he can't exactly go public with his accusation. So he handles it the way he handles everything else - discreetly. Only this time it has disastrous results.

"Sometime after you killed him, and the investigation seemed to be gettin' nowhere, you somehow found a way to conveniently plant the photograph in order to get rid of it while focusin' suspicion on me."

"For all this intriguing speculation," Reynolds sneered, "you don't have one iota of proof!"

"Oh, it's there all right. They'll be real curious about that little inscription I wrote Peggy on the back of it, especially since I haven't had access to it in over forty years."

Reynolds calmly walked over behind his desk and opened the right-hand drawer. He produced a snub-nose revolver and pointed it at Dusty.

"I don't know how you figured it out," he said, "but I'm afraid we'll just have to keep that little matter between ourselves."

"Are you going to kill me, too," Dusty asked.

"You just *wouldn't* go along with the program," Reynolds said caustically. "You had the whole world offered to you on a silver platter and you wouldn't take it. No, you wanted to have everything your way! You damn fool!" he muttered shaking his head. "You should've wised up while you had the chance!" He parted the curtain and glanced over his shoulder out the window.

There was now a wild look in Reynolds' eyes.

"He was so *smug*! He expected everything done at the push of a button. When he found out about that stupid little picture, he was going to fire me. He called me a thief over one *lousy* picture while *he* was stealing credit for the whole project! Sure I called on him that night. I begged him to reconsider, but he wouldn't back down. He had all that power and he was going to ruin me. I worked hard to get where I am... *damn* hard! And I'm not about to let *him* or *you* or *anybody else* take it away!"

His mind now began grasping for a plan to deal with his immediate problem.

"You were a prowler... that's it!" he continued. "We've had a lot of burglaries and assaults here lately and I had to protect myself. I didn't know it was you or even *expect* you to come by here. Just one more in a series of tragic misfortunes which has been dogging you since you came back.

"Now get up!" he said motioning with his gun. "Real slow now... over here by the sliding door."

Dusty's eyes fixed on his adversary's as he complied.

Reynolds' lips tightened as he raised his arm to take aim. "Don't worry," he smiled grimly. "This'll be over real quick!"

"Drop it Reynolds!" commanded Folsum emerging from the kitchen with his own gun extended at full arms' length and aimed at Reynolds' head.

Reynolds froze in his tracks and suddenly turned white.

"I said, **'Drop it! Now!'**"

The gun dropped to the floor. Reynolds' hand began to twitch as he reached up to his forehead, then slowly and jerkily pulled it over his face.

Presently two uniformed officers came forward to handcuff him. He was subsequently read his rights and taken away.

Folsum put his hand on Dusty's shoulder. "You really stuck your neck out, guy," he said.

"Yeah, I know," the pilot said heaving a weary sigh of relief. "I know."

"You've done enough for one night, son," said the detective. "We've got it all on tape. Go home and get yourself a good night's sleep. We can wrap all this up in the morning."

Just then Mark bolted through the doorway and greeted his grandfather with a hug.

"We really did it, didn't we, Dusty!" the boy proudly proclaimed.

"We sure did, Mark," Dusty smiled. "I could never have done it without you."

Then putting his arm around the boy's shoulders he said with a tired smile, "It's all over, son. We can go home now."

Chapter 31

It would be a long time before Dusty could fully accept that his ordeal was finally over. The recurring nightmares would continue to haunt him for many months.

His heart would never completely accept the reality of his transition. He would always be the stranger, the outsider; and the loneliness, the bouts of depression, and the inner longing for a familiar world long gone would never be far away.

When he awakened from his long sleep the first thing he did was to call Peg. She could barely contain her excitement as she awaited the return of her two men. Dusty assured her that it would only be a couple of days while he tied up a few loose ends.

Albert Folsum tended to be something of a cynic. Having seen so much of life at its worst, he had long ago forsaken the idealism of his youth. His heroes, such as Martin Luther King, Joe Louis, and the many black servicemen who had fought for their country abroad while fighting prejudice at home, seemed at times to be distant figures to him.

The mainstream heroes of the twenties - the Babe Ruths, the Lindberghs, and the Dempseys — these were all white men's heroes of a time noted for its oppression of black people. It was not an era Folsum regarded historically with any fondness.

But if anyone could give him cause to reevaluate his beliefs it was the pilot who had cracked the case for him. Folsum now saw Dusty as a man who had overcome so much in the pursuit of what he believed to be right. Out of his element, the latter had pitted his own intuition against the collective might of misguided authorities and had won. It exemplified courage of the highest order.

"I still can't get over how you managed to pull it off fooling Johns with that phony bootlegger's code book," marveled the detective. "That's certainly a new one for me."

"It was the only way I thought I could force the stalemate," Dusty replied.

"But wouldn't all the ensuing media hoopla have defeated your purpose? You were zeroing in the artillery on your own position."

"It was a risk I had to take. The moment the story hit the headlines, I would've explained it all, and Johns would've have come out lookin' like the jackass that he was. That's the way it was *supposed* to happen. Of course though," added Dusty, "this all had depended on his bein' alive."

Folsum shook his head. "Why didn't you come forward with this crazy scheme before? You could've gotten yourself killed going it alone like that."

"Who would have believed me," replied the pilot. "Everybody was sure I was guilty. Besides, like the rest of you guys, I had assumed that Johns had been killed over the code book, and it seemed best to wait and see what the killer was gonna do with it. The irony was that it worked too well. How could I convince everybody that it wasn't real after I'd gone to all the trouble makin' 'em think that it was? Once you set somethin' like this in motion, it's almost impossible to bring it to a stop."

Folsum still had a bit of difficulty following the pilot's peculiar line of reasoning, but it no longer mattered now.

"Tell me, Dusty," he asked. "What put you onto Reynolds?"

"It was the picture in the paper. I couldn't figure out how it got there, what with Johns takin' such pains to guard 'em all. Then it dawned on me that maybe it was never *with* the others; he had either overlooked it, or somebody stole it from under his nose. From that point it was a process of elimination as to who else might've had access to it. Besides," he went on, "somethin' else about Reynolds rubbed me the wrong way."

"What's that?"

"The way he stood out. I don't think any of you guys would've noticed it because you weren't really tuned into what was really goin' on. You see... with all the other players, at least I knew where they were comin' from: Halleck, Abrams, even Verneer with all his eccentricities. But Reynolds, he was different. He was always tryin' to be my friend, offerin' me advice on how to make my life easier."

"Playing the 'good guy' against the backdrop of the 'bad guys', huh?"

"Somethin' like that."

"And that made you suspicious? I'd think most folks in that kind of situation would welcome such a gesture of friendship."

"Maybe," Dusty acknowledged. "But there was one thing nobody bothered to notice, and it was one of the main reasons I could never have gone along with Johns at all. Remember how methodical he was in always checkin' everything down to the last detail?"

"Yes."

"Well, when he and Reynolds went back to Claremont to check out my family, they must surely have found out about Joe's big land deal, and his scheme to cheat Peggy out of all her property. Don't you think that a true friend would've tipped me off about that?"

"Yes," nodded the investigator. "I see your point now."

Folsum opened his desk and produced the small black notebook, which he tossed to the pilot.

Dusty examined at it as if it were an old friend.

"Dusty, this code book here.... How were you able to make it look so authentic?"

The pilot looked at him curiously. "What do you mean, Lieutenant?"

"Well, it just seems to me that only someone with an intimate knowledge of such things could've pulled off something like that. Tell me for my own curiosity... not that it matters very much at this point... were you ever engaged in bootlegging?"

Dusty gave a mild chuckle. "I suppose most people in my line of work knew it was goin' on. Even if you weren't in on it yourself, you usually knew of somebody who was, so the current price quotes were fairly common knowledge, just like cars and houses."

Folsum cast Dusty a long sideways look. This was not the answer to his question, and he sensed that the pilot knew more than he was letting on. But at this point he chose not to pursue the matter any further.

He then reached behind his desk and produced a package about the size of a large hatbox, which he handed over to Dusty. "I think you might find this interesting," he said.

Dusty lifted the lid. His eyes widened in amazement.

"My stuff! The pictures... my letters... *everything*! They're all *here*!"

He looked up at Folsum and asked, "Where did you find these?"

"Johns kept 'em in a strong box he had hidden behind his wall unit. I figured that, since he didn't really trust anybody, he would've most likely kept them close by."

"It sure would've been bad if Witt had gotten ahold of these."

"Yes I suppose it would've," agreed the detective. "That's why I never told him."

Dusty took several minutes to look over the contents of the box, and what he found brought tears to his eyes. They included all the photographs of Peg and himself together in their youth. There was even a poster from his barnstorming day with a picture of the group including his friend Jim. A flood of dreams and lost memories had suddenly come alive once again.

He looked up at Folsum. His face took on a more solemn look as he once again reflected upon the close call he had come through.

"Lieutenant, let me ask you something. How come you didn't rush to judgment on me like everybody else?"

The detective leaned back in his chair and lit his pipe.

"Johns' death was too convenient for a lot of people. Everybody was running around half-cocked, out to make a name for themselves while trying to protect their own turf. Since they were all so bound and determined, the least I could do was head 'em off for awhile and buy the forces of reason a little more time."

Folsum went on. "Remember when Witt was so sure you were guilty and he and his men set out to arrest you? Well, I thought he might try something like that so, unbeknownst to him, I had your place under surveillance. When you had gone out of your apartment, I left that marked unit there to warn you off."

"*You* did that?" said Dusty.

Folsum nodded. "I also made sure Witt didn't get ahold of your booking photos after that little flying escapade.

"I kept trying to tell him that it was premature to make any arrests; there were too many loose ends. But he was bound and determined to do it his way. If I had tipped you off directly, I would have broken the law for obstruction of justice, so I played the role of bumbling cop instead."

Dusty looked at Folsum in amazement.

"I guess it just goes to show that sometimes you never know who your friends are," acknowledged the pilot. "When I think how close it came to goin' the other way…"

Folsum smiled in the gentle manner of a wise man giving counsel to his son.

"Try not to dwell upon it anymore," he said. "What matters most is that we were able to put the genie back in the bottle - at least until such time as you're ready to let it out."

"By the way, Lieutenant, what happened to Witt?"

"Oh, didn't you hear?" he smiled. "It seems our friend got himself transferred somewhere - South Dakota, I think… one of those out of the way places."

"You're kiddin'!"

"No, it's the God's honest truth. In all his zeal, he made the FBI look like the Keystone Kops. From what I understand, the agency came out with quite a bit of egg on its face; and, oh yes, I got a call this afternoon from a man who would like to see you tomorrow, some high-level mucky-muck from Washington."

"What does he want," Dusty asked.

"I can't say for sure, but from what I gather, he's rather anxious to cut some sort of deal with you."

When they rose to say goodbye, Dusty warmly extended his hand to his friend.

"Good luck," smiled the detective. "I hope you and your grandson have a happy future."

He looked on as Dusty walked down the hallway. When the pilot got to the end, he turned and waved back in a final salute before he opened the door and walked out.

Thomas White was a man in his mid sixties. Six feet two with a full head of white hair, he had a distinguished presence. Although somewhat taciturn in his initial demeanor, he proved to be quite congenial and amiable once one entered his circle of trust.

White had been sent in as an administrator/troubleshooter, with the immediate tasks of untangling the mess at the ICR and minimizing, to the extent possible, any potential fallout that could prove embarrassing to the government in this post Viet Nam/Watergate era. While Dusty did not want any sensational publicity brought upon himself, it turned out that the government wanted it even less.

It did not take long for both men to establish rapport. A meeting for all concerned parties was scheduled in two days to take place in the main conference room. Dusty was advised to bring legal council with him.

A formal agreement was passed around for them to sign, the basis of which was as follows:

Those who had either worked on, or had direct knowledge of the Recovery Project were free to write up their own works, *provided* they refrained, directly or indirectly, from making any references to Dusty or his family. This restriction would remain in effect until such time as he himself elected to go public. Should any of the participants violate this agreement they were about to sign, any money earned from such disclosures would revert to Dusty as royalties, plus the offending participant would be subject to any legal action Dusty might choose to bring.

In return, restitution to a number of these people would be considered on a case-by-case basis. Reuben Abrams was to be restored to his position in the Life Sciences Department, as would many of his former team members, as part of the government's effort to correct some of the inequities from Johns' regime. Halleck and Johns' other political cronies were encouraged to take an early retirement.

Dusty's attorney studied the agreement and gave his approval. The others promptly concurred.

All that is, except the psychiatrist, Ronald Verneer. As a consultant, he had no position to be restored to him. He had managed to retain copies of his notes before he was fired, and he wanted to expand and capitalize upon them.

"We all put considerable effort in this," he protested, "and if we are not permitted to go into the specifics it will look like fiction. No one will recognize their scientific validity. Besides, you can't really enforce this since there is no legal precedent of this nature concerning the rights of someone already declared legally dead."

The others joined in a collective rebuke of Verneer as Dusty looked him straight in the eye.

"If you want to fight this, Verneer," he said, "go right ahead. But just remember, it works both ways. You go public with this and, so help me, I'll see to it that your own duplicity is brought out too! It's up to you. Now take it or leave it!"

Verneer, his dignity ruffled, grudgingly added his signature to the agreement.

When the meeting was over, Dusty and White went to the latter's office where, behind closed doors, the acting director opened his briefcase and handed him some additional papers.

"There," White declared. "You are no longer a nonperson. You will find these papers authenticated to reflect more contemporary dates, which should prove helpful in such matters as obtaining credit and finding a job. You'll also find included a letter of reference, which I think you'll find will go a long way. Should you choose to resume your former occupation, you'll probably have to undergo instrument qualification and upgrade your skills. Perhaps this will help."

He handed Dusty a check for fifty thousand dollars. The pilot gazed at it dumbfounded for a moment, for he was not accustomed to seeing that kind of money.

"Call it back pay and wrongful termination damages," White smiled. "Oh, and one thing more; the reckless flying charges against you have been dropped, and all records pertaining to your arrest have been expunged.

"But remember," he cautioned. "You are free to go public with your story at any time. However once you do, the others will no longer be bound by the constraints of the agreement. They will be free to do so as well."

"I don't see myself doing that in the foreseeable future," the pilot said solemnly.

White developed a deep respect for this honest and straightforward man who had made his own job considerably easier than he'd had a right to expect. However the senior official, accustomed to the political world of wheeling and dealing, found himself puzzled by Dusty's motives.

"I just don't understand," he said. "Movie stars, generals, athletes - even ex-presidents - these people can't *wait* to cash in on their celebrity status, to write their memoirs, to go on speaking tours and commercial endorsements. Yet you, who have undergone one of the most incredible experiences of all time, don't seem to want any part of it. Could you explain to me why?"

Dusty paused for a moment before he spoke. When the words came there was a sadness to them.

"Everyone seems to think that what happened to me was some kind of heroic exploit. It wasn't. It was a freak chain of events. There's no glory to wakin' up one mornin' to find out that all your friends are gone and the whole world has passed you by. Everywhere I look, I'm constantly reminded that I'm out of place here, like some kind of relic from a distant time.

"From the moment I woke up in that hospital," he went on, "...I saw nothin' but greed and selfishness. It will be a long time before I get that bad taste out of my mouth.

"No, Mr. White... there's quite a few issues I gotta work out before I can even *think* about those things. Do you understand what I'm talkin' about?"

"Yes, Dusty," White said kindly, "I think I do."

As the pilot rose to leave, White imparted to him one final thought.

"I can never begin to comprehend the magnitude of what you must have gone through," he said. "This immense feeling of isolation must indeed be a tremendous burden to bear.

"But you should always know that the memories of your friends and the world you once knew will forever remain a part of you, as well they should, for you are so much richer for having them. I do believe, however, that with the passage of time you will find a place for yourself in this world too. It may be a big challenge, but I think you have the inner strength and resiliency to handle it.

"There is one thing I would like to ask. Try not to judge us too harshly. As with any institution, your government may have its bad apples from time to time, and we try to root them out as we find them. In the long run we do try to respond to the needs of our citizens, but sometimes it just takes a lot of persistence in pointing us in the right direction."

White then offered his hand.

"Good luck, Dusty," he smiled, "and Godspeed."

The flight home was uneventful. As he and Mark walked along the concourse, Dusty looked out at the many giant sleek jetliners lined up along the tarmac. The decades of advances in aviation had totally transformed it into something he could no longer recognize. Gone were the dreams and romance of the early days, having given way to the myriad complex daily mechanical routines which had come to characterize modern life.

He was dismayed by the strong presence of uniformed security personnel, and he momentarily balked at having to pass through the metal detector booth. Unaware of the recent developments necessitating such measures, he regarded them as yet one more example of how modern society was being transformed into a police state. It took several minutes for his grandson to explain these things to him before he began to understand.

Once they were airborne, he was likewise disappointed when he was refused permission to see the cockpit with his grandson.

"The price of progress becomes too high," he sadly noted to Mark, "when common people can no longer become intimate with its workings."

Before long, however, their minds moved on to happier thoughts.

"Dusty, did you tell Lieutenant Folsum about the taxicab driver in the trunk?"

"No," replied the pilot. "That subject never came up."

"I guess that's another one of those things he probably knew, but didn't think it was necessary to talk about," Mark said with a wink.

"Yes, you might say so," smiled Dusty.

One chapter was closed and another was about to open. They talked of a new world in which would be merged the best of the present with that of the past. Since the future was their generation's to shape, perhaps its prospects needed not to be so glum after all.

Upon their arrival they had not expected a welcoming committee. They had no sooner made their way to the baggage area of the main terminal when they were met by Foster Westwood, the preservation activist.

His face was pale and somber. Dusty and Mark quickly sensed something was wrong.

"Dusty, come with me right away," Westwood said. "It's Peg!"

Chapter 32

As the three rushed down the hospital corridor, Dusty's heart pounded. His head was numb with shock and disbelief. This was one more crazy twist in a bizarre, continuing nightmare. He felt a heavy guilt wondering if he himself had brought this upon her by causing her all the anxiety and worry which had overtaxed her strength.

When they came to the nearby waiting room, Lynn spotted them, ran up and tightly hugged each of them.

Dusty touched her chin and looked into her eyes. "When did it happen," he asked gently.

"This afternoon," she replied in a tear-choked voice. "She was apparently up and about when she suddenly collapsed. The nurse who happened to stop by found her lying on the floor."

"Is she conscious?"

"In and out. The doctor gave her a sedative to help her rest better. She doesn't seem to be in any pain, thank God."

Lynn then broke down completely and Dusty gently eased her into a chair. It was several minutes before she recovered sufficiently to go on.

"Mother was so happy," Lynn went on. "It seemed for once that everything was going right for her."

Just then a nurse emerged and came up to them. "It's okay," she whispered. "You can come in now."

Dusty looked over at Mark with concern. Perhaps all this might be too much for a lad his age, but the young man rose to his full height, looked at his grandfather, and solemnly nodded.

The room was dimly lit, yet there seemed to radiate from Peg a certain light of her own as she lay there peacefully.

"It's good you could come," the doctor whispered. "She's been calling for you."

A few moments later her eyes fluttered open. She looked up at the faces around her and when she recognized her two young men, she brightened into a smile. Feebly she reached up to Dusty who knelt close beside her, took her hand in both of his, and pressed it to his cheek.

"When did you get in," she asked.

"About an hour ago," smiled the pilot.

"You did it," she said. "You really did it."

"Of course we did," Mark piped in. "Did you think we wouldn't?"

"No, no...," she sighed. "It's just an old lady's nature to worry over these things." Then turning to Dusty she said, "I guess I underestimated you."

"In what way, kitten?"

"You've always managed to make it back, no matter what. From that day when they carried you into my father's house, I knew there was something special about you. Behind that boyish innocence I could see a deep inner strength... a quiet determination that never failed to come through when it was needed most. Now... from here on... the rest should be easy."

"First we've got to get you out of here, hon," he said.

"In awhile...," she sighed. "In awhile. Right now I just have to rest a little... that's all."

"Sure, kitten... sure. Would you like us to come back later on? We'll just be outside if you need us."

"No, no...," she smiled. "Just stay here with me awhile. We've been apart too long as it is."

She closed her eyes for several minutes, then awakened again.

"Was it rough out there," she asked.

"Nah," he shrugged. "There were never any problems; Mark here saw to that."

She nodded contentedly. There was a gentle smile on her face as she looked around at her loved ones. Then once again her eyes focused on him.

"Dusty?"

"Yes, kitten?"

"Tell me about California."

He knew that she was not talking about the sprawling metropolis from where he just returned, with all its congested freeways, the monster buildings and the smog. She was thinking of the California they used to talk about so long ago, a dream they would someday fulfill.

"It's real neat, Peg," he described in a dreamy voice. "First you come to this vast range of gray, snow-capped mountains, the most majestic mountains you've ever seen, reachin' halfway up into the sky. It almost takes your breath away as you fly over them. You have to fly low so you can skim over the beautiful blue lakes up close.

"Then they fall away into this great valley… stretching out like a golden carpet for as far as the eye can see, with rivers and streams gently winding their way through the fields and the gently rolling hills, all studded with oak trees and grazing cattle. It's kind of a special place, like it was set aside by God Himself. And there's no more beautiful and more peaceful place in all the world."

Just then her eyes closed. She heaved a long sigh and he felt her gently slip away. Tears rolled down his cheeks and his voice choked up for a moment, but somehow he managed to recover himself and continue.

"Except maybe where you are right now, hon, with no more pain, and no more sufferin', … and your family and friends whom you haven't seen for long time are all waitin' there to give you a big welcome home. You're free now, hon."

He remained with her for several minutes. Then he tenderly kissed her goodnight.

Not much was said in the weeks immediately following the funeral. Other than the perfunctory courtesies at mealtime, they mostly sat in silence or wandered off on their own separate ways. Lynn, for her part, tried to avoid the issue by losing herself in answering the many letters of condolence that continued to pour in. But in spite of everyone's efforts to avoid it, the looming question would not go away.

It finally came to a head one morning while Mark was out. Lynn wandered by Dusty's room to find him packing his belongings into his duffel bag.

"Were you planning to leave without saying goodbye," she said somewhat stiffly.

"It's better this way," he explained. "I've never been a burden on anyone and I don't intend to start now."

"That's not what we're talking about here, Dusty, and you know it. In fact, I'd say it's more of a copout."

Her brazenness took him aback, and he was not quite sure how to respond. But Lynn's pent-up anger, once unleashed, took on a will of its own.

"Let's tell it like it is, shall we!" she cried. "You feel your job here is finished and so now it's time to slip out quietly like the way you slipped in!"

"Lynn... I-"

"*Don't*... say anything," she interrupted. "I'm not *finished*! You... you just go on ahead if you want to. We'll manage. But I think you're forgetting something. You have a family here! Your grandson thinks the sun rises and sets with you. For the first time in his life he has a real feeling of pride and accomplishment... and now you're about to take all that away from him! If you couldn't be there for me when I was growing up, at least you could be there for him!"

Dusty stood dumfounded as Lynn walked out of the room. Presently she returned with a white envelope which she handed to him.

It was in Peggy's handwriting. On the front was written *Dusty*, spelled out in simple letters.

He sat down on the bed, his hands trembling slightly as he carefully pulled apart the seal. It had been written the week before he came home.

Dusty Dear,

A moment never goes by when I don't think of you, and rejoice for the day when the two of you will march through the door. As I write this I can only hope that this joyous moment will not be far off.

I would like to take a moment to express some thoughts which have been of deep concern to me.

I know it will be difficult for you to put the pieces of your life back together. I can easily appreciate that once this mess is over with, the aftermath can be difficult and painful. But, knowing you as I do, and in light of what you have already overcome, I'm sure that given time, you will handle this too.

The Claremont Preservation Project is off on its own now, thanks in no small part to your efforts. It has been a source of considerable pride and satisfaction to me watching it take root from a fragile dream to an actual reality.

Lynn has played a big part in carrying out the work we have begun. You are the head of the family now. Lynn also wants it that way. Just be there for her when she needs you.

And above all, be there for Mark. His curiosity and high spirits may, at this time in his life, require occasional guidance now and then, but his heart is in the right place and he'll always be there when he's needed.

Please don't ever feel any guilt or remorse over what happened with us. You did not desert us; you did what you had to do and had the foresight to see that we were taken care of. I don't know how we would have made out otherwise. You have given these last months added meaning for me. And what's more, it's not every woman who can live out her years with the contentment that a part of her will go on after her.

I have no regrets. If I had it to do all over again, I would do exactly as I have done, and I wouldn't trade my memories of you or our years together for anything in the world.

May the years you missed out on be restored to you and may they also be many and happy. God bless you, Dusty, and thank you for all the joy you've given me.

All my love,

Peg

He laid the letter aside, put his hand over his eyes, and wept. Lynn came over and picked it up. And when she finished reading it, she wept too.

When she was able to speak, she said to him, "Papa, you have nothing to feel guilty about. Her last days were happy ones... meaningful ones. Her heart was filled with joy knowing that you and Mark were on your way home."

Then she added, "You know, Papa, when she heard the news, she contacted her attorney. You're in charge of her estate, now."

"No," Dusty said. "I don't want that."

"It's what she wants, Dusty," she said. "It's what we all want."

"As far as I'm concerned," he replied, "You're runnin' things here just fine."

Dusty and Mark said little to each other as they drove through the countryside. The vast expanse of passing fields and farms cast an hypnotic spell over them as if time itself had stood still.

The pilot's thoughts wandered back and forth to people and events of the past, distant and not so distant, randomly and independent of their actual chronological occurrence.

After awhile they turned off onto a dirt road and proceeded for a quarter mile when the airport came into view. It was a primitive little field, with a couple of weathered corrugated hangars and a windsock. The only paved surface was the narrow 2400-foot runway.

They walked along the row of parked aircraft, where presently they came to a Stearman.

Mark regarded the aircraft with awe and wonder. He was so excited that it was difficult for him to speak.

"Dusty... you -?"

"It's okay," grinned the pilot. "After all, if you're gonna learn to fly, at least you oughta start out right."

After making a careful inspection of the biplane with his grandfather, Mark placed his right foot upon the root of the lower wing, pulled himself up and carefully made his way along the fuselage the way Dusty told him to. He grabbed the hand-hold grip at the midpoint of the upper wing, then hoisted himself into the front cockpit.

Dusty gave him some instructions, then walked to the front where he swung the propeller through a couple of times. After untying the ropes which tethered the plane to the ground the pilot climbed up and eased himself into the cockpit.

"You know what you're supposed to do," he called out.

"Yeah," Mark hollered back with enthusiasm.

"Okay then... *Brakes!*"

"Brakes," Mark resounded.

"Give it a couple shots with the throttle, now."

The young man complied.

"Throttle cracked," Dusty called out.

"Throttle cracked," Mark repeated.

Now came the awaited word.

"*CONTACT!*"

"*CONTACT!*" Mark called out.

Dusty engaged the starter and the propeller slowly began its revolutions. Then suddenly oily smoke belched forth from the exhaust as the radial engine coughed into life. At first Mark jiggled the throttle to keep it going, and then the master pilot took over, guiding the lumbering biplane across the taxiway. After stopping for a minute to perform the final engine and ground checks, the plane slowly entered onto the runway. Then Dusty eased the throttle forward and the Stearman began to roll. When she had picked up enough airspeed, she gracefully rose from the runway and ascended majestically into the sky.

For Mark it was a whole new experience. The coordinated turns and stalls came a bit awkwardly at first, but it would not be long before, under his grandfather's guidance, he would come to master these maneuvers on his own with a timeless grace.

For Dusty, it was the return to a more familiar world where once again he found himself in his natural element, with the wind whistling through the wings.

The late afternoon sun painted the giant puffy cumulus clouds in a brilliant orange hue. One cloud in particular made him suddenly sit up in his seat, and he looked upon it with awe and wonder; for as they flew by he could clearly make out the distinct features of a familiar looking young woman, smiling and waving to them as they continued on their way.

2183354

Made in the USA